THE PRICE OF TEMPTATION

THE PRICE OF TEMPTATION
BY
M.J. PEARSON

Seventh Window
Publications

First Seventh Window Publications edition: September 2005
cover illustration © 2005 Sean Platter – studio splatter – all rights reserved

Excerpt from "When We Two Parted" by Lord Byron (1788-1824)

Published in the United States of America by:
Seventh Window Publications
P.O. BOX 603165
Providence, RI 0206-0165

Library of Congress Control Number: 2005930940

ISBN-13:   978-0-9717089-3-8
ISBN-10:   0-9717089-3-2

For Aunt Billie

ACKNOWLEDGMENTS

I'd like to thank my agent, Sharene Martin, whose enthusiasm kept me going; Ken Harrison, my publisher, for taking a chance; my first readers Pat, Erich, Tracey, Kris and Keith for their comments and support; Aidan for being there; and especially Paul.

Chapter One

*J*amie Riley had been lonely for so long.

He stood in Hanover Square and looked up at St. Joseph House with happy anticipation. Four stories tall, the London town house of the Earl of St. Joseph looked more welcoming than imposing, its red brick edifice glowing warm in the October sunshine. The building's painted white columns and classical-inspired pediment above the door spoke of a relatively recent construction: probably within the reign of the current George, but some years before his unfortunate circumstances forced the accession of his son as Regent. Jamie paused to admire its clean lines, and shake his head at the small paved courtyard, so much more practical in the big, dirty city than the cheerful front gardens he was used to back in Yorkshire.

The main attraction of the house, of course, was the family who lived within. Robert and Mary Clair, the Earl and Countess of St. Joseph, had reared three delightful and energetic boys, who were now of an age to require a tutor to both oversee their learning and attempt to keep them in hand. Jamie's dimple flickered as he smiled to himself, looking forward to the challenge. Life from now on would be very different from the quiet existence he had known, just he and his ailing mother scraping by in their rural cottage near Wheldrake. A shiver ran down his spine, and he firmly put those thoughts behind him. Now was not the time to look back to his mother's long illness and the dreadful months that had followed her death; it was the time to look forward to his new post, filled with bustle and cheer.

With a deep breath to steady his nerves, Jamie closed the wrought iron gate behind him, and climbed the wide marble steps to the front door. He rang the bell, and the door was soon opened by a tall, white-haired gentleman of an almost uncannily stiff posture. The butler, of course. Jamie's acquaintance in Yorkshire hadn't included much experience with the breed, but this one's hauteur fit his expectations admirably.

"Yes?" The butler flicked his eyes over the young man standing before him, and Jamie wished that he hadn't needed to sell his overcoat to help pay for the trip to London. Still, his black super-fine jacket, handed down from the vicar two years ago, was as well-tailored as his mother's clever needle could make it, and his neck cloth was neatly tied. Surely he was imagining the contempt in the other man's visage. Butlers were supposed to be stony-faced, after all.

Even so, Jamie stood up straighter. "Good day, sir. My name is James Riley, and I've come to take up my position with his lordship the Earl of St. Joseph"

The information did not soften the butler's countenance in the least. He regarded the valise clutched in Jamie's hand with faint astonishment, then looked back at his face, eyes narrowing. "His lordship is installing you here? In the household?"

Jamie widened his own eyes in surprise. "Where else? It is, after all, where I'll be performing my duties."

"Rather young for this, aren't you?"

"I'm well-suited to my trade, I assure you." A smile flickered on Jamie's face as he thought of his first meeting with his charges some months back. Good boys, but rambunctious through and through. "I can imagine at times I'll need a young man's energy and stamina just to keep up."

The butler, looking pained, put up a hand. "That's quite enough. Follow me."

Stephen Clair, Earl of St. Joseph, was playing euchre with his valet Charles when his butler, Mr. Symmons, entered the room and stood ramrod straight, by his side. Since the stakes they were playing for included ownership of the last half-bottle of contraband brandy in the earl's London home, neither player acknowledged the interruption with more than a grunt. Napoleon's defeat last year at Waterloo had allowed good French brandy to become more available, but the ruinous taxes on the legal stuff made the continuation of smuggling inevitable, and a win today especially desirable.

Mr. Symmons exuded disapproval while he waited, perhaps even less pleased than usual. If such a thing were possible.

Stephen sighed and sat up straighter, one hand rising of its own accord to neaten his cravat. His butler had that effect on him. "Yes, Symmons?"

"Gentleman to see you, my lord," Mr. Symmons announced.

"Egad; it isn't Julian, is it?" A moue of distaste marred the earl's generous mouth as he played his next card.

"I believe I said *gentleman*, my lord."

Stephen let the insult slide, intent on studying his opponent's face. Charles was a worthy card player, or would be if he could keep every turn of fortune from registering on his plump, kindly face. Suddenly Charles' expression brightened, causing his lordship's to darken to a corresponding degree. Hell. He needed that brandy. Aunt Matilda had been cursed ungenerous since he'd missed her birthday party, and quarter-day was over two months away.

"My lord?"

Maybe the day could yet be saved. "Not a creditor, is it?"

"I don't believe so, my lord. Certainly not one of the usual bunch."

"Does he have a name?"

"Doubtless, my lord."

Charles played the queen of hearts, taking the trick, then laid down the king, beaming. Stephen looked at his remaining cards, and they didn't look encouraging.

"Might he have shared it with you, Symmons?" Stephen plucked at a card as if he were about to play it.

"A Mr. Riley, I believe he said, my lord."

Stephen fiddled some more with his cards, fine, dark brows pulled together in a frown. "Did he say what he wanted, Symmons?"

"He said, my lord, that you had offered him a position."

Charles said something in an undertone, and they both snickered while Mr. Symmons bristled.

"A position of *employment*, my lord."

"Surely not." His lordship frowned again. "Almost surely not. Was I at all incapacitated when you put me to bed last night, Charles? No, don't answer that. Of course I was," Stephen said, tossing his cards onto the table with relief. "Perhaps I should see him after all, and find out what I had in mind. A replacement for the lovely Julian, I suppose." And then to the butler, "Well, Symmons? Is he at all in the Golden One's league?"

"I am *hardly* the man to judge, my lord."

"All right, then. Charles?"

Charles walked over to the door and peered out into the hall with interest, coming back to make his report. His transparent face showed a struggle to put the best spin on the news, and at last he smiled as something positive occurred to him. "Well, my lord, I'm sure he'd be much less a drain on the pocketbook than Mr. Julian."

"That bad?"

"Oh, no, my lord. His features are quite regular, I'm sure." He considered further. "Sort of a cute nose."

"Ha. Plain as a pikestaff, you mean."

"Nice fair skin."

"Whey-faced," the earl interpreted. "Hair?"

"Oh, yes, my lord," Charles said. "Quite a lot of it, even." He paused, then admitted, "Comes almost to his shoulders."

"Hardly fashionable, then," said the earl, running his hand through his own ebony curls, cropped à la Brutus. "Blond? Brunet?"

"Neither, really. Sort of lightish brown."

"Mousy, you mean. Good lord, what was I thinking? What about his eyes? And don't tell me, yes, two of them. Unless he doesn't have, I mean."

"In which case I would hardly say—" Charles broke off as Stephen used his own two eyes to advantage, glaring darkly. "Sorry. Couldn't really tell, due to the, er, spectacles. Tinted, I'm afraid they were."

"Spectacles." Stephen sighed. "Doesn't sound like my type at all. Unless... built like a stevedore, is he?" the earl inquired, but at this point without much in the way of hope.

"Not *quite*, my lord. Medium height, I'd say. Slender as a reed."

"Scrawny."

"I didn't say that, my lord."

"You didn't have to. Lord, I must have been three sheets to the wind." The earl reached for his discarded hand, resigned to losing the brandy after all. "Symmons, tell the gentleman I am not at home."

"Wait, Stephen."

The butler, standing near the door, harrumphed his displeasure at the valet's flagrant breach of formality, but the other men ignored him.

"It doesn't really seem fair to just — I mean, if you did lead him to believe—" The valet brightened again. "Besides, when I first opened the door, he was looking at that painting of your mother. On the far wall?"

"Yes. And?"

"*Really* lovely arse, my lord."

At that Mr. Symmons stalked back out of the room, slamming the door behind him.

Jamie Riley had been cooling his heels for some time in his lordship's hallway, but he had yet to become bored. There were so many things to look at. He marveled at the expensive flocked wallpaper, took his time examining the paintings. Two pretty watercolor landscapes and an oil portrait of a lovely woman with dark hair. Not the current countess as he remembered her, perhaps the dowager? An exquisite table with finely carved legs—surely French? —with a China bowl of delicate, blush-colored roses gracing the top. Expensively out of season. Jamie closed his eyes and once again inhaled their perfume. Bliss. Especially after the last few days of travel, crammed into poorly-sprung, musty coaches with too many fellow travelers

Here at the front of the house, the hall opened on either side into the two largest rooms of the residence. A stiff, formal drawing room was to the right, the delicate tables fluted and gilded, chairs and sofas upholstered in an ice-blue silk. Should the furniture be pushed back to the walls, it was spacious enough to allow dancing room for at least eight couples. Across the hall, Jamie peeked into an equally large dining room. The enormous mahogany table and matching sideboards were of a sturdier, older design than the French Empire décor of the drawing room, too handsome in their own right to be discarded for the vagaries of modern taste.

Two other doors, closed just now, flanked each other across the hall further down, and beyond them a smaller, plainer door probably led to the kitchens. Jamie looked forward to exploring the house later: as the boys' tutor, he would have daily access into rooms the lower servants would visit only to clean. Incredible that this lovely place was his home from now on. It was still difficult to believe his luck, but he supposed that it would all become real to him once he began looking after the children.

Jamie wasn't yet concerned that the earl hadn't come to greet him, assuming him to be a busy man with many duties, but he did wonder at the quiet of the house. With the three young boys in residence, the house should be full of laughter and noise. The young man shrugged to himself. It was a fine, brisk day, perhaps they were out working off some of that energy at a nearby park. Too bad they hadn't taken the sour-faced butler with them. Might have cheered him up a bit. And who was the plump man who had opened the door briefly and stared at him? Another servant, perhaps. Jamie shrugged again, and went back to smelling the roses.

A slamming door startled him out of his reverie. It was the butler, back at last, narrow-eyed and looking like he'd been sucking on a lemon.

"His lordship will see you now."

Jamie smiled and said "Thank you," very politely, but the effort seemed to be wasted as the butler stomped ahead of him into the next room down on the right.

"Your Mr. Riley, my lord." It was almost a snarl, and the countenance the butler turned on Jamie was cold. "I believe you already know the Earl of St. Joseph." With that, he marched from the room, slamming the door behind him.

Jamie blinked at the still-vibrating door. "Goodness," he said.

"Yes, well, I'm afraid Mr. Symmons doesn't like me very much," said a rich, warm voice. If hot chocolate could speak, it would be in tones like these.

Jamie turned toward the voice, adjusting his spectacles. He seemed to be in a morning room: smaller and more intimate than the formal drawing room, this was where the Countess doubtlessly received her daily visitors. The décor here was Grecian, with lyre-backed chairs and a low, rose-silk sofa with scrolled arms set comfortably near the fire. Nearer to the door, two men rose from a round table, its top inset with a classical honeysuckle pattern, partially obscured just now with a litter of playing cards.

One of the pair was the plump young man who had inspected him while he waited in the hallway; the other was a complete stranger. Tall, correspondingly broad, thirty-ish, very handsome, dark hair, very dark eyes. Fashionably dressed in buckskins so tight they looked painted on, and a coat cut with such inevitable simplicity that it must have cost... Jamie had no idea what such a garment would cost, just that it was well beyond his means. He smiled uncertainly and looked around. The earl was not present: a huge, benevolent bear of a man, his size and beaming face were unmistakable.

"I understand I offered you employment?" the dark-haired man said.

"I... no, there must be some mistake. I'm looking for the Earl of St. Joseph."

The man raised his brows. "Speaking."

Jamie stared in confusion. "There must be some mistake," he repeated. "The man who hired me... who *said* he was..."

"Was someone else?" The earl let out his breath in obvious relief. "See, Charles? Not so bosky after all. I'm sorry. I don't know who's played this cruel trick on you—" his eyes narrowed. "Wait a minute. This man who pretended to be me. Did he have guinea-gold hair and sea-green eyes?"

Jamie shook his head, dazed. It was an effort to find his tongue. "No, my lord. He was tall, and dark like you, but even bigger." He groped for a better description. "Bear-like. Not so well-dressed. Oh my," his eyes, indeterminate in color behind the lightly tinted spectacles, widened. "Maybe that should have warned me. His jacket didn't fit nearly so well, and surely a true lord...? But he was so... so nice." He stopped, as the real St. Joseph groped blindly for his chair and sat, mouth drawn into lines of pain. The round-faced man was staring open-mouthed.

"Speaking of cruel tricks," said his lordship, dark eyes blazing, "Are you trying to tell me you've seen my brother Robert recently? Because that is quite, quite impossible."

"No," Jamie whispered, putting it together. "Brother. And you're the earl now. So he's—but there were boys—if you've inherited—" Jamie felt sick. Those laughing, mischievous, bright-eyed children... The room swayed, and Jamie felt himself being led to a cushioned chair. He looked up, and the round-faced man was looking at him, concern in his warm brown eyes.

"I'm Charles West, his lordship's valet. Do I understand that you had an arrangement with the *previous* Lord St. Joseph?"

"It seems so," Jamie said. "We met last winter in York. He was staying with mutual friends, on his way back from Scotland. He had read my paper on the Rose Villa—the Roman villa, in Yorkshire, with the rose mosaics?—and we got talking for hours. His lordship offered me a post, on the spot, to tutor his boys. I mean, I went the next day to meet the Countess, to get her approval, of course, and I met the children..." Jamie stopped and swallowed. "They were wonderful people—I liked them so much. They were all so excited about being able to go to the Continent, now that Napoleon is safely tucked away. They wanted me to go with them, but my mother was ill, so they said when they got back in October..."

The earl closed his dark eyes for a long moment, then opened them and gazed steadily at Jamie. "It's just as well you couldn't go with them. Their ship went down in the Mediterranean three months ago. Everyone on board..." He looked away for a moment, then met Jamie's eyes again. "I'm sorry. I wish I could do something for you, but I have no children for you to teach. Likely never will. Do you need a few pounds to get you back home to Yorkshire?"

As Jamie sat, tongue-tied with disbelief and despair, Charles spoke up. "Stephen?" he said. "Perhaps you do have a position to offer."

The earl looked at his valet with something approaching horror.

Charles flushed with amusement at his lordship's consternation. "Not *that*. I mean, when you missed your great-aunt's birthday? You did say that if you'd had a personal secretary to keep track of your correspondence, then you never would have lost the invitation."

"Yes, well..." Stephen ran his fingers through his curls, obviously hesitating to speak freely in front of a stranger.

Charles was less circumspect. "If you're worrying about the expense of another servant, may I remind you of what a *costly* mistake missing Aunt Matilda's party was? Especially if she remains annoyed with you?"

Stephen bit his lip and drummed his fingers on the table for a few seconds. "Can you write a fair hand?" he asked Jamie.

"Oh yes, my lord." Through his shock, Jamie was daring to hope.

"Keep track of dates, appointments, and the like?"

"Of course, my lord. I am a historian, after all. We do rather specialize in keeping track of—"

The earl interrupted. "Suppose it had just been brought home to you that you had greatly annoyed a very wealthy relation. Do you think you could compose a suitable letter of apology?"

"I suppose I could, my lord."

"Well? How would you go about it?"

Jamie thought, pulling his mind together with effort. "I suppose—I suppose it's best to keep as close to the truth as possible. And grovel abjectly, of course."

"Of course," the earl agreed. "Well, in this case the truth is I happened to be out of town with... a very particular friend. One she used to find rather amusing, in an appalled sort of way, but since I've come into the title she doesn't think I should be consorting with people like that. She'll assume I was with him, there's no getting around that. I think it's why she's so angry."

"Where did you go?"

"To a prize-fight in Hampshire. Aunt Matilda hates boxing, too." He sighed. "This is not an exercise she would approve of in the least."

Jamie nodded. "And is there anything in Hampshire your aunt would approve of you doing?"

"What?" The earl looked confused, so Jamie clarified.

"What are her interests? What can you tell her you saw or did there that might interest or amuse her? Does she care for racing? History? Architecture?"

"Oh. Oh. I get you." Stephen's dark brows creased in thought. "Well, Aunt Matilda does fancy herself a patroness of the arts. But is there any art of note in Hampshire? If there is, I certainly didn't notice it."

Jamie stared. "Not notice Castle Ord? Not only is it architecturally unique for this part of England—the round tower is a feature almost never found outside of Ireland in the eleventh century— but Lady Gregg has a collection of medieval religious paintings that's quite enormously famous. One couldn't possibly have passed through Hampshire and not heard of the Saints Gallery at Castle Ord."

"Yes, but one couldn't possibly know me and think I would visit such a place."

"How well does your aunt know your particular friend?"

"They've met, but I wouldn't call them cozy."

"Well then? Try something like this: *My dearest Aunt Matilda, I was absolutely devastated when I realized I had missed out on your birthday party.*"

"Your eightieth birthday party," the earl added glumly.

"Oh, dear." Jamie paused. "*You must know me well enough to imagine my chagrin that I was not in attendance to give you my felicitations on such a glorious occasion.* Lay it on thick, then be honest enough so you aren't insulting her intelligence. *You also know me quite well enough to imagine that instead I was up to no good with someone who should remain nameless in polite company, much less to someone I cherish as I do you.* Is *cherish* too much, do you think?"

"Oh, no. Auntie M. will eat it up. And the truth is, I really am very fond of the old bi—er, besom. We get along quite well. Usually."

"Good. That will help. Where were we? *I meant to return in time for the celebrations, of course, but instead found myself dragged against my will to Lady Gregg's Saints Gallery. I expected to be bored out of my mind, but was quite diverted instead. Did it never occur to you that Van Lorn's St. Sebastian is the very image of Member of Parliament Burdett? Assuming one can imagine him stuck quite full of arrows, something I feel sure is well within your powers.*"

"Now that, Mr. Riley, is brilliant," the earl said with awe. "However did you deduce Auntie's opinion of Francis Burdett?"

Jamie shrugged. "She's a rich, elderly aristocrat—what would she think of a radical MP?"

"Go on. Please."

"All right. *It wasn't until I saw Paoli's*—hmm, better make it that *Italian bloke's St. Joan lit up like a birthday candle that it occurred to me that I was missing your party. If you would deign to allow me to apologize in person, I could tell you who I think St. Catherine's face reminds me of, but it isn't something I would write in a letter, so please, please don't beg. Your own favorite saint, if in name only, St. Joseph.* How's that?"

Stephen looked impressed, Charles smug. "Mr. Riley, I do believe you are hired," said the earl. "How much was my brother going to pay you?"

"Fifty pounds, my lord."

"Fifty per quarter?" The earl frowned. "That seems a bit high."

"Oh no, my lord, not—" Jamie hastened to correct the mistake, but Charles was quicker.

"— Not when you consider he was to have three charges, after all, and is, of course, a historian of note." The valet shot a warning glance at the confused young man. "But perhaps since he's only got you to worry about now, and is untried as a secretary, we might persuade him to accept forty per quarter?"

The earl turned to his new employee. "If that's not an insult, Mr. Riley?"

Jamie swallowed. "Not at all, my lord."

Chapter Two

*T*here was something unsettling about this household.
Jamie looked around his new room, finding little to fault
here. The iron bedstead was narrow, but so was he, and
the mattress, when he tested it, was thick and soft. A colorful rag
rug warmed the wood floor. There was a sturdy wooden wardrobe
for his meager clothing, and a washstand with a pretty flowered
ceramic bath set on it. He pushed his spectacles up his nose and
peered at the latter, thinking it looked rather fine for a servant's
room. The wash basin was intact, but a large chip in the rim of
the pitcher told the story: once damaged, the set was unsuitable
for family use, but still too good to be thrown away. He nodded
approval at the economy.

A small desk and chair of simple design completed the furnishings, and above them, facing east, was a window with a panoramic
view of London spreading out before him. First, Hanover Square,
quiet and dignified, with its stately town homes and newfangled
gas lamps. To the north, Jamie could see the bustle of Oxford
Street, lined with elegant shops, and in the other direction steady
maritime traffic thronged the Thames. The never-ending pall
caused by thousands upon thousands of coal fires was thick today,
but through the autumn haze he could just make out the turrets of
the Tower of London, not two miles to the east.

London. He shivered in excitement to be living here, and in such
relative comfort. But such a strange household! A rude, haughty

butler. An over-familiar valet, who calls his employer by his first name. And the housekeeper! White of hair and pleasant of feature, a smile on her face would have made her the very image of a kindly grandmother. But she was as sour-faced as the butler, and he was not surprised when Charles introduced her as "Mrs. Symmons."

She had sniffed loudly when presented with the latest member of the household. "Oh, this one's to live here, is he? Personal secretary, my eye."

"We do have a room, don't we, Mrs. Symmons?" Charles had asked.

Why is everyone so tolerant of these unpleasant people? Jamie wondered. Surely an earl's staff could be held to a certain level of civility.

"Aye, not that it'll see much use, will it?" grumbled the woman. "Up the stairs here, I'm putting you at the top. " Mrs. Symmons paused for breath on each landing. On the first she shot a glare at Jamie. "His lordship's rooms take up the east side of this floor, with the guest rooms across the hall. You're to keep away unless you're specifically called for, understand?"

"Yes, of course." Jamie stiffened to think he might be suspected of snooping, or worse—theft.

The housekeeper nodded and continued up the stairs, pausing again at the second landing. "The upper servants have always had their rooms here, up with the—the nurseries." Her bottom lip quivered with the last words, and Jamie felt another stab of pain for the loss of the Clair family. How much worse for those who had known them well, served them daily. Watched the boys grow. "We've since moved the rest of the staff here, to save from heating the attics, but I'll not have our sleep disturbed by any of your shenanigans."

His sympathy fled. Shenanigans? This was too much. "I beg your pardon?"

Mrs. Symmons tightened her lips. "You come down these stairs at night, you creep like a mouse, hear? Assuming you use the room much at all."

What in Hades was going on? Obviously Mrs. Symmons had serious reservations about his character, and didn't expect him to stay long. What could cause her to think so? The question niggled at him as he followed her up the last flight of stairs and into his new room. He set his valise on the floor and looked around. "This isn't so bad," Jamie said in relief.

"Chimney smokes," Mrs. Symmons reported with dour satisfaction. "Should you ever light the fire."

"Why wouldn't I?" It just burst out of the bewildered Jamie.

"It's already getting cold at night, why wouldn't I light the fire?" The housekeeper fixed him with her steely gaze. "Mayhap you're as innocent as you pretend to be, and mayhap you're not. But if you are..." she paused for dramatic effect. *"Lock your door. And that's all I have to say on the matter."* With a swish of skirts, she was gone.

Jamie stared after her, open-mouthed. Mrs. Symmons' taste in literature must lean toward the very worst of the popular gothic novels. "What evil walks the corridors of St. Joseph House at midnight? Headless monk, displaced banshee, or the devil himself?" he droned to himself, attempting a sepulchral tone. Too bad, of course, that this was a thoroughly modern town house, not thirty years old, and if it was haunted by anything, it was memories of warmth and laughter.

Jamie unpacked slowly, drawing out the task. He hung his second-best jacket, another woolen hand-me-down from the vicar, in the wardrobe, added two rather shabby white linen shirts, an extra pair of trousers in practical black, and a comfortably-worn flannel dressing gown. In the drawer at the bottom he placed a few pairs of well-darned stockings, two pairs of gloves, some undergarments and neckerchiefs. Jamie's six remaining books he set with reverence in a row on the desktop, then he frowned and moved them to the broad mantle above the fireplace. If the chimney really did smoke, he would have to have the window above the desk open frequently, and it wouldn't do to expose his meager library to the London weather.

The last item in the valise was a small portrait of his mother, taken on the occasion of her come-out. Jamie touched the painted face gently with one finger. Such a lovely face, full of hope, eager to please. Too eager, as it turned out. All at once Jamie felt overwhelmed with sadness, for his mother, for the previous earl and his lost family, for himself and the post he had looked forward to with such anticipation.

"Life rarely turns out as we expect, does it, Mama?" he said. Just then there was a tap on the door, and his lordship's valet poked his head in.

"Mr. Riley? Is there anything you need? I brought you some flowers." In his plump hands was a small bowl of roses. Jamie flushed with pleasure.

"Thank you, Mr. West. Do come in."

"Charles—please." The valet transferred the bowl to one hand, extending the other, and Jamie shook it gratefully.

"I'm James. Most people call me Jamie, though."

"Well, Jamie, we dine in the kitchen at six. Unless you'd prefer a tray tonight? You must be tired from your journey." Charles was looking around with avid curiosity, and Jamie was embarrassed at the shabbiness of his things.

"No, I'll be happy to join you downstairs. I'd like to meet the rest of the staff."

The other man moved to set the flowers down on Jamie's desk. "Not that there are many of—oh! How lovely!" He picked up the miniature and tilted it to better catch the light from the window. "Your mother?" Charles looked from the painted features back to Jamie. "You must take after your father."

"I suppose I must," Jamie agreed. "I fancy a quick wash before dinner. Do you think I could have some water sent up, or should I fetch it myself?"

Charles put the painting down reluctantly and moved toward the door. "I'll have some sent up. Six o'clock, then, and don't be late, or Alex will have all the potatoes."

Jamie paused with his hand on the kitchen door half an hour later, gathering his courage. What would the rest of the servants be like? Charles had been nice to him, and Betsy, the twelve-year-old maid who'd brought his water, was cheerful enough. But the Symmonses... He shuddered, and opened the door.

Despite its considerable size, the kitchen was warm to the point of stuffiness, heated not only by a fireplace large enough to stand up in, but by a modern coal-burning cook stove. Hanging copper and iron pots filled one entire wall, and the others were lined with cabinets and work tables. By the hearth, an enormous iron cauldron and folded drying racks awaited laundry day. He had never seen the item next to them, but thought it might be Mr. Beetham's celebrated patent wringer.

In the center of the room, the huge rectangular kitchen table, old and scarred from decades of use, was more than adequate for the insufficient staff that gathered around it. Mr. Symmons had the head, with his wife to his right. The seat to his left was empty: no one else, apparently, dared claim worthiness enough to sit next to the haughty butler.

Charles rose from his chair, halfway down one side of the table. "Come sit by me, Jamie. I'll introduce you. I believe you've met the Symmonses?"

Jamie nodded to the elderly couple, receiving frosty stares in return.

The valet waved at the person sitting next to Mrs. Symmons, a hawk-faced woman whose long, grey-streaked black hair was confined in a tidy braid down her back. "May I introduce Mrs. Sawtell? She and her son Alex look after the stables."

"Abby," the woman said, holding out a large hand. Jamie shook it, surprised at her strength. She looked competent, indeed, capable of handling any livestock smaller than a water buffalo. But still, a woman in charge of the stables? It seemed very odd. Her son Alex, although only ten years old, was similarly craggy of face and dark of hair, and looked well on his way to outstripping her height. Jamie bowed to both of them.

"Pleased," Alex mumbled. Neither he nor his dam seemed much in the way of conversationalists.

"And our cook is Rebecca Wyss."

Cook? From her youth, Jamie had assumed the woman setting out the meal was a kitchen maid. She appeared to be no more than twenty, and was as truly stunning a girl as he had ever seen. Pale gold hair, flawless skin, wide sky-blue eyes. "Hullo, Mr. Riley." Her smile was warm.

He smiled back. "Mrs. Wyss."

"Please, just Rebecca." She rolled her eyes as she slipped into her seat across from Charles. "Mrs. Wyss sounds like a sneeze."

There was only one other place set at the table, presumably for the still-absent Betsy. Jamie counted: just eight servants, including the stable hands? Surely an earl's establishment should be much grander. A few footmen at the very least, some scullery maids. How odd. Unless—Charles had emphasized what a costly mistake the earl's missing his aunt's birthday had been. Could his lordship be having financial difficulties? Jamie felt another qualm of conscience over the enormous salary he was to be paid. But the Earl of St. Joseph's finances were not his concern, and he should keep to his own affairs.

Betsy arrived just slightly late, rosy-cheeked and out of breath from running an errand. "Well hullo, Charles. I thought you'd be over to Sam's. Himself coming home again tonight, is he?"

"I suppose it depends on how things are going with-ah—" a swift glance at Jamie— "on how things go this evening. But I'll wager half-a-crown he's back by midnight."

"Does the earl spend much time away?" Jamie asked.

More glances were exchanged. "Not so much as he used to," offered Charles.

Betsy piped in, "That's because he's getting tired of —"

"Late nights," Rebecca cut in smoothly. "Mr. Riley, would you care for some more bread?"

"Yes, thank you. It's excellent." He wished he could praise the young cook's other efforts, but the roast was overdone to his taste, while the potatoes roasted with it had a distinct crunch of rawness in their middle. Alex Sawtell didn't seem to mind: true to Charles' prediction, he was methodically working his way through every unclaimed comestible on the table. Well, it's not like he stopped to talk. He and his mother Abby barely spoke throughout the entire meal, but seemed taciturn by nature, not unfriendly.

"Sam made the bread. He's the finest baker in town," Betsy said. "He made me a cake for my birthday. Oh, it was lovely! And so big even Alex couldn't finish it all. First birthday cake I ever had. When's your birthday, Mr. Riley?"

"October twenty-seventh," Jamie admitted.

"But that's just a few weeks away! Charles, do you think Sam will make a cake for Mr. Riley?"

"That's really not—"

"Of course he will, poppet," said Charles with a smile. "And there'll be Christmas puddings in December, and a Twelfth Night cake after that. You'll be so fat by Easter we'll have to roll you to church."

Betsy giggled. "That's what happened to you, Charles. I bet you were a scarecrow before you and Sam—"

"Sam is Charles' best friend, Mr. Riley," Rebecca interrupted.

"They both used to work for the Duke of Enderton, until— Ow!" Betsy, within kicking distance of Rebecca, rubbed her leg beneath the table and changed her mind about what she was going to say. "Cor. A duke. What was that like, Charles? Is they much richer than earls?"

"Richer than this earl, I'm sure," Mr. Symmons muttered from the head of the table. Perhaps his lordship was in straits after all. But if so, why the expensive flowers everywhere? Nothing seemed to make sense in this household.

Rebecca ignored him. "I'm sure it's bewildering to find yourself in the middle of conversations about people you don't know. Now, if Betsy might stop chattering for a few minutes, perhaps we could get to know you a little better. You're from Yorkshire, Mr. Riley?"

"Please, Jamie. Yes. I wasn't born there, but my mother and I lived near York for many years."

"And does your mother still live there?" Rebecca passed the bread basket again, and Jamie paused while he cut off another slice.

"No, I'm afraid she passed away in the spring."

"How awful!" Betsy's eyes got huge in her thin face. "My mum died, too, but I don't really remember her, 'cept that she wouldn't wake up no matter how hard I shook her. But that might have been when she was still alive, because they say she drank blue ruin 'til her liver rotted out. Was your mum like that?"

"Betsy!" Rebecca exclaimed, aghast. Charles, on the other hand, looked to be holding back inappropriate laughter.

"It's all right, Rebecca, she doesn't mean any harm," Jamie said. "No, Betsy, my mother had consumption." The young girl looked bewildered, so he tried putting it in her terms. "That means her lungs, er, rotted out, but it wasn't from anything she did. She just got sick."

Betsy nodded in comprehension. "Uncle Tony says as how the earl's sick, but he sure looks fine to me."

"Uncle Tony?" Mrs. Symmons deigned to enter the conversation for the first time. "We do not discuss that man here. Mrs. Wyss found Betsy crying in the street about a month ago, and brought her into our household. So far, we've been unsuccessful in our attempts to track down any of her legitimate relatives."

Something in her voice, and the grim look on Rebecca's face, made Jamie doubt they had looked very hard.

Mrs. Symmons was right: the chimney did smoke, Jamie found when he went up to bed. He tried opening the window, but the draft then pulled the smoke directly across his face. Jamie burrowed under the covers and tried to sleep anyway, only to wake up sometime later overheated and gasping for air. With a cough that ended in a long sigh, Jamie got up and closed the damper, smothering the fire. He could do without it tonight, but when winter came this was going to be a problem.

As Jamie crossed over to the window to close it, he became aware of a commotion outside and groped for his spectacles to see what was going on. An ornate landau, much too flash in design for Jamie's taste, was pulled up at the earl's gate, and in the light of its lanterns Jamie could see two men arguing passionately, their words indistinct but the tone obviously heated. The height and build of the taller man gave him away as the Earl of St. Joseph. The second man was a little smaller, but still finely built. Lamplight glinted off his hatless golden curls, and silhouetted his chiseled profile. The golden man was apparently trying to get the earl back into the carriage, and the earl was refusing to go, his voice rising almost to a shout before he looked around and lowered his tones.

They conversed more quietly for a moment, and then the smaller man seemed to be pleading coquettishly with the earl. Jamie watched, mouth open, as with a gloved hand the man reached up and caressed the earl's face, stroked his hair—like a—a *lover* Jamie was thinking, and just as Jamie's numb brain formed the word, the earl bent suddenly and kissed the other man full on the mouth. The golden man clung to him for a long moment, and then the earl stepped away, breaking the kiss, his head shaking in negation. The other man stamped his foot and called something, but the earl walked swiftly through the gate and up the stairs, and even at the top of the house Jamie could feel the vibrations from the slam of the front door. The carriage door closed with an answering bang, the vehicle sped away into the night, and then silence descended on the house.

Well. That explains the servant problem, Jamie thought, running his fingers through his hair in bemusement. He sat at the desk and lay his head on his folded arms, thinking. He supposed he should be shocked, and on some level he was. As a historian, he was aware that such matters were in some places and times tolerated, even encouraged. Ancient Greece, of course, being the classic example: Alexander and Hephaistion. Socrates and Alcibiades. Zeus and whomever he could get his godly hands on. Later times, too. Wasn't Michelangelo supposed to have loved men?

Here in England, there was poor Edward II and his Piers Gaveston — and look what his countrymen had done to them. Jamie closed his eyes, recalling something even closer to home. What was his name? The seminary student who had come to help out Mr. Caswell, the vicar, the summer before Jamie had turned seventeen. William Parks. He had been charged by the vicar with showing Will around the area, and they'd quickly become close. Once, caught by a summer storm, they had squeezed together under a hedge for shelter: even now, he could feel the heat of the other man's body pressed close against him, recall the breathless moment when he'd been sure Will was going to kiss him, the heart-stopping combination of confusion and delight he'd felt. But the clergyman-in-training had remembered himself in time, and the moment passed.

Jamie chuckled to himself now, thinking of Mrs. Symmons' doleful warning. Lock your door, indeed. If the golden man in the landau was at all representative of the earl's taste, Jamie felt he should be quite safe from his lordship's attentions. Which was, in its own way, something of a pity: Stephen Clair was a damned attractive man.

He shook his head at the ridiculous thought and went back to bed.

Chapter Three

*T*he next morning, Charles opened the door across the hall from the morning room with a flourish. "You'll be working here, in the library."

Jamie tried not to gape. His senses duly noted the beauty of the room: rich, dark red velvet draperies echoed the chief color of the intricate Turkey carpet on the floor; the great mahogany desk standing proud on clawed lion's feet; a few library tables set near the fireplace for comfortable study. But his main impression was of books. There must be hundreds, perhaps even thousands of them. Tall bookcases lined the walls, all mahogany to match the desk but otherwise a blend of old and new, glass-fronted and open, some reaching to the ceiling and some barely shoulder-high. He looked at the abundance of volumes with hunger. Surely, he could take some time to browse, but not yet.

Jamie dragged his eyes away from the bookcases and looked at the clutter of paper and envelopes in haphazard piles all over the surface of the desk. An ink pot had spilled its contents over half of them, and he shuddered to think that the lovely wood beneath must be stained as well. Perhaps Mr. or Mrs. Symmons might have a preparation that could clean it? "Good heavens. Where shall I start?"

"Oh, wherever." Charles waved a careless hand at the mess. "See what you can do with the correspondence first. I did some rough sorting of it for you. Stephen—his lordship has been missing important engagements. He desperately needs some sort of schedule."

"Right. I'll see what I can do."

Still, the valet hesitated in the doorway. "Um, did you sleep well last night?"

"Fine, thank you."

"No disturbances?"

"Oh." Jamie thought of the scene he had witnessed from his window and flushed, not knowing what to say.

"I would hate to think you might leave us quickly because you— because you don't approve of—ah, having your sleep disturbed." Charles' face was not created for stealth: his worry showed clearly.

"There was a bit of an argument outside," Jamie said cautiously, "but I don't consider his lordship's personal life any of my business."

Charles sagged with relief. "Some are more judgmental. Like the Symmonses. They were with Stephen's brother, and are set to get a generous pension if they make it to thirty years' service. They despise him, but he still hasn't the heart to get rid of them. Besides, Stephen has had difficulty keeping staff, even when he can. I'm afraid the rest of us are here because we'd have trouble getting posts elsewhere."

That made sense. Betsy, the street urchin. Abby Sawtell, the female coachman. Rebecca Wyss, too beautiful not to be a threat to any mistress. And Charles himself? He had an idea about that, and decided to test it out. "His lordship seems to have a big heart. But in your case, I should imagine a good reference from the Duke of Enderton would get you a post anywhere you liked."

The valet grinned. "I should imagine it would, if I had one." He put up his chin. "I'm afraid Sam and I were found together, and sacked immediately. It put Stephen's back up when he heard gossip about it, so he hired me and convinced his Aunt Matilda to stake Sam for the bakery. One of the best investments she's ever made, and that's saying something."

"Well, if last night's bread is anything to go on, I'm sure he's wildly successful. Good for him."

"You're very understanding." There was a hint of a question in the remark, and a discreet pause for an answer.

Jamie took a breath. The valet had certainly been honest with him. "I suppose I do understand. For half my youth I thought I had a crush on the daughter of the local squire—and then our vicar acquired a handsome young assistant, and suddenly Miss Loring wasn't quite so important. It was all fantasy, of course: he was as out of reach as the squire's daughter, so it didn't seem any more wicked to dream about him."

The valet nodded understanding. "So, Jamie-me-lad, that's our little household of misfits. Think you can stomach it? "

Jamie thought about his answer. "There's a lot to like here," he said at last. "And for the rest, I have a simple philosophy. If I see something I don't like, I try to make it better."

Charles smiled. "Oh? Any plans yet?"

"Wait and see, Charles," Jamie said. "Just wait and see."

"I like him." Charles wasted no time tracking down Rebecca, finding her polishing the silver in the pantry off the kitchen.

"He seems a nice young man," Rebecca agreed, handing him a cloth. "Too bad he's not better-looking. Get his lordship's mind off that dreadful kept man of his."

Charles obligingly began work on a chased silver teapot. "Julian Jeffries is on his way out, they're always fighting now. It's just a matter of time."

"Yes, and if his lordship scrapes up the funds to pay off Mr. Julian's contract, we won't get our salaries this quarter, either." She held a spoon up to the light, looking for spots. "And the next one might be even worse. I don't care how gorgeous they are, his lordship's got dreadful taste in men."

"I've been with him a long time," Charles reminded her, "he'll make it up to us eventually, and then some. Stephen's especially generous when he's feeling guilty. But you're right, I've often thought it would be better for all of us—especially him—if he'd only settle down with some proper young man. And our Jamie's quite pleasant looking," the valet offered, and Rebecca laughed.

"He's a little sparrow, and you know it. And his lordship prefers peacocks, no matter how they screech. Besides, he comes across as such a respectable young man. It's doubtful his tastes even run in his lordship's direction."

Charles grinned, thinking of the vicar's assistant. "Without betraying any confidences, on that point you might be mistaken. And as to his looks—as a wise man once said: *If I see something I don't like, I try to make it better.* There's definitely room for improvement. A nicer haircut, better clothes. Maybe get rid of the spectacles."

Rebecca shrugged. "He'll still be a sparrow. But it can't hurt to try."

After the valet took his leave, Jamie sank into the leather chair with a sigh of contentment. There was a lot to do, but he liked a challenge. He reached for a stack of envelopes. Charles, in an effort to be helpful, had sorted the envelopes by size and then color, which, Jamie thought, was not in the end of particular use. He sighed. Who were all these people, and why on earth didn't they date their invitations? With much searching, Jamie found a few blank pieces of paper and began to make lists of names on one, and to rough out a calendar on another. Just after noon he was satisfied enough with his progress to get up, stretch his legs, and finally allow himself to browse the books that lined the library in neat, orderly rows.

In which, he quickly realized, the books were sorted by size, and then color, with absolutely no consideration of subject or author. Jamie groaned.

"Giving up already?" his lordship said from the doorway.

His secretary waved at the shelves. "Do I recognize the hand of Mr. West?"

Stephen shrugged. "I leave the decorative touches up to him. He has an eye for them."

"Books are hardly for decoration, my lord!" said Jamie, appalled. "How on earth can you find anything in here?"

"I have a foolproof system, Mr. Riley. I simply don't read." The earl burst into laughter. "You should see the look on your face! And yet Charles just informed me you're hard to shock."

Jamie ignored him. "You have a wonderful library here, my lord. It just needs to be organized properly, and perhaps catalogued."

"Seems like a waste of time to me, Mr. Riley, but if it pleases, then go ahead."

"Especially the rare books."

"The what?" Suddenly he had the earl's attention.

Jamie cleared his throat. "There are some lovely items here, my lord. First editions, a Second Folio of Shakespeare, an early English bible. Not Tyndale, but not much later. Even a few illuminated manuscripts."

"And these are worth money? Books?" His lordship sounded skeptical.

"Oh yes, my lord. Quite a lot, some of them. Surely you've heard of the sale of the Duke of Roxburghe's library?"

"Yes, he lived right here in Hanover Square. Didn't something go for some ungodly sum?"

Jamie nodded. "One volume, a Boccaccio, fetched more than two thousand pounds. And there was a second that sold for over a thousand. I'm not saying you have anything quite so rare here, but in aggregate —"

"Then what are you waiting for, Mr. Riley? I believe my library needs cataloguing."

Jamie smiled. "Right away, my lord. But first, since you're here, I have some questions about your correspondence."

"Oh, I suppose. I was just going to dine with Julian. He can wait."

"I won't keep you long, I promise."

The earl grinned. "Serve him right if you do."

They spent a quarter hour going over the list of names Jamie had compiled, establishing who was whom, and ranking them by the order in which their invitations should be accepted.

"There, are we through?" Stephen inquired at last.

"Well, my lord, that would about cover my questions about your social correspondence." Jamie hesitated.

"Yes?" The earl raised his dark brows to effect.

"There were a number of other notices among the invitations, my lord. Most of them reminders about accounts due."

Stephen sighed. "Bottom drawer on the left, Mr. Riley. I'll deal with them when I can. Now, are we finished?" He glanced toward the door. "The Golden One awaits." For someone who didn't mind keeping his lover waiting, he certainly seemed eager to get to him.

Jamie nodded, and with a courteous "Good day" the earl swept from the room. Once alone, the young man sighed, gathered the dunning letters into a neat pile, then reached for the designated drawer. It stuck for a moment, and he had to tug hard to get it open. It was easy to see why — once opened, the drawer was revealed to be crammed to overflowing with bills. He pulled out a handful, and blanched with shock as he started to add up the sums involved. The earl's finances were none of his affair, he had told himself yesterday. But they had to be someone's, or they'd all be in the street before long. Jamie sighed, and reached for a fresh sheet of paper.

Chapter Four

"*A* personal secretary? What the devil do you need a personal secretary for?"

Julian Jeffries' allure was such that despite their recent troubles, Stephen's first impulse was to kiss the petulance off his face. The dining room of White's club was hardly the place for kisses, so he settled for a verbal response. "I suppose I don't, really," he admitted. "Although if he helps keep me from forgetting important events like Aunt Matilda's birthday, he'll pay for himself in a fortnight."

"Really, Stephen, how often does Auntie M. have a birthday, anyway?"

The most perfect pout becomes tiresome in time, especially when coupled with such nonsensical speech. "She does invite me to other events, you know. And Robert hired Mr. Riley to teach his boys. I felt responsible." Stephen paused to allow his companion the opportunity to express sympathy for the loss of his family. Julian's lack of commiseration didn't just annoy, it hurt. Didn't Julian care for anything beyond himself?

But once again, the actor missed his cue, leaning forward over the starched white tablecloth with a wicked gleam in his eyes. "So your secretary's the donnish type, is he—spectacles and thinning scalp?"

"Spectacles, indeed," Stephen said. "But he does have a full head of hair."

The waiter arrived with their post-prandial brandy, and Julian was distracted into a discussion of whether there wasn't something better available in the cellars. With prodding, the servant admitted to a very fine, hundred-year-old cognac.

"We'll have that, then," Julian said. "Just bring the bottle."

Stephen winced, and the waiter paused to give him a chance to overrule the decision. Oh, hell, what did it matter? He couldn't afford the more pedestrian choice, either—and the fight that ensued whenever he tried to deny the Golden One anything was never worth it. He waved agreement to the waiter, who nodded and left. Still, it would be nice to puncture Julian's vanity, if only a little, and by now he knew the actor's weakest spot. "Mr. Riley does have the nicest skin," he allowed, "but they do tend to glow at that age, don't they?"

The sea-green eyes narrowed almost to slits. "A mere boy? You didn't mention that."

"Beyond the spotty phase, of course. But he can't be twenty-four, if that."

"Ha. I thought you meant much younger. I myself have barely turned twenty-seven."

Stephen let that one slide. In the forgiving illumination of the club, it might almost be true. Give or take half a decade.

Jamie sat at the large kitchen table at luncheon, barely fiddling with his soup, which was thin and tasteless anyway. How could the earl have got his finances in such appalling order? Still puzzling it over, he hardly noticed the others at the table until with a purposeful glance at Charles, Rebecca suddenly skidded her elbow sideways, neatly dumping the remainder of her bowl over the front of Jamie's shirt.

"Oh! How clumsy of me!" Rebecca cried, wiping at the greasy stain with her napkin. "I'm so sorry—I've quite ruined your shirt. What are we going to do?"

Charles picked up his cue. "Don't worry, Rebecca," he said, before Jamie could brush off her concern. "I'm sure I can replace it, if Jamie doesn't mind a hand-me-down?" He turned to the dripping Jamie and smiled hopefully. "I'm a dab hand with a needle, really, and Stephen is always giving me his cast-offs to make over for myself and Sam. If you would allow me?"

Rebecca widened her pale blue eyes. "Oh Charles, that would be perfect! Jamie?"

They both turned to Jamie with such eager faces that it would have been churlish to refuse. "That's very kind of you," he said. "But really, I don't want to put you to the trouble—"

"It's no trouble at all," Charles assured him.

Rebecca allowed a frown to trouble her perfect features. "That takes care of the shirt. But I'm the one who was clumsy, I should do something to make it up to you." She clapped her hands, as if an idea had suddenly occurred to her. "I know! Christopher, my fiancé, lets me cut his hair for him — he says I do a fine job of it, too. Jamie, if you'd let me—I notice yours is getting in your eyes a bit?"

Again, it was impossible to say no. In the blink of an eye, it seemed, Charles had whisked Jamie away upstairs to change into one of his other two shirts, taking the soiled garment to use as a pattern for the new one. Then back down to the kitchen, where Rebecca was waiting with a towel and scissors. She draped the towel over Jamie's shoulders.

"There, now. Let's have those spectacles out of the way," she said.

Jamie obligingly slipped off his tinted specs and set them carefully on the table. "Ready," he said with a smile, lifting his unprotected eyes.

"Oh, my," Rebecca said softly.

Charles closed his jaw with an effort. "Perhaps a waistcoat, too," he mused. "Something *blue*."

After his haircut, Jamie remembered to track down Mr. Symmons, for advice on how to deal with the ink stain on the library desk. He found the butler in the morning room, polishing a collection of Meissen figurines, handling each fragile piece with delicacy and grace. "Oh, there you are, Mr. Symmons. If I might have a word?"

He glowered at Jamie's interruption. "Mr. Riley?"

Jamie smiled. "Yes, Mr. Symmons, I'd like to speak with you... oh, my. How lovely." He reached for a tiny shepherdess, only to have his hand knocked away with surprising violence.

"Please don't touch those, Mr. Riley. They belong... *belonged* to the Countess."

"His lordship's mother? Or Lord Robert's wife?" Jamie asked, nursing his hand.

"Lady Mary," the butler said, picking out another figure with care.

The last countess, then. "I met her, you know," Jamie said. "She was a lovely woman, very kind to me. And to see her with her children..."

"They were all lovely. A lovely family. Lady Mary. Lord Robert. And his little lordship, the viscount, although we only ever called him Master William. Master Peter—such a devil." His voice shook. "Master Stephen, you can guess who *he* was named after. His stammer was just beginning to— All of them. To think they're gone... all of them *gone*... and that *creature* in their place."

"I suppose they disapproved of him as well," Jamie guessed, his tone sympathetic.

The butler, regaining control over himself with an effort, shook his head brusquely. "They adored him. They were that good, to overlook his many faults." He looked Jamie full in the face, suspicious. "Oh, I see. I suppose you think I should show more respect to him, for their sakes?"

"No, Mr. Symmons," Jamie replied. "We all grieve in our own ways. Honor their memory as you see fit." He paused, to let that sink in. "But if you have a moment, I'd like to ask you about ink stains, if I may."

Chapter Five

*I*f I see something I don't like, I try to make it better. Three days in St. Joseph House had taught Jamie that he had a lot of work in front of him, but he remained optimistic. If the reduced number of slamming doors was anything to go on, Mr. Symmons was already rethinking his attitude toward the earl, and that not-insignificant victory gave him the courage to take on other matters. This morning, his fourth in the house, he set his chin with determination as he made his way down to the kitchen for breakfast.

He'd lingered up in his room, and now, as he'd hoped, Rebecca was the only person present, the rest already busy with their morning tasks.

"Good morning," Jamie said, taking his place at the table.

"You're up late this morning." The cook set down her chopping knife and crossed to the iron cook stove, scowling down at a copper-bottomed pot. "I'm afraid the porridge wasn't improved by standing. Not that it was much to begin with. Luckily, Sam sent over some of yesterday's pastries again."

Jamie shuddered to think of what their lot would be like if Charles didn't have a baker for a lover. His contributions of pastries and meat pies were keeping them all alive. "You know," he said casually, "my mother always added salt to her porridge. And she swore by stirring it constantly while it boiled. I never remember a single lump."

"Salt? Really?" Rebecca glanced up. "I'll write that down." She pulled a small book and stub of a pencil from her apron. "How much? A half cup?"

"No, just a pinch." Jamie held up his fingers to demonstrate, and she nodded and wrote it down. He burrowed into the basket of pastries on the table, emerging with a lemon tart. Bless Sam. "You, um. You're new at this, aren't you?"

Rebecca poured them each a cup of coffee and joined him at the table. "I suppose it shows. But I am getting better."

If so, Jamie felt very sorry for what the household must have endured previously. "If it's not too personal a question, how did you end up with the post?"

"Oh, that." She bit her lip, looking like an illustration in a children's morality primer, under 'Guilt.' "I had to leave my last post, as a lady's maid for Miss Feldspar, because her brother — well, anyway, I was to receive a good letter of recommendation. The Feldspars had to let their cook go at the same time, and somehow the envelopes got switched. Once I realized I had the letter for Mrs. Crosby, and that 'Cook' was never mentioned by name, I decided to claim it for my own. I hoped that spending all my time in the kitchen might keep me out of sight of the sorts who made my life difficult at my other posts." Rebecca smiled. "As luck would have it, I found a place with Lord St. Joseph, so that's rather moot anyway." The smile faded. "But if I can't get up to snuff, I'll be sacked the first night his lordship decides to stay in to dine."

"Doesn't he? Ever?"

"Not yet, but I've only been here two months."

Jamie blinked, trying to imagine a world where one dined out every evening. "I think Sam would help you out if you asked him. And can't you get a cookbook? There are several excellent ones available in the shops."

Rebecca stared into her coffee. "His lordship was a little short last quarter-day, so I haven't two farthings to rub together. And all my savings, such as they are, are invested. Christopher—that's my fiancé—he and I are saving up to buy an inn some day."

"Couldn't we buy a cookbook from the household money? It seems a reasonable expense."

"Heavens, no. We need every bit we can scrape together just to—" She flushed, breaking off suddenly.

Jamie thought of the overstuffed drawer in the library desk. "Keep the creditors from repossessing the silver? It's a mess, I agree."

"I wasn't sure you knew." She blew out a sigh of relief. "It's worse than a mess. And we're so short-staffed that everyone has to pitch in to keep the house in order—unless we can find another housemaid, I'll be too busy cleaning windows to ever learn how to cook properly."

"I have some ideas about economy, if his lordship will listen to me. I think we can even squeeze in another housemaid or two just on what the butcher's been overcharging us. But as to you: let me search the library. There are likely a few cookbooks in there."

Rebecca's blue eyes widened. "Borrow a book from the earl? I wouldn't dare!"

He looked at her in surprise. The Earl of St. Joseph was really quite nice, but then again, Rebecca probably hadn't had the opportunity to speak with him very often. "Don't worry, if anything happens to it, I'll take full responsibility."

"If you're sure..."

"I am."

"Then, thank you." Rebecca gave him a sidelong glance, a slow smile spreading over her face. "You know, I'm a bit nearsighted myself. I'd have a hard time reading a cookbook, unless, perhaps, I could borrow your spectacles from time to time?"

"Anytime you need them," Jamie vowed, and wondered why Rebecca looked so pleased.

"Well, hello Mr. Riley." Stephen swept into the library later that day, and found his secretary perched on a rolling wooden ladder, examining some dusty old tome of Robert's. He watched with appreciation as Jamie descended: Charles had been right about the young man's chief asset.

"Yes, my lord?" Jamie seemed nervous to be the center of the earl's attention, but the resultant pink flush lit his features nicely.

"I got a letter from Aunt Matilda! She's ready to forgive me, so *who* does St. Catherine look like?"

Jamie looked away. "It doesn't really matter, my lord. Pretend you have a secret and she'll be all the more intrigued. But if you really want to lay it on thick—"

"Yes?"

"St. Catherine has the most exquisitely beautiful face I've ever seen. You might say her bone structure is exactly like your aunt's."

Stephen laughed in delight, and clapped Jamie on the shoulder. "You're a treasure, Mr. Riley." He looked around the room, thinking it was an attractive place, and really should be used more often. "How's the cataloguing going? Find anything that will, uh, add to the kitty?" And help him pay off Julian's contract, if decided he needed to. Keeping a lover on call, especially one as skillful and enticing as Julian Jeffries, had its definite advantages, but the actor's tantrums were wearing thin.

"Over here, my lord." Jamie hurried over to a table near the window, where several items were neatly stacked. "Here's that Shakespeare I mentioned before, and a first edition of Donne. They're both in wonderful condition, but very replaceable, should you ever be in a position—"

"Why bother? I haven't cracked a book since Oxford."

Jamie let out a sigh. "You went to Oxford?" he said with quiet reverence.

The earl's full lips curved into a wicked smile. "Only because my father wanted desperately for me to go to Cambridge." He shrugged. "I quite enjoyed it, however. I'm not a total idiot," he added parenthetically, "I just seem to have other things to do with my time. What else do you have here?" He picked up a small leather-bound book, and Jamie, perhaps thinking of Mr. Symmons and the shepherdess, took it away from him gently.

"This, my lord, is a medieval manuscript, a Book of Hours. Look at the hand-lettering, and the illustrations — masterfully done." He opened the book to demonstrate. The pictures inside were stiff and colorful, with a preponderance of blue, red and gold. They seemed to alternate between religious scenes and illustrations from daily life: on one page the Annunciation; on the next a lively country fair. Jamie pushed his spectacles up his nose, his eyes shining. "It was possibly made in York, even, if this cathedral meant to be York Minster. But it's hard to tell, the pictures aren't necess—"

"Worth anything?" the earl cut him off.

Jamie stared. "Worth quite a lot, my lord," he admitted with obvious reluctance. "Even with the broken binding. But, unlike the others, it's quite irreplaceable."

Stephen felt a flash of pain, remembering how proud Robert had been of his collection. He could picture his brother here at the mahogany desk, glowing with pleasure as he turned the pages of the Book of Hours. His secretary had that same look now, as he gazed down at the small volume in his hand. "Irreplaceable? Well, then. We don't have to sell them all at once," he said at last. "Could you put together enough old books to the value of, say..." What did he owe on Julian's contract? "...a thousand guineas, without dipping into the irreplaceables?"

"Oh, yes, my lord, I think so. And I haven't been through a quarter of your collection yet."

Stephen smiled. "Well, get back to work then." He was almost to the door when Jamie put up a hand to stop him.

"Wait, my lord," he called out. The earl turned back, an elegant black eyebrow lifted. Jamie flushed. "Since you're here. I've been wondering if I might make some suggestions. About the household budget."

"I wasn't aware there was one, Mr. Riley," the earl admitted cheerfully. "I assume, if there is, it's Mrs. Symmons' province. But you have my blessing to speak with her, if it pleases you."

"Thank you, my lord, I shall. I think some economy might be in order."

His lordship's frown was mocking. "Put me on bread and water, will you? Well, as long as the bread is from Sam's—"

"Please, my lord, be serious for a moment," Jamie begged. "If you would just listen to a few of my ideas?"

The earl hesitated, then nodded, deviltry lurking in his eyes. "I will, but not now. According to the schedule my frightfully efficient personal secretary has created for me, I'm nearly late for a musicale at Aunt Matilda's. Since my librarian has kept me longer than I expected, I'm afraid I don't have time to meet with the household steward right now. Perhaps tomorrow, after lunch?"

"Yes, my lord." Jamie smiled in gratitude, giving Stephen his first glimpse of the dimple.

Not so bad, thought the earl with approval. Not my type, of course, but that smile— "Have a good evening, Mr. Riley," he said, once again heading out the door. "And tell Charles not to wait up." If he were going to be able to rid himself of the Golden One soon, he may as well get some use out of him tonight.

Lady Matilda Clair stood at the top of the wide marble staircase that led down to her ballroom, bemoaning to herself the high-waisted, slim gowns of these modern days. Practical to conserve fabric considering the years of war they'd just been through, but the dress of the last century had been impressive indeed. There was a time—she didn't want to think of the exact year—she'd had panniers so wide her skirts had brushed both sides of the stairway as she descended. Now *that* was an entrance. Still, the light reflecting from the crystal beads on her bodice gave off a pleasing sparkle, and her painted India fan would be the most fashionable in the room.

Matilda raised her opera glasses and surveyed the room below. A longtime veteran of society campaigning, she knew to scout the terrain for intelligence before advancing. Signorina Isabella di Sarno, the lovely Italian soprano who would be making her London debut tonight at Matilda's musicale, was throwing back her head to laugh at something Lord Lovington was whispering in her ear. Isabella would be the toast of the town: the silken swirl of ebony hair coiled on top of her head was rumored to reach her knees, and not an eye in the room would be able to tear itself from her mobile, cherry-ripe lips once she began singing. It was rumored that she could even carry a tune. From the possessive manner in which Lord Lovington held her arm, it was clear the soprano had made her English debut of another kind in his boudoir last night. Matilda hoped Lovington had enjoyed himself, for he was unlikely to get a second private performance: Signorina di Sarno's wide black eyes were busy searching the crowd for her next conquest.

Tonight, the ballroom was set up for the performance to come: the wide expanse usually reserved for dancing was arranged with low couches on which her guests could comfortably flirt behind their fans under cover of music. Matilda was well-satisfied with the stage she had designed for Signorina di Sarno at one end of the room: she had borrowed several prop columns from the Theatre Royal, festooned them with ivy, and strategically placed a number of her own classical busts among them. A grateful artist, whose investments she had been directing for some time now, had provided a painted backdrop of moonlit Italian mountains, and the effect was that the soprano would be singing among the ruins of a Roman temple deep in the Italian countryside.

Most of the guests were still on their feet and mingling, but a number were already taking advantage of the couches to pursue their evening's goals: Major Burke was, as always, seeking a warmer bed than that provided by his wife; Patrick Howard a discreet loan to cover his rocketing gambling losses. Matilda thought it was time to take the Howard lad in hand: if he had anything left of the impressive inheritance he'd received from his second wife, she had just the opportunity for him to buy into. Perhaps they would talk privately later.

And there, just arriving, was her great-nephew Stephen. She sighed. Stuck to him like a boil was that dreadful Julian Jeffries. Her nephew, too, was in desperate need of financial advice, but he was in no shape yet to take it. Always a bit of a playboy, in the months since Robert's death he had thrown himself into vice with a vengeance, and she calculated that it would already take some years to settle the ensuing debts. At least he would always have the St. Joseph estate to back him. Matilda had helped her brother, Stephen's grandfather, tie the capital up into so many legal knots and entails that even the owner couldn't get his hands on the principle without years of court battles.

It was time to make her entrance. Matilda signaled to the orchestra, and they struck up a fanfare to announce her descent. Even at eighty years of age, she could hold a crowd's attention. Good carriage was a must, of course, but the diamond tiara she had copied from an ancient Roman original for the occasion didn't hurt. She quite expected to see many more like it in the coming weeks.

Matilda made her way through the crowd, stopping for a word here and there. By God, she would have made twice the duchess of Lady Alice Bywater, if she'd consented to marry George when he'd asked her. Lady Bywater still dressed like the simple country lass she'd been fifty years ago, and it seemed too late to change her now. Inevitably she found herself in front of her nephew. "You're looking peaked, my boy," the grand doyenne told Stephen. "Perhaps it's the company you keep."

Julian, resplendent in a new waistcoat embroidered in a delicate green to match his eyes, smiled with faint reproof at his lover. "I've been telling him he'd be happier if he'd just pay more attention to me. His neglect has been shocking."

Stephen shrugged. "Still trying to get my household in order. I don't know how Robert and Mary managed so well on the allowance from the estate. I've heard the harvests were especially good this year; I don't suppose there's any chance—"

"There isn't," Aunt Matilda said. "You've a very generous portion, Stephen. If you weren't gambling like a fool, and spending every loose farthing on entertainments that are well beneath you—" She cast a significant glance at the actor.

"Oh, come now, Auntie," Julian said, with the smile that doubtlessly fluttered hearts in the cheapest rows. "The gambles you've taken in your investments are legendary. Surely you can't begrudge a man for emulating you?"

Matilda prided herself on having a remarkably stiff back for a woman of her years. "I took calculated risks on business ventures that I knew had a good chance of success. I never risked a fortune on the flip of a card."

Stephen seemed relieved to see a friend approaching, suggesting that his luck had failed to turn yet again at the faro tables last night. "Excuse me, Aunt Matilda—I haven't seen Drake since the wedding, and need to offer my congratulations. Julian?"

The actor tossed his golden curls. "Not just now. Auntie and I can have a comfortable coze." When they were alone, Julian leaned his head closer to Matilda's. "Darling, you are so wonderful with financial advice. I'm really at my wits' end."

"Not such a long journey, was it?"

He smiled brightly. "Such a tease you are, Auntie. I fear I must speak plainly: as much as I adore Stephen, it's difficult to make ends meet lately. He would be so heartbroken if I were forced to look elsewhere for help. Isn't there anything you can do, for the sake of his happiness?" He batted his remarkable eyes.

"You know, Julian, perhaps I can help." One crabbed hand delved into the reticule she always wore on her wrist, and emerged proffering a single coin.

Julian's smile faltered. "Half a crown? What am I supposed to do with that?"

"Oh, but *darling*," Aunt Matilda said, "as you well know, it's the fee for an hour's rental of one of the freelance rooms at Madame Novotny's. You won't get the price you commanded twenty years ago, but a couple of nights on your knees should see you back on your feet."

Julian was speechless just long enough: probably trying to decide which was the greater insult: the implication, however true, that he had begun his career in a brothel; or the insinuation that his age was somewhat greater than he claimed. Not giving him the chance to come up with a stinging reply, Matilda pressed the coin into his palm and patted him on the arm.

"Run along now, *darling*," she murmured. "There's enough left of the evening that you could even pay for that dreadful waistcoat yourself."

"Look at us," Julian said later that night, in the house in Floral Street, having refused to take Aunt Matilda's excellent advice. It wasn't hard to follow his direction: as soon as Stephen had installed him here, the actor had festooned the bedroom with mirrors, allowing them to view their activities from a variety of clever angles. Stephen approved of the effect, less so of the many shades of red satin, silk and velvet Julian had upholstered every available surface with. It was meant to be sensuous and erotic, he supposed, but it was rather like living inside a surgeon's tent. "See?" the actor said again, "We look so good together."

It was hard to disagree. Even fully dressed, the contrast of Julian's golden fairness with his own dark smolder was striking, and once they were naked it would be even more so. Striking. Titillating. Arousing. Stephen watched in the glass as he bent his head to lick at Julian's neck. "I need you tonight," he whispered, nuzzling one perfectly-formed ear. "I need to lose myself inside you."

"Inside me?" Julian laughed. "Not tonight, sweetheart. You were so rough last time, I don't feel quite recovered even yet."

It was your idea to play Mad Captain and Innocent Cabin Boy, Stephen wanted to point out. But it wouldn't do any good. Julian, as a lover, practiced a very studied unpredictability, and part of his allure was that Stephen never knew what would be forbidden or insisted upon on any given occasion. He sighed. "What did you have in mind?"

"Oh, I'm feeling particularly generous tonight." Julian's smile was arch.

Then give me what I want. He held his tongue. No need to pick a fight. "Meaning?"

The Golden One tugged at Stephen's cravat, undoing Charles' careful work in an instant. "You've been far too tense lately. So first, I'm going to relax you with a nice massage. Then I've been saving a little surprise for you." He stopped undressing Stephen long enough to remove an object from a drawer in the bedside stand.

Stephen stared. The form was something he was quite familiar with, but it was disconcerting to see it detached from its usual place. The size and shape were exact, to the very veins and wrinkles. It even had a slightly perceptible curve to the left. "That looks exactly like —"

"Me, of course." He pressed the dildo into Stephen's hand.

"How in Hades did you make it?"

"I had my dresser Bertie help me make the mold from plaster of Paris, then we cast it with pink beeswax. Incredibly lifelike, don't you think?"

"I've had no complaints about your stamina, Julian." He picked his cravat up from the floor with his other hand, stuffing it into his pocket. "A dildo is really not necessary."

The actor's lips tightened. "We've used toys before. I thought you'd be pleased."

"Pleased? I'm wondering if it isn't more that this way, you don't even have to make love to me yourself. In which case I'm hardly getting my money's worth."

"To get your money's worth," Julian said, gritting his teeth, "there would have to be some money involved, wouldn't there?"

Stephen thought of the mounds of bills cramming the desk drawer in the library at home. "The house, the carriage, the endless *clothes*, for God's sake. They don't count for anything?"

"You haven't paid my allowance in six weeks."

"I haven't paid my staff in six months."

Julian stamped his foot. "Oh, bugger your staff!"

In response, Stephen tossed him the dildo, not certain why he was so angry. "Julian, bugger yourself."

Chapter Six

Stephen sat at the library table after lunch the following day, thinking Mr. Riley was looking quite well. He had done something to his hair, of course, but what else? Perhaps the blue satin waistcoat. It was cut close to the secretary's body, emphasizing the elegance of his build. And the lace on his shirt, falling down to brush his knuckles, drawing attention to the small, fine-boned hands. Very distracting indeed. But it was chiefly the animation in the young man's face that drew his eye, the rapt attention he gave to the columns of figures on the table in front of him. *If Julian gave me that much attention,* he mused irrelevantly, *I'd fight dragons for him.* With an effort he dragged his mind back to what Mr. Riley was saying.

" —so even with the new housemaid, we're that much better off."

Jamie looked expectant, so he nodded. "Yes, I see. Very good, Mr. Riley, please go on." What had he been saying? Something about saving enough money by switching butchers to afford another mouth to feed. Which sounded deuced odd, but if it brought such pleasure to his secretary, he wasn't going to quibble. Maybe, if he was lucky, he'd get another glimpse of that intriguing dimple. The lace slipped down over the back of one hand, and Jamie pushed it away with the other. Well, you know what they say about small hands. Small nose, too, but hang it, the boy was compactly built all over, it wouldn't be surprising if—

"There are several other areas in which Mrs. Symmons and I think we can save considerable expense," Jamie continued. "For instance, your brandy."

Stephen blinked, aghast. Was he joking? "I need my brandy, Mr. Riley. I know it's expensive, but you can't expect me to become a teetotaler overnight, just to save some blunt."

"I don't, my lord. In fact, I was going to suggest buying more brandy in bulk, not less."

"Buying in bulk? That might save us something in the long run, but the smu — ah, traders I deal with insist on cash payment. It would be awkward to come up with the necessary sums."

Jamie hesitated. "Actually, my lord, I had something else in mind. From the evidence I've gathered, one doesn't really taste a liquor much after the first few glasses. Is that true, my lord?"

Stephen nodded. "Yes, I suppose."

"Then wouldn't it make sense to have a second decanter, next to the first? Nothing too dreadful, of course, but a nice *English* brandy, perhaps?"

He sighed, supposing he should make an effort. "All right, Mr. Riley. Two glasses of ambrosia, and then I'll drink myself to sleep on the second-best."

"And then there are the roses, my lord."

"Not negotiable."

Jamie looked up. "But surely—"

"No, Mr. Riley. Go on, please."

"My lord, Charles buys fresh roses for the household every day, year round. The expense is enormous. If we must have fresh flowers, it seems to me—"

"I can imagine how it seems to you. But Charles did me a particular favor once, and I promised him the reward of his choice."

"Perhaps, if you asked him, Charles would understand."

Oh, no. They were never going to discuss that incident again, if Stephen could help it. "I made a promise, Mr. Riley. I will not go back on it now."

"Admirable, my lord," Jamie said, sighing and crossing out a line on the sheet in front of him. "I'm sure there are other items we can economize on, instead." He looked back at his notes. "Like candles, my lord."

"Candles?"

"Yes, candles. Right now we have wax in every room, when tallow would do just as well in some places. Some of the servants' rooms, for instance."

"Some? Why not all?"

"Well, Charles sometimes sews in the evening. And Rebecca has been studying her cookbook—her eyes aren't strong, so she needs good light for that."

"And you, Mr. Riley? Don't you read in your room at night?" A picture came unbidden into his mind, of Jamie curled up in bed in his nightshirt, lace falling over his hand as he turned a page, face rapt.

"Not usually, my lord. My chimney smokes, so I tend to read in the library."

"Does it really? Perhaps it just needs sweeping. I'm sure we could afford that."

Jamie shook his head. "I tried poking an umbrella up there, to see if there might be a bird's nest or something blocking the flue. Several bricks fell out instead. I'm afraid part of the chimney has collapsed, and it will be quite a job to repair it."

"Do we have another room?" Stephen asked. There were five spacious bed chambers on his own floor, four of them unused, but surely the secretary knew what he meant. Those rooms were hardly appropriate for servants. No matter how sweet their hands.

"Not really, my lord. I like being up on the top floor, and besides, it wouldn't be suitable for me to be on the hall below with the girls. There are other rooms up top where I am, my lord, but they're being used for storage, my lord."

Oh yes. Robert and Mary's possessions, and the boys' too, of course. Five lifetimes of things Stephen couldn't bear to look at, not just yet. The change in his expression must have been apparent.

"It's all right, my lord," Jamie hurried to assure him. "I don't mind. And I've learned that if the peat is very dry, it doesn't smoke nearly so bad. I have to avoid coal, of course, which is a pity, because it's much cheaper, but on the other hand, since I'm not in there until I go to sleep, I hardly need wax candles, do I?"

Stephen found himself smiling, despite the stir of painful memories, and without thinking he reached out and squeezed Jamie's hand. His secretary wasn't such a bad sort. For a mouse.

It was cold that night, so Jamie attempted a fire again, feeling foolish. *Like this time the chimney's going to decide to draw.* Still, the peat was dry and should burn cleanly, and if he kept the blaze small, he might not get smoked like a winter ham. And in fact it wasn't too bad, at least when he first went to bed. He lay on the narrow mattress, unable to sleep. Counting his victories, wrestling with the challenges still unmet. So far, the food was better, thanks to Sam's coaching of Rebecca and a first edition of Susannah Clark's *The Frugal Housewife* he'd dug up from the library. And cheaper, too: he'd been right about the butcher, and had his suspicions about the dairyman as well. They were saving enough money just there to pay the wages of the new housemaid, Maisie. She was a find: a thin, grey ghost of a woman who worked like Sisyphus on any task put in front of her. She and Betsy got on well together, which wasn't that surprising when you consider that Betsy was motherless and Maisie had recently lost her only daughter. Maisie's presence relieved the burden on the other servants, but didn't put them ahead—yet. Where else could the household trim expense?

The candles, the brandy; why wouldn't his lordship compromise on the roses? What could the favor Charles did for him be, that he had to reward it at such expense? The cost was so enormous for the out-of-season blooms, that it would be cheaper to build a damned greenhouse and grow them at home.

He sat up in bed. Why not? It really would be cheaper, in the long run. There was plenty of room in the back garden. A billow of smoke from the fireplace cut off his ruminations. "Blast," Jamie muttered, rising to close the damper. There was a sound from somewhere below him in the house. Someone else up late? He paused to listen, ears intent, and heard the unmistakable *creak-click* of the door to the kitchen garden. Charles, deciding to join Sam? Or Rebecca, sneaking out for a rendezvous with her footman fiancé? But both were open enough about their activities that they should have ventured out at a more sensible hour.

Maybe one of them woke up with that sense of longing, he thought. *The one that hits you in the middle of the night, when you just can't stand being alone anymore...*

Lucky Charles, lucky Rebecca. To have someone to go to, when they needed it.

A few days later, the earl stopped in briefly to change his clothing before going out to dinner. Charles found dressing his master twice the task it usually was, and by the time they had decided on an ensemble the dressing room attached to Stephen's bedchamber was littered with cast offs.

"Sorry, Charles." Stephen picked up a discarded cravat from the surface of the dressing table, searching for something. "But I have to look my best tonight—I need confidence for the task ahead. Where's the box with my cufflinks?"

"Here. Did you want the jade ones?" Charles rifled through the carved wooden box, a present Robert had sent from a visit to India.

"Yes, perfect. How do I look?"

Charles regarded Stephen in the full-length mirror, satisfied with his efforts. The new jacket, of dark green wool crepe, was so tightly fitted to the earl's form that he had been sweating with exertion when he had finally shoehorned his master into it. Stephen had been vague so far on his night's plans, but said he wasn't going anywhere formal, so after some discussion they had eschewed knee breeches for a pair of sleek fawn trousers. Any dandy would be proud of the paisley waistcoat, its dark blue and green pattern discreetly enhancing the color of the jacket he wore over it. And it had taken nearly a dozen tries, but Stephen's cravat was a triumph: Charles had mastered the difficult Waterfall at last.

The valet nodded, handing over a fresh pair of gloves. "Can't remember when I've seen you look so well."

Stephen looked at his reflection, straightening his back. "Good. Expect me home by midnight. Now ask me why."

"All right, Stephen, why?" The valet held his breath while he waited for an answer.

"Because it's over with Julian—and I mean it this time. Almost certainly. Lord, what a scene." Stephen put a hand to his temple. "Any headache drops, Charles?"

"I don't think so. I can ask Mrs. Symmons. Mr. Julian—he's moving out of the house on Floral Street, then?" Charles tried not to sound too hopeful.

"Well, not just yet—the man does have a contract, after all. Just get me a brandy, will you? The good stuff, too."

Charles poured a generous measure, from the decanter with the gold tag, not the silver one. "If you aren't feeling well, why not stay in tonight? Rebecca's got a nice leg of mutton." *And Jamie's wearing the blue waistcoat,* he added to himself. *Get your mind off that yellow-haired tart.*

Stephen shook his head, and winced slightly. "No, I'm committed to Aunt Matilda's tonight, for dinner and cards. The company should be good, and I can hardly afford to offend her."

"As you please." Charles gave Stephen's coat a final brush. "There you are. Perfect as always." Time for plan B, then. "Stephen? I didn't expect you'd be home tonight, and Sam's feeling poorly. Would you mind putting yourself to bed?"

"I think I can manage," the earl said, pulling on his gloves. "Anything else I can do for you?" he asked, with exaggerated politeness.

Charles refused to be baited. "Yes, actually. Check the library on your way upstairs. Jamie's been falling asleep at the desk lately—"

"Oh, all right. I'll see he gets to bed. Tell Sam I hope he feels better."

"I'm sure he'll be over it soon," Charles replied. The valet smiled wickedly as his employer strode purposefully from the room. *Seeing as I made it up on the spot.*

Later that night, the earl opened the library door quietly and peeked inside. As predicted, his secretary was sound asleep at the desk, head pillowed on his arms, a book still open beside him. The earl tiptoed over, rather unsteadily, and sitting down on a chair next to the desk, contemplated the sleeping Jamie. The light from a single candle flickered over his face. His skin glowed in the candlelight, flushed from sleep, rose-pink lips parted slightly. Stephen examined those lips with a critical eye. Upper a bit short, but he'd never noticed how pleasantly full the lower one was. Temptingly full. He stretched out his hand, brushed one finger over it. The boy—how old was he, anyway, twenty-two, twenty-three?—stirred in response, as if seeking to re-establish the contact.

The earl scooted his chair a little closer. "Jamie," he whispered.

Jamie opened his eyes, and the earl drew back in surprise. His secretary blinked in confusion. "My lord?" he said, his voice husky from sleep.

"Where on earth are your spectacles, Mr. Riley?" Stephen asked, recovering slightly.

Jamie blinked again. "Oh. Rebecca borrows them sometimes. I don't really need them to read, and she —"

"Blue," marveled the earl. "There's really no other word to describe them, is there? Not so deep as sapphire, nor as light as the sky. Not even a hint of green, or grey, or violet. Just blue."

Jamie flushed deeper. "I think you've been drinking, my lord."

"I know I have," agreed his lordship. "But I don't think you realize how rare those eyes of yours are. I've only ever seen that particular shade before once in my life."

"Just once?" Jamie seemed intrigued by the idea that he possessed any sort of quality that might be considered rare.

"Oh yes." Stephen reached out a finger and delicately traced the corner of Jamie's eye. "My first lover, in fact," he said. "You don't know what it's like, Mr. Riley. Can't imagine." He shook his head. "You hate yourself. Think you're wicked, evil to have such thoughts. Such unnatural thoughts, but they won't go away... and then you meet a man. An older man. A good man, a noble man — a lord, yes, but noble in the truest sense of the word, and if he's like that too, then maybe, just maybe you aren't such a monster, either."

The earl paused, his finger traveling down Jamie's face, brushing again over his lip. "The first time he kissed me, I cried. And the first time we made love, I knew I'd found heaven."

Stephen leaned forward, giving his secretary every chance to stop him. But there was no attempt to evade the kiss, and the earl's generous mouth brushed gently over Jamie's. Jamie still didn't pull away, even when Stephen's hand crept to the back of his head, pulling him in closer, lips more demanding now. The earl's tongue caressed Jamie's lower lip, and Jamie gasped, allowing the tongue to slip inside his mouth, and begin a slow, thorough exploration. The young man tasted of the tea he'd been drinking, and cinnamon; so much more appetizing than Julian's usual sour-wine tang. Shyly, Jamie's tongue met his, and Stephen couldn't help a moan of surprise at the jolt of pure desire this small gesture evoked in him.

But the sound seemed to bring his secretary back to himself. Jamie's chair overturned with a crash as he jumped to his feet with a cry, wild-eyed with dismay.

"I—excuse me, my lord, I have to—"

Stephen closed his eyes wearily and laid his head down on the desk, the sound of footsteps echoing in his ears as Jamie ran blindly up the stairs.

Chapter Seven

*J*amie walked west on Oxford Street the next morning, in search of a glazier the London City Directory listed over on Adams Street, near the coach manufactory. He was putting together a proposal for the greenhouse, and while he could have sent a letter inquiring the price of the necessary glass panels, Jamie needed a chance to get out of the town house for a while, to clear his head after last night's incident.

He shivered despite the warmth of the late autumn sun, still unable to believe that the earl had kissed him. It was lowering to think that on Sunday he would turn twenty-two years of age, and yet had never been kissed. The close call with the vicar's assistant had been as near to it as he'd been. There had been rare opportunities when a coy glance or smile from one of the neighborhood girls had hinted that liberties might be allowed, but he had never taken advantage. At the time, he'd supposed he was being noble, but the truth was that none of the girls he'd known had ever stirred him the way Stephen Clair had last night.

His heart beat faster as he remembered Stephen's dark eyes, liquid in the candlelight as his face had moved closer... Stephen's full mouth claiming his... the first electric brush of tongue on tongue...

"Pardon me!" A liveried footman, over-laden with packages, glared at Jamie, and he sidestepped quickly to avoid collision.

"Sorry," he called after the retreating figure. Oxford Street was

not the place to lose oneself in reverie: one of the main thorough-
fares into town, it was becoming increasingly busy as the morning
lengthened. Jamie paused to get his bearings, surprised to realize
he was already on the edge of Hyde Park. Perhaps for his own
safety, he should remove himself from traffic until he'd got his
thoughts under control. He waited for a gap in the endless stream
of carts and carriages and dashed across the road, seeking the wide
expanse of the park. Exciting as the city was, he was country-
born, and this green oasis among the cold stone and brick was
instantly soothing.

Jamie settled himself under a tree. On another day, he might
have been interested in the slow trickle of finely-dressed men and
women on horseback, the brass buttons of their military-inspired
riding habits gleaming in the sunshine as they arrived for their
morning ride. It would have amused him to wonder who they
were, and why they were up and about so early for society denizens. Today, however, he was consumed by the kiss.

Just for a moment he allowed himself the indulgence of reliving
it. It couldn't have lasted more than a few seconds, perhaps half a
minute at most, from the first touch of Stephen's lips on his to his
panicked dash from the room, fleeing from a confusion of arousal
and shame. The flickers of attraction he'd felt for his employer
had been acceptable when Jamie had been certain the earl was out
of his reach. But now he had to face the harsh reality: it was no
use mooning after the Earl of St. Joseph, no matter how exciting
the kiss had been. Even if his employer's attraction to him were
anything more than a brandy-induced lapse, Jamie could never,
ever become the plaything of a lascivious lord.

Because that's exactly what his mother had been.

And it had destroyed her.

His mother had told him the story before she died, wanting him
to understand. Maria Riley had visited her aunt in London for the
Christmas season following her come-out, and caught the attention of a handsome young viscount. Although she had no title of
her own, the match was not impossible: her father was the Earl of
Thornleigh's youngest son, and her dowry was substantial. And
while she hadn't boasted of it, Maria had been beautiful. Even
twenty years later, her face aged prematurely by worry and illness, enough trace of it had been there to convince Jamie that
the portrait he treasured of his mother had not exaggerated her
loveliness.

Her eyes had been faraway as she'd described the night he'd
been conceived. "I was supposed to go back home to the country
early in January, but I kept making excuses to stay. To be near him.
London is fairly quiet at that time of year, which means instead of

the dozen social entertainments to choose from every night during the Season, one scrapes by on that many in a week. The Perkins' ball in celebration of the English victory at Toulon was the chief event of the month. I'd made my debut the spring before, so I was allowed to wear colors. My gown was peach peau-de-soie, and I wore my grandmother's pearls. I thought — I thought he was going to ask me to marry him."

She had fallen silent for a long moment, and Jamie hadn't pressed her. At last, she continued. "We were allowed two dances together in an evening. Any more was considered scandalous—perhaps it still is. A couple might choose to sit out one of the dances together, to spend the time in conversation. He asked if we might have a private word together in the orangery. Of course, I thought—and when he asked me to be his, I was sure he meant—oh, Jamie. I won't lie to you about it. He didn't force me, didn't coerce me in the least. I gave myself to him, there among the orange trees, with the moonlight streaming in the glass walls. It was the most wonderful experience of my life, and what happened after can't take that away from me. I loved him so much, and I was sure he loved me."

A long bout of coughing interrupted the narrative, and Jamie hastened to fetch the drops Dr. Roundtree had prescribed for his mother's condition. "Please, Mother. If it taxes you, you don't have to go on."

She shook her head. "You deserve to know, before it's too late. The day after a ball, he always sent violets, a little nosegay with a charming note. When they didn't arrive the next morning, I assumed it was because he'd be calling formally, to ask for my hand. I cancelled my engagements and waited. And waited."

"He never came." Jamie couldn't help the bitterness in his voice. "The scoundrel."

"We were so young, Jamie, neither of us even eighteen. I was too mortified to approach him about it, at least until I realized the trouble I was in."

Then, she had sought the viscount out, begged him to do the right thing. He denied he was the child's father, said she'd probably had a dozen others since they'd been together. Cruelly, he'd told her that his wife would someday be a great lady, and he was damned if the position would go to some roundheels who would lift her skirts in the shrubbery for any man who asked. Once her increasing belly had advertised her shame to the world, her father had cast her out of his house in only the clothes she had on her back. Maria sold the jewelry she'd been wearing and took a cheap room, determined to find a job somewhere. But at seventeen, unmarried and pregnant, with few skills beyond the rudiments of embroidery and watercolor-painting thought suitable to young ladies of her class, she had nothing to recommend her to potential employers.

She had been desperate when a friend of the viscount's tracked her down in her cheap lodgings. A baron of middling wealth, he might have offered for her hand himself, once, if he'd thought he stood a chance. Now, he had another offer to make. And to keep herself alive, to provide food and shelter for the child growing within her, she'd taken it. Become his mistress, first kept lavishly in a large house on his estate, then, once he'd married, shunted off to a tiny cottage in Yorkshire and all but forgotten.

In the small village of Wheldrake, the neighbors were more inclined to accept her story that she was a widow, despite the occasional visits the baron still made from time to time. But she'd never cared for him, and the stress of her position and what everyone would think of her and her son if they knew wore away at her. When Jamie was fourteen, she'd come down with a bilious fever, and her lungs had never recovered. It had taken several more years for her to waste away to nothing, coughing her life out bit by bit.

No. The kiss had been extraordinary, and Jamie's whole body thrilled to the memory of it now. But Stephen Clair was another like his father, a man who took his pleasures where he would and then moved on without a backward glance. He would never share the shame that had killed his mother.

Jamie stood up from beneath the tree and brushed off his trousers briskly. It was time to visit the glazier.

Stephen made a face at himself in the ridiculously ornate mirror he'd purchased when he'd inherited St. Joseph House, a huge bronze monstrosity festooned with sphinxes and pyramids. The earl's chambers had needed redecoration at once — he could hardly bring himself to sleep in Robert's and Mary's marriage bed — but it occurred to him now that he'd been careless executing the change, choosing a popular Egyptian theme almost at random and allowing his decorator a free hand. The result had been amusing at first, but it was starting to grate on him. He stared at the palm tree legs of his dressing table with a frown, pulling his train of thought back to the conversation at hand. "I was drunk and sentimental, that's why," he said, lifting his chin so that Charles could scrape the razor over his neck. He would have shaken his head, but the delicacy of the operation precluded it, so he settled for a sigh. "That colorless little mouse."

Charles made a noncommittal sound, which his lordship chose to take as encouragement. "Not entirely colorless," he admitted.

"You wouldn't credit it, Charles, but he has the loveliest eyes behind those dreadful spectacles."

"Really?" For some reason, the look on his valet's face was almost a smirk.

"Really. The very definition of blue. Lashes Julian would kill for, and without a speck of paint, either. And that smile! Such a prim little thing, though."

"Who, Mr. Julian?"

"Very funny, Charles. But Julian doesn't need candlelight to bring out highlights in his hair."

"No," the valet agreed, "just bleach. What highlights?"

"Red. Gold. The lad is a cache of hidden treasures. If I were the poetic sort, I'd compare his hair to an autumn grove—you think it's all brown and lifeless until the sun comes out, and then—oh Christ, this is why I'm not a poet." The earl sat glumly for a few moments while Charles navigated his jawbone. "Half an hour with Julian should sort me out."

"I thought you said it was over with you and Mr. Julian?"

Stephen grimaced. "I tried, but what's the point? I'm paying for him anyway. I might as well—besides—oh, blast." He scowled, unable to explain the actor's attraction, even to himself. Maybe he was like this bedchamber, exotic and fun, but not especially meant to be restful. "It was a hell of a fight last night, but we didn't quite end it. If Julian freezes me out for a while, I may be able to pick up some temporary respite elsewhere. There's a new baritone in the chorus over at Sullivan's Music Hall — auburn hair and cheekbones that could cut glass. I hear he's open to offers."

The razor slipped just a little, but no damage was done. "Perhaps you should get to know Mr. Riley better, first," Charles protested. "He's a very good sort."

"Mouse," muttered the earl. And then, in disbelief, "Charles? Are those *tallow* candles?"

Early that afternoon Jamie heard a familiar voice, rich as Sam's sherry trifle, outside the library door and tensed. A moment later the owner of those tones appeared in the doorway, looking back into the hallway with confusion.

"What do you make of that, Mr. Riley? I swear... Mr. Symmons was downright *civil* to me."

Jamie did not look up from his accounts. Why bother? He knew exactly what his lordship looked like. "Perhaps he's had a change of heart."

"Well, let's see if it lasts."

"Mmm."

"Am I bothering you, Mr. Riley?" the earl asked, with a touch of asperity.

Jamie still didn't look up. "Not at all, my lord."

"I wanted to talk to you about something."

At that, Jamie pushed his spectacles firmly up his nose, and at last met his employer's gaze. "Yes?"

"There are tallow candles in my room."

Jamie let out the breath he hadn't realized he'd been holding. "Oh. Yes, there are. I told you—"

"Mr. Riley, is this not my house?"

"Yes, but it's not like you spend much time in your room."

"Charles and Rebecca get wax, and I get tallow?"

"They need the light, and you don—"

"Mr. Riley! Am I not the head of this household?" the earl snapped.

Jamie snapped back. "And therefore should have the most interest in balancing your accounts!"

Stephen closed his mouth. "You're right, Mr. Riley," he said in quieter tones. "My apologies. And since I'm apologizing—"

Jamie colored some more. "No need, my lord. You were very drunk indeed."

"I'm sorry I was drunk, and I'm sorry if I made you uncomfortable. But the kiss itself—I can't be sorry for that. It was a very sweet kiss, indeed." And, softly, as Jamie turned an even more vivid scarlet, "Wasn't it, Jamie?"

Jamie decided quickly that his best refuge was the truth. "My lord," he said with unmistakable sincerity, "It was quite the worst kiss I've ever had."

Stephen's face flickered with shock, hurt, and then settled into anger. He turned on his heel and stormed out of the library, slamming the door hard enough to shake the house. Jamie balled up a piece of paper and threw it after him. "Worst kiss, indeed. It would have to be, you idiot. And the best, too." But he knew that it would never occur to the earl, that anyone could reach the ripe age of nearly twenty-two without ever having been kissed.

"Oh, God, Julian. I've missed you so." Stephen stroked the golden curls hovering just above his lap. It was easy to be contrite when Julian was being so agreeable. He arched his pelvis, ready for the actor to pick up the pace, but Julian held his hips steady, keeping to a slow, maddening rhythm. "Oh, that is so good."

How could he ever have wasted time thinking about that little mouse at home, when he had access to such skill? No matter how attractively his secretary colored up when he was angry, how his eyes flashed fire even behind the muting spectacles... But Julian, of course, *enjoyed* his kisses. Just for a moment, he imagined Jamie's mouth busy where the other man's was now, and had to bite his tongue, hard, to keep from coming on the spot. *Why?* he wondered. *Next to Julian, he's nothing. Just a mouse, just a little*— "Jamie," he whispered, and with a soft cry he ruined Julian's careful ministrations, which should have gone on for an agonizingly long time.

Julian lifted his head, green eyes narrowed. "Did you say 'Jamie?'"

Stephen thought fast. "No, of course not. I said, 'you shame me.' I don't usually lose control so easily." He held his breath, but Julian's vanity carried the day, and the actor believed his clumsy lie.

The Golden One relaxed back onto his heels, his smirk holding triumph as he wiped his mouth. "Such passion," he said. "I don't know what you'd do without me."

Stephen closed his eyes. "I can't imagine."

Jamie shifted from one foot to the other in the hallway outside the morning room. His lordship was probably still angry after yesterday, but a curious encounter with Abby Sawtell made it necessary to seek him out now.

Abby had emerged from the stables behind the house and visited him in the library, her rough clothes and raw bones looking out of place in the refined room.

"Mrs. Sawtell? What can I do for you?"

"Lordship ain't the horsy type," she'd said without preamble, seeming to expect him to get her point at once. It took a while to extract the necessary information from her sparse words, but once he'd understood the problem, Jamie had assured her he'd take care of it.

So he'd best screw up his courage and do so. Jamie opened the door to the morning room, finding the earl engaged in his evening ritual of playing a game of cards with Charles before going out to dine.

"Bloody hell!" Stephen threw down a card. "Lucky at cards, my arse. I've been having the damnedest luck in both love and—" He broke off as he noticed his secretary in the doorway. "Mr. Riley." His tone was decidedly cool.

Charles took the final trick. "Euchred again!" The effort it was costing him not to gloat was transparent on his face, further annoying the earl.

"Blast it," he said. "All right, Charles, what's the damage?" He scowled in Jamie's direction. "What the devil do you want?"

"Twelve shillings," replied Charles generously, the actual total being somewhat higher.

"I have some financial matters to discuss with you, my lord," Jamie said. "I was talking with Abby Sawtell—"

"Liar," growled the earl, pulling his wallet from an inside pocket and tossing a pound note at his valet. And when Jamie's back stiffened, "Oh, not you, Mr. Riley. Please, sit down."

Charles rose quickly from the table. "I'll just—um, many things to..." he trailed off, neither of the others paying the least amount of attention to him, and slipped quietly from the room.

Jamie sat down. "Abby Sawtell had some ideas to save money in the stables. She thinks you have more horses than you need, which makes the feed bills unnecessarily high. Plus, of course, you could raise some funds by selling the extra horses. And... your nephews' ponies. She thinks they'd be better off, and happier, at your country estate, where they could be put out to pasture, and perhaps the stable boys could ride them occasionally. Alex used to be able to exercise them in Hyde Park, but he's grown too large to ride them anymore."

The earl lifted both eyebrows in amazement. "Abby Sawtell said all that?"

Jamie grinned. "Well, not in quite so many words."

"I'll bet." The earl nodded. "Makes sense, though. Consider it done." The corners of his mouth quirked. "And then, of course, do it."

"Yes, my lord." *How does one go about the sale of horses?* Jamie was wondering, when the earl spoke again.

"Lord knows I could use the blunt." He stretched and glanced at his pocket watch. "I have a dinner appointment with a gorgeous redhead, and foresee many expensive presents in the very near future."

Not surprisingly, Jamie's hackles went up. "My lord. Quarter day is coming up, and not only does your household prefer to be paid, but a new batch of bills is sure to arrive. Perhaps you could consider—"

"Certainly, Mr. Riley... if in turn you could suggest a more economical manner in which to satisfy my desires? Perhaps someone closer to home?" And as Jamie turned pink, "No? Well then, I'm forced to seek the company of those who actually enjoy my kisses."

"Oh? And how would you know? You pay for your companions and, since they tend to be actors anyway, hasn't it occurred to you that they might be acting?"

"That's quite enough," the earl hissed, stung. "I know an honest response when I get it, even from you, and you're about as cold as they come. Unless you care to deny...?"

"I'm not —" *cold*, Jamie started to say, but realized instantly that pursuing that particular argument would only lead to trouble. "—not denying that you—that I—was half-asleep, and you took me by surprise," he ended lamely. He ran his fingers through his hair, and, straightening his back, moved on to surer ground. "I'm not sure you comprehend fully the state of your finances. You are deeply, deeply in debt. Whatever you do, and I'm sure you'll do exactly as you please, could you please keep that in mind?"

"I'll keep it in mind," the earl said, settling down. "And, of course," he added with poisonous politeness, "I'm always eager to hear your next *unusual* idea for saving money. The candles quite had them all in stitches over at White's."

Jamie couldn't suppress a smile. "Then I have one you'll dine out on for weeks. If, as you say, fresh roses daily are a non-negotiable—"

"And they are," his lordship said.

" —then why not build your own greenhouse? Charles could grow roses, my lord, for a fraction of what they cost to buy."

"Build a greenhouse for my valet?" The earl laughed. "People will think I'm totally mad."

"Yes, it does seem odd. That's why I hadn't brought it up before." Jamie hesitated. "Well, one of the reasons."

"There are others? Amazing."

"Just one, really. I've done some thinking about this—it's not totally impractical. There's plenty of room in the back garden, and a nice southern exposure. There are gardening books in your library, with greenhouse plans, even. And you know, don't you, that Charles dreams of growing flowers?"

"I didn't. But I'm not surprised, he does like to fuss over things." He thought about it for a moment. "You're right, it doesn't sound so far-fetched."

Jamie nodded. "The major obstacle is the start-up cost. I'm sure the greenhouse would pay for itself within a year, but the construction expenses wouldn't be cheap, and neither would the plants themselves. I'm not sure where we would come up with the money."

"There is that." Stephen sighed. "I never had to be responsible before—you know that?" He looked at Jamie. "All my life, someone's been bailing me out — my parents, my brother. Aunt Matilda. Who has thawed considerably toward me, thanks to you, but even she seems to think I should start looking after myself."

"It's not just yourself," Jamie reminded him. "There are nine more of us in this house alone, not to mention those at your Scottish estate, and God knows what other properties you have."

"Oh, the estate takes care of itself. My grandfather and Aunt Matilda—she was his sister—set it up that way," Stephen said. "Keep any of us from wasting the capital—I can't touch that. All I get is my quarterly allowance. And until recently I had the freedom to treat that as pocket money."

"But surely, it did increase when you came into the title?"

"Oh yes, considerably. Which just seemed to me like that much more to fritter away—and the loss of my brother and his family like a good excuse to do it." Stephen shut his eyes. "So, here I am, thirty-four years old, and with nothing to show for my life but a mountain of debts and a title I never wanted in the first place." He opened them again and laughed. "Sorry about the self-pity. I think I desperately need to get lai—" Somehow it didn't seem right to get too coarse around Mr. Riley. "To get uh, into the company of the sort of men you disapprove of. Unless," he said politely, with a wicked gleam in his dark eyes, "you wished to make the supreme sacrifice, for the good of the household?"

Jamie tried very hard not to blush, shaking his head mutely.

The earl glanced at his watch again. "Well then, I'm off. Do tell Charles not to wait up, won't you?"

Chapter Eight

*B*ut as it was, his lordship was home before midnight, and in a foul mood. Luckily, his valet had the foresight not to take the night off and go over to Sam's, having a premonition that the evening might not go as planned. Whether he realized it yet or not, Stephen was tiring not just of Julian, but his sort entirely: replacing one glittering male courtesan with another would no longer suffice. Charles hummed as he cleaned up the usual mess caused by dressing his employer, straightening the dressing room and then moving to make sure the earl's bedchamber was prepared should he return home later. His and Rebecca's plan was working: the kiss with Jamie was a definite good sign. Stephen had certainly been affected by it. He grinned to himself as he replaced the burnt-out candles in the obelisk-shaped candlesticks by the bed. Still tallow—Jamie had won that fight, and eventually he would win Stephen as well.

Charles laid out silk pajamas and turned down the bed, then retired to his own small room adjacent to the bedroom, just to the right of the dressing room. He was dozing lightly over Tod's *Plans, Elevations and Sections of Hot-Houses, Green-Houses, an Aquarium, Conservatories &c.* when he heard the earl return. He set the book down and came out, blinking a little, and greeted his employer pleasantly.

Seeing Charles was home did not improve his lordship's temper.

"Didn't you get my message? You weren't to wait up," the earl snarled, throwing his gloves in the general direction of the dressing table. Charles patiently retrieved them from the floor and moved to help his lordship with his boots.

"Well, it was possible you wouldn't come to an immediate agreement with—with—"

"Mr. Kendall Ambrose, but don't bother remembering the name. What the deuce was I thinking? His hair wasn't auburn—it was orange."

"Like that lovely shade of Titian red-gold?"

"Like carrots. And his face was all bony and angular. Nothing subtle about him in the least."

"Oh, dear," said Charles, suppressing a smile. So much for cheekbones that could cut glass. Perhaps Stephen was coming to appreciate a more subtle form of beauty. "Wasn't he at all charming?"

"I don't know," Stephen said. "Charming enough, I suppose, if not very bright. I don't think I could ever have a real conversation with him."

"Yes, and we all know how important that's been to you in the past," murmured Charles.

The earl glared at him, but didn't rise to the bait—yet. "I kissed him goodnight, but it was no good. He was so bloody practiced."

"What, unlike Mr. Julian?"

"You know damned well who I'm talking about. Help me with this cravat, I'm being strangled."

Charles freed the knot, unwinding the starched neck cloth. "How should I know? You kiss so many."

"The mouse, idiot." He punctuated his words by snatching the cravat and throwing it on the floor.

"My, you are in a state." Charles just managed to keep a smile from his face.

"And why shouldn't I be? Ever since he came into my house, everything has been topsy-turvy. The meddling little—"

"His meddling has improved things tremendously around here—or haven't you noticed?"

The earl dragged a hand over his face wearily. "I've noticed. He's doing all the things I should be doing, and he doesn't even like me."

Charles put a hand on Stephen's shoulder. "He likes you."

"He said he didn't like kissing me!" There was genuine hurt in the earl's voice.

"And you can't think of any reason he might prevaricate? Think, Stephen! Jamie is so capable that it's easy to forget that he's just a simple lad from the country. And young, too. He probably thinks he's over his head. Maybe he needs time, maybe he needs—"

Stephen looked up, his face hardening. "Money. What else do I have to offer someone like him?"

"You can't think to—to buy Jamie?" Charles was aghast. "Please believe me, I know him well enough to know he would have an absolute horror of that."

"Everyone has a price. If not cash... let me think." He bit a nail. "He does adore books, doesn't he? And there was one in particular he seemed very fond of indeed. It had a torn cover, gilt edges, and very bright, rather stiff pictures."

"Not your brother's Book of Hours?"

"Yes, that's it. He said it was worth quite a lot, but of course it won't cost me a penny. Perfect, isn't it?" The earl had the gall to look pleased with himself.

The valet shook his head. "Please don't. It would be a big mistake."

"Then what does he want? You tell me."

"I wager he wants what we all want." *Love, you dolt.* But how to bring Stephen around to that? Charles thought about himself, and Sam. "He wants to be listened to. Respected. Admired. He wants help when he needs it, and the privilege of being leaned on in turn. He wants to feel special, and important. If you think he doesn't like you, make him like you."

Stephen stared. "Egad, what a lot of work." He waved his hand. "Just feel him out about the book, will you? And be a good lad and send the damn thing out to be rebound. I can hardly give it to him in that condition."

There was no one to turn to but Rebecca. "It seemed like such a good idea," Charles said, over a cup of tea in the kitchen late the next morning, "to get Stephen interested in Jamie. Now it's a disaster. You should have seen the look on Jamie's face when I told him about Stephen's offer."

"I can imagine." Rebecca shook her head. "But it can still work out. Have you seen Jamie's face when he looks at the earl? He's no good at hiding his feelings. And his lordship must be desperate for our lad—that book must be worth hundreds."

Charles waved a hand. "No, that's just what he's used to. In all the years I've been with Stephen, he's never had a real romance— from things he's said here and there, I think he was burned pretty badly in his youth. I figure that purchasing his pleasures keeps him in control of the situation, so he doesn't get hurt again."

"Well, what's past is past. His lordship needs a good man to settle him down, and Jamie could use some stability in his life. If they just let the attraction develop, fell properly in love—"

"Ha," said Charles. "I tried just *hinting* to Stephen last night—" He took another sip of tea and shook his head. "I want him to settle down, too. I just don't know if he's ready."

Rebecca poured more tea, then stirred her cup. "They need to spend more time together. We know that they're perfect for each other, they just need to figure it out. What can we do?"

The earl took the news of Jamie's refusal, and Charles' suggestion that he give his secretary time, with apparent good grace. Well, why not? Worst kiss of his life or not, Jamie *had* kissed him back. There was fire in the little mouse—and unlike with Julian and his ilk, he didn't have to wonder about its authenticity. It shouldn't be too difficult to seduce his secretary, and worry about the arrangements later. And, thanks to Charles, Stephen knew that Jamie frequently fell asleep in the library...

Jamie was wide-awake, however, that night when Stephen stealthily poked his head around the library door. Damn. The earl had left his card party early, and for once luck had actually been with him. He started to withdraw, but just then Jamie looked up, and smiled. Like a filing drawn to a magnet, Stephen entered the room after all, and walked over to the desk.

"What's that? Greenhouse plans?" He leaned in for a better look, his shoulder brushing Jamie's slightly.

"Yes, my lord. I've been trying to figure exact costs. I went out to a few glaziers, to price the panes." The secretary reached over for some papers on his right, leaning away from the earl, who took the opportunity to perch on the left arm of the chair. When Jamie straightened up, it was to find himself in very close proximity to Stephen's thigh. He stared at it and swallowed. "My lord?" he said with gentle reproof.

Stephen sighed and moved off the chair. "Don't you find me in the least bit attractive?" he coaxed, more teasing than plaintive.

"I'm sure I'm one of the two people in the room with the highest opinion of your looks," Jamie said. "But that's neither here nor there. I like being your secretary. I like my work, and I'm very happy in this household. I want to stay here for a very long time."

"And somehow that precludes us being together?"

"Doesn't it? Let's talk economics again. I cannot afford to give in to you, my lord. As small as the chance is that I'll actually be paid come quarter-day, I need the security of having a position. Once you're finished with me, do you think it's likely anyone else would hire me? And don't you dare suggest that I turn such a thing into a career."

"You wouldn't need to. Jamie, do you have any idea what I settled on Julian? A man—if you don't happen to actually *be* Julian—could live quite comfortably on what he's getting from me. Do you imagine I'd be any less generous with you? You could get your own house—"

"Damn you." Jamie picked up one of the heavy ledgers on the desk and threw it on the floor. "Oh, *damn* you. Do you know what I do in here from morning to night? I *work*. I catalogue your library, handle your correspondence, plan your social calendar, manage your household and placate your staff. I'm trying desperately to find you the means to discard your current lover, and then there's your debts—Julian's debts, and his predecessors' as well—remember them?" He took a sheaf of papers from the front of a second ledger. "Hector Quinn? Anthony Basingstoke? There were two Elphinstones—brothers, I assume?"

"Twins," confirmed Stephen.

"And remember Daniel Post?" Jamie brandished a sheet of paper. "Because his tailor certainly remembers you."

"Oh, Danny had the longest tongue in Christendom. I could hardly forget him."

Jamie stopped dead in the midst of his tirade, looking confused. "What good is—"

The earl laughed. "I'll wager you don't actually want to know. But believe me, it was well worth—" he plucked the paper from his secretary's hand and frowned at the crabbed writing "—seven hundred pounds? Jesus."

Jamie snatched it back and continued. "I've been tearing my hair out trying to come up with the means to pay these off, on top of everything else I do. And yet you have the gall to tell me I'm worth more to you if I'd only—if I'd—" Lacking both the vocabulary and will to continue, Jamie expressed his anger and frustration by throwing the second ledger, sending the enclosed bills scattering in a satisfying arc.

The earl stared, appalled. "I—I'm sorry, Mr. Riley. I know you do a lot for me, I just never put it together quite how much. Perhaps a raise?"

"Oh, Jesus." Jamie's voice was weary. "No, I don't want a raise. Good night, my lord."

When he was gone, the earl stooped and picked up Jamie's ledgers and papers, placing them slowly and neatly on the desk. Somehow, he'd managed to blow it again. There was an ache in his throat as he thought, again, of the brief kiss they'd shared. Its sweetness, its passion. Stephen closed his eyes, imagining Jamie's hands caressing his flesh with that same tender shyness.

"Jamie. My mouse," he whispered. "What the hell do you want from me?"

Chapter Nine

*J*amie was hard at work in the library the next morning when he heard voices in the hall. Mr. Symmons, speaking to an unknown visitor, sounded frostier than ever. He craned his head to try to see who was calling.

"Mr. Riley has his lordship's schedule. Perhaps he can help you." The butler tapped on the open door. "Mr. Riley?"

The visitor nodded with an air of condescension the Prince of Wales could only aspire to. Jamie took in his appearance with a sinking heart. Guinea-gold curls, artfully arranged, framed a chiseled countenance that might have been sculpted by Phidias himself. It was the first time he'd seen the actor since the one distant glimpse on the night he'd arrived, but it could be no one else.

Julian Jeffries' smile did not warm his lovely green eyes. "The Earl of St. Joseph was supposed to meet me this morning for a ride in Rotten Row. Is he very ill?" The implication seemed to be that only a deathbed might be sufficient excuse for the lapse.

"I—I believe he had an emergency to attend to." With effort, Jamie kept his eyes from flicking to his copy of the earl's engagement schedule, which clearly showed a late breakfast with the Johnstons this morning. If there had been an appointment with Julian, it had probably been crossed out after one of their many fights.

The actor advanced with enviable grace. "You're the secretary, of course." The smile grew a trifle broader. "To think I worried about his having a fresh young man in the house."

Jamie couldn't help but be stung. "I beg your pardon?"

"Oh, that was no comment on your looks." The dismissive flick of the sea-green eyes belied his words. "Although, you don't seem to be quite Stephen's type, do you?" Julian caught a glimpse of himself in the mirror above the mantelpiece and preened slightly. "I just meant, of course, that you seem the quiet, bookish sort."

With reluctance, Jamie regarded his reflection, next to Julian's, in the glass. With his spectacles and ink-smudged fingers, he did look like the bookworm he was. Quiet, colorless. Almost invisible compared to the actor's physical brilliance.

It hurt.

Julian squeezed his shoulder in commiseration. "I hope he doesn't bother you anyway, out of sheer proximity. Just hold your ground if he does, he'll soon lose interest."

"You should know." As soon as the words slipped out, Jamie wished with all his might he could take them back. "I mean, knowing him so well."

The actor allowed his smile to show pity. "I do know Stephen well, in ways you can only imagine. Or... perhaps not." He made a show of consulting the expensive gold watch dangling from a fob. "Oh, dear. I'll have to hurry if I'm going to make my tailor before luncheon. So nice to meet you, Mr. O'Reilly."

"Indeed, Mr. Jefferson." Jamie immediately regretted playing Julian's spiteful little game. Julian had no reason to get his name right, but as Stephen's secretary it was his responsibility to know the actor's name. Pretending otherwise only made him look foolish. Julian's self-satisfied smirk as he left drove the point home nicely.

Once Julian was gone, Jamie decided to treat himself to a day out. Well, it was his birthday. One year ago, in honor of his twenty-first birthday, he and his mother had hitched up their pony cart and driven the six miles from the village of Wheldrake into York. It had been one of his mother's good days. She had been able to join him for a tour of York Minster and even walk a short bit of the ancient city wall with him. They'd concluded their day with a special birthday tea in a cozy teashop on High Petergate. Jamie's smile of remembrance faded. This year, he was without family, and his birthday excursion would be solo.

He wrapped up some of Sam's bread, leftover from last night's dinner, and a hunk of cheese, and went out to explore London properly at last. The earl's townhouse was on Hanover Square, just off Oxford Street, so it was a reasonable walk to the center of the city. St. Paul's Cathedral looked just like the etching the vicar had of it, but was even larger than he'd imagined, Wren's magnificent edifice looming benevolently over the City. Jamie admired its clean lines and airy interior, but it was the dark and ancient Westminster Abbey that stirred his soul. Here were entombed the great figures from English history: the kings and queens who had shaped this green and pleasant land.

Edward I, Hammer of the Scots, who had pilfered their sacred Stone of Scone and brought it to captivity, to rest beneath the Coronation Chair near the High Altar. Henry VII, the Welsh opportunist who had staked a bloody claim to England at the Battle of Bosworth, lay beyond in the Lady Chapel, his Yorkist bride at his side. Nearby were his polar opposite granddaughters Bloody Mary and Good Queen Bess: the intolerance of the former driving the country to the brink of religious civil war; the good sense and crafty politics of the latter bringing years of peace and prosperity.

Jamie spent a good deal of time in the Poet's Corner, able to forget about the earl's tangled finances, smoldering eyes and unpleasant paramour while he stood in reverence before Chaucer's grave. The painted letters of the inscription on the grey marble monument were flaking badly, but he could make out the date the poet had died: October 25, 1400. Four hundred sixteen years and two days ago. Stephen's brother, like Jamie, had adored Chaucer; there were at least six different editions of *The Canterbury Tales* alone in the library, not to mention a miscellany of other works and a number of commentaries. Someday, when he had time, he would delve into the collection properly. But not now—there was simply too much to do. Three weeks of dedicated labor had barely made a dent. Jamie sighed, thinking he had best get back to the town house and get to it. He left the dark sanctuary of the Abbey for the tumultuous streets outside.

Even on a grey, foggy day London was a riot of color and noise—maybe just a bit too much noise, Jamie thought, nursing a slight headache as he finally made his way home in the late afternoon. He was pleasantly tired when he opened the kitchen door, in search of a cup of tea.

Jamie stopped, just inside the threshold. He hadn't expected the kitchen to be so busy at this hour, but it seemed the whole household was present, with some additions as well. Sam was over at the huge iron cook stove, supervising Rebecca as she stirred something with care. At one end of the table, Mrs. Symmons was sitting with Betsy and Maisie, folding some linens which had dried on a rack near the fire. Charles and Mr. Symmons were at the other end of the table, enjoying tea and arguing amiably over some gardening books with a third man, tall and brown-haired with an engaging smile. Jamie hadn't met him before, but he was almost certainly Rebecca's sweetheart Christopher. Abby Sawtell wasn't there, but her son Alex was sitting in a quiet corner, dark hair flopping over his face as he contentedly worked his way through a plate of biscuits. Well, he doubtlessly needed the fuel: the boy was only ten years old, but was growing so fast he'd nearly reached adult size already.

Rebecca was the first to notice him. "Happy birthday!" she cried, handing her spoon to Sam and crossing over to kiss Jamie on the cheek. "And welcome home."

Home. Jamie breathed in the homely scents of cooking and fresh laundry and the damp wool of the coats on the rack by the door. And Rebecca had remembered his birthday. His headache eased immediately, and he smiled as he looked around, waving a hand at the stranger seated at the table. "Is this your Christopher?"

"Yes, of course. Lady Feldsham gave him the afternoon off. Chris, this is our Jamie."

The young man held up a fragrant wafer. "Come try the almond biscuits, Jamie."

Rebecca nodded. "I finally got them right—"

"Took her three batches," Chris volunteered, exchanging a teasing smile with his fiancée.

"Alex is gracefully taking care of the rejects," Mrs. Symmons added.

"He don't mind," snorted Betsy. "I bet the real reason the feed bill is so high is that Alex eats all the oats."

"Betsy," Maisie's voice was little more than a whisper, but the gentle reproof was evident.

"Oh, I'm sorry," Betsy said, contrite. "I didn't mean no harm." But over in his corner Alex just nodded cordially, and stuffed another biscuit in his mouth.

Home.

"Could I try one?" Jamie's dimple flickered. "Of the good batch, that is."

"Over here," Charles called. "Grab a cup, Jamie, the tea's hot."

"But mind you don't spoil your appetite," Rebecca warned. "There's a nice joint, and Sam's teaching me how to make a lovely sauce. And wait—just wait until you see your birthday cake!"

"Cake?" Jamie felt his smile grow wide, and foolish.

"Of course." Charles was positively beaming. "Didn't I say Sam would make you one? But don't get a swelled head over it—we try to find occasion to stuff Betsy with as many sweets as possible."

Jamie collected his tea and sat next to Charles. The valet and the others had been arguing about greenhouses, much as Jamie had thought. He listened with half an ear as they debated everything from east-west placement in the garden, to whether fewer larger panes were better in the long run than more smaller panes of glass.

Then of course, there were problems of drainage, and protection from trees and other hazards.

"No, Charles, we can't put it in that corner, unless we dig out the walnut tree. And you are fond of walnuts, aren't you?"

Jamie let the conversations wash around him, more content than he could remember being for years, perhaps even before his mother had taken ill. Just this morning he had told himself he was without family. It seemed he had been mistaken.

After a magnificent birthday dinner, including Sam's towering cake, a many-tiered confection trimmed with marzipan roses, the party broke up. Jamie staggered up the stairs to his room on the top floor, his arms laden. His friends had even given him presents. Maisie and Betsy had knitted Jamie some fine white stockings, and Abby pushed into his hand a small figure of a horse which she had whittled herself—it was roughly carved, but she had caught a vitality and sense of motion a more technically-adept artist would have traded five years of training for. The Symmonses provided him with a greatcoat, probably not new, but warm and in perfect repair. There was clothing, too, from Charles, who had made over three more of his lordship's discarded shirts, another waistcoat, and a lace-trimmed nightshirt for him. Rebecca gave him a new volume of Lord Byron's *Poems*, elegantly bound in blue morocco.

"Rebecca! You shouldn't have. This must have cost—" He'd flushed in consternation, but the cook had just laughed.

"Don't worry about that. Three of Lady Feldsham's, um, admirers gave her copies of the same book. She told Chris he could have one. He gave it to me, but I knew it would suit you better. I mean," she gave him a sidelong look, "assuming you like the romantic stuff?"

"Thank you, Rebecca, I love it. I can't wait to read it," Jamie said. "Thank you all. This is the most wonderful birthday I've ever had."

Now, Jamie put his new clothing away in the wooden wardrobe and set Abby's carving on the desk, admiring its rough beauty. The book of poems he kept in his hand. Once again, the night was too cold to keep to his room; it would have to be the carpet in the library for him tonight. He didn't mind. The library was cozy, and he relished the chance to read by the fire for a while. He flew lightly back downstairs, poked up the fire and stretched out, supporting himself on one elbow and opening the new book of poems. But despite Byron's best efforts, Jamie's attention wandered.

Julian Jeffries had stood right here by the hearth just this morning, catty and sly, picking deliberately at Jamie's confidence. Could the actor possibly be jealous? Of him? It seemed ludicrous, unless... Perhaps the earl had dropped a hint about the kiss.

Jamie's eyes were drawn back to the desk, its mahogany surface glowing in the firelight. The earl—Stephen—had kissed him there. He dropped his head down onto his arm, sleepy and warm. What if there were a reason for the actor to be jealous? It had been quite a kiss, after all. Jamie's lips curved into a smile, even as he fell asleep.

For the earl, perseverance paid off. Peering into the library that night, he at first thought the room was empty. Then, out of the corner of his eye, he noticed what looked like a foot on the floor. It was a foot, shoeless and clad in a much-mended white stocking, peeking out from crumpled black trousers. His eye following up the graceful curve of a leg, his lordship perceived that it was attached to his secretary, who was stretched out on his side on the rug in front of the fire. Not surprisingly, even in sleep his hand was curved over a book.

The earl removed his own shoes, and, creeping over to the sleeping Jamie, carefully arranged himself on the floor next to him, propping himself up on one elbow. As he had before, Stephen could not resist brushing a fingertip over Jamie's lip. And as before, Jamie stirred in his sleep, head moving slightly as if trying to keep contact with the earl's finger. *I shouldn't*, thought the earl. *But I'm going to.* He brushed his lips over Jamie's, then pulled back slightly. Jamie gave the slightest of moans, and turned his head, seeking. His eyelids fluttered, but didn't open.

"Jamie," whispered Stephen. "My sweet Jamie." He placed feather-light kisses on the sleeping—was he still sleeping?—man's face, forehead, cheeks, chin. That ridiculously perfect nose. A slight hesitation, then back to the mouth. Gently, oh so gently, he nibbled on Jamie's kissable lower lip. Again the other man stirred and moaned, and the earl lost the battle with his conscience. He began kissing Jamie in earnest, and then Jamie was kissing him back, one of the secretary's arms sliding around the earl's back, pulling him closer.

Jamie's lips parted instantly under Stephen's gentle probing, and a shiver ran the length of his body as their tongues met. Jamie was no expert at the art of osculation, but the earl showed him how it was done, teaching him how slow, deep, and delicious a kiss could be. The lesson went on for some time before Stephen felt a gentle but determined hand in the middle of his chest, pushing him away.

Reluctantly Stephen obeyed, rolling off Jamie and back onto his elbow, staying very close beside him. He looked down at Jamie's eyes, huge in the firelight, and smiled gently.

Jamie's return smile was tentative. "Hello, my lord."

"You taste like marzipan. And there's the remains of a honking great cake in the kitchen. What was the occasion?" He licked the side of Jamie's neck, making him shudder.

Jamie flushed with mingled confusion and pleasure. "It's my birthday, I'm afraid—" he rolled over and squinted near-sightedly at the clock on the mantle, "—or rather, it was."

"Happy birthday, then." Stephen pulled Jamie back into his arms and kissed the corner of his mouth. The dimple appeared, and he kissed that, too. Several small, teasing kisses to Jamie's lips, swollen deliciously from his lordship's previous attentions, until Jamie couldn't stand it anymore and pulled Stephen down for a proper kiss.

After a long moment Jamie's hand came up again. Reluctantly. "We need to stop. Please."

"All right," the earl agreed. Jamie still hadn't moved away from him, which was a very good sign, no matter what he said. "So, how old are you?"

"Oh, ancient. Twenty-two," Jamie admitted. "Do you see my spectacles?"

"Yes, but I'd rather see your eyes, at least for a few more minutes. Mind terribly?"

"I—all right," he said. Jamie steeled himself and looked up into the earl's eyes. A man could get lost in those eyes, get lost and never even try to find his way back—warm, dark, liquid. Mesmerizing. *Oh God, is this what it feels like to fall—to fall—?* He couldn't even think it. Jamie shook his head in desperate negation, rolling away and burying his face in his hands.

"Jamie," the earl spooned up behind the young man, and stroked his hair. "Don't turn away. I want you. You want me," he whispered. "What's the problem? Come upstairs with me now. Let me make love to you."

Jamie shook his head mutely.

"Come on, sweetheart," urged the earl. "Let me show you what it's like. A scholar like you should want to try it for the experience alone—"

Jamie looked at him then, and tears were welling up in his blue eyes faster than his impossibly thick lashes could blink them away. Those were hardly words of affection, were they? Julian was right. He was just convenient to the earl. "Stop it," he repeated. "I can't." He rose awkwardly to his feet and looked around blindly. Stephen took pity on him, and retrieving Jamie's spectacles and book, stood up and handed them over.

"Thank you," murmured the boy, not looking at him. "Good night."

"Good night, my sweet Mouse," whispered the earl, but Jamie was already at the door, and probably didn't hear him.

Up in his room, Jamie wrapped his arms around himself and shivered, reliving the feel of being held in the earl's arms. He told himself that it was just desire he felt. Stephen Clair was gorgeous to look at, and his voice was a delightful cross between velvet and a cat's purr. But there was little else to admire about him, certainly not to — to —

Love. That was the word he was avoiding, and he made himself say it out loud. "I do not love the Earl of St. Joseph. Lord Stephen Clair. Stephen." The name became a verbal caress, quite against his will. Jamie blinked and shook himself. His employer was a drunk, a libertine, arrogant, careless. Spendthrift.

And... warm-hearted, a collector of misfits like himself, broken-hearted over his brother's death. So good-natured, too: he laughed off his troubles with an ease Jamie envied, and refused to take offense for long. Sensuous. Jamie shivered again, thinking with longing of the kisses they had shared. Not to mention, the only person in the world who had ever looked at Jamie with lust. Ah, there it was. "See? It's just desire." If he said it enough, it might turn out to be true.

Chapter Ten

*S*tephen stared up at the bedroom ceiling in the house in Floral Street, feeling restless and unsatisfied. Perhaps he should have pursued the red-haired singer more assiduously, just for a little variety on the side. Julian was a devil in bed, there was no denying that, but no matter how inventive their romps, more and more something had been lacking. But the baritone would have been just the same in the end, wouldn't he? They all were.

Perhaps this mood was just annoyance over his failure to seduce his mouse. In the weeks since their last encounter, Mr. Riley had been avoiding him as much as possible, and in their necessary meetings concerning his schedule the secretary had kept his demeanor formal and distant. Stephen scowled at Julian, sprawled next to him, his bare skin golden in the light of at least a dozen wax candles. How Jamie would squawk over that extravagance.

"I'm bored." Stephen winced to realize he had spoken the thought out loud.

Julian sat up and looked at his reflection in one of the many mirrors festooning the walls, patting his hair back into shape. "It's early yet. We can still make the card party at Lord Kerrigan's."

It didn't sound intriguing. "I'd have to go home and get dressed first."

"Nonsense. You wore evening clothes out to dinner, and Bertie can help put you back into order."

"The play's bound to be deep. We should drop in at the John-stons' instead—Eddie and Pamela know all the best gossip."

"Don't be so tight-fisted, Stephen." Julian rose from the tangle of sheets and rang for his dresser. "Besides, the deeper the play, the more you'll take home if you win. This losing streak of yours is bound to end sometime. Which reminds me, the boot-maker sent his reckoning here by mistake. Shall I send it over to you, or just throw it on the fire?"

Stephen sighed. "Just give it to me. I'll take it back for Mr. Riley to add to the list."

"That dreadful little man. You said once you really don't need a secretary. If you're so concerned about expense, why not sack him?"

"That is hardly your concern."

Julian's eyes were cool as he climbed back onto the bed, creeping with the grace of a panther until he was on all fours directly above Stephen, his naked form elegant and sinuous. "To hell with Kerrigan's. Let's stay in tonight. I can make you forget all your troubles."

With difficulty, Stephen extracted himself from the bed. "But I'd still have them, wouldn't I?" There was a knock on the door. "Here's Bertie. Let's get dressed."

The card play that night was even worse than he expected. Marcus, Lord Kerrigan, was a confirmed bachelor with no interest in his surroundings. His slovenly staff barely kept the house livable, and Stephen frequently found his sleeve sticking to the tabletop in the game room when they played cards. In previous days, the exciting play had more than made up for the squalor, but tonight the room seemed populated with a combination of the worst of London's pleasure-seeking bucks and dead-eyed professional card sharks. Between them, they cleaned out his purse twice over, and it was only a single lucky run as the faro bank that kept him from having to write out an IOU.

After, he allowed Julian to talk him back to Floral Street to demonstrate a new delaying cream that the actor's apothecary had made specially for him. The effect, Stephen thought, was to lengthen the session without improving its quality. And once more he found himself staring blankly at the ceiling, thinking *I'm bored. I'm truly, truly bored.*

Charles and Rebecca were not about to let their plans slide. As November sidled toward December and the earl still spent too much time away, they put their heads together to come up with a good reason to keep him home. The week after Lord Kerrigan's card party, they put it into action.

"Your game, Stephen." The valet smiled brightly as he began to count out the hand's winnings.

The earl stared in disbelief at the cards on the table, suspicion storming in his eyes. Their nightly pre-dinner game had most decidedly been in his favor this evening. "You wouldn't let me win, would you, Charles?"

"Certainly not," Charles waved one of his plump hands in dismissal. "You just have the devil's own luck tonight. Perhaps you ought to stay in for a few more hands?"

"You're not very good at deception," said Stephen. "What is it? Is there something you wanted to talk to me about?"

"Well, now that you mention it..." Charles hesitated. "I wonder if we could talk about the greenhouse."

The earl frowned. "It's a good plan, Charles, but I don't see how it's possible right now."

"I was looking over Jamie's figures, Stephen, and I was thinking, how much did you lose at Lord Kerrigan's card party last Wednesday?"

Stephen looked startled at the sudden change in topic. "What does that have to do with anything?"

"You did lose, didn't you?" Charles asked. "And you paid your vowels in cash?"

"I certainly did. A gentleman doesn't welsh on his gambling debts, it just isn't done. But if it makes you feel better, it was only what I had with me. About seventy pounds."

"You played cards again on Friday?"

"Friday?" The earl thought. "I broke even, or nearly. I may have lost twenty or thirty pounds."

"One hundred pounds then, just last week. And you usually play more than twice."

"So what?" Stephen sounded irritated. "Is everyone in my household going to hound me about my expenses? These are trifling sums for gambling debts—last week at White's, Lord Derby lost over twenty *thousand* pounds. And I do win occasionally."

"Just not lately," Charles said. "You're right, of course. Never mind. I guess I just thought—it just seemed to me—that in a very few weeks, the money you usually spend on gambling... " He shrugged, dejected.

The earl smiled. "Could pay for your greenhouse? Now, that's a plan worthy of Mr. Riley himself." He sat and thought for a moment. "I promised you roses, Charles, when you saved me from that preposterous bout of self-pity all those years ago. If you prefer to grow them, that's your affair. Mine is keeping my promise." He paused. "All right then, I'll be a good boy and put, say, twenty pounds in a kitty for the greenhouse for every night I stay home."

Charles beamed. "Thank you, Stephen. You have no idea how much this means to me."

"Yes, well, consider it your job to entertain me on those evenings. Deal the cards, Charles."

"Of course. I hope you don't mind? Jamie was going to read to me tonight, while I worked on some sewing. Would it be too distracting if he did so while we play?" Charles looked hopeful. "I'm keen to hear some of this Lord Byron's poetry."

The earl was feeling magnanimous. "As you please. Come on, let's play."

His lordship's night home turned out to be quite pleasant. Lady Luck proved even-handed, so neither he nor Charles had much to be disgruntled over there. After the first hour or so, Jamie took a break from his accounts to come and read to Charles, and despite his initial surprise at the presence of the earl, was quickly persuaded to stay and entertain both men. The earl wasn't so very interested in poetry, but his secretary read well, and his voice was pleasing, soft but clear.

Another hour passed, and Rebecca brought in a tray of tea and biscuits, staying for a moment to pour for them. "My, don't you all look cozy."

Charles winked at her behind the earl's back. "You should stay and listen to Jamie read. Such a lovely voice he's got."

Stephen felt an irrational twinge of jealousy that Charles should have noticed. "Yes, by all means, let's put him on display for everyone."

The valet and cook exchanged another glance. It sounded as if their employer wanted to keep Jamie for himself, didn't it? How promising. "No, I'd best get back to the kitchen, my lord," Rebecca said. "Good evening, gentlemen."

Jamie continued to read while the card players took a break to enjoy their snack. One particular poem definitely caught Stephen's attention. *When we two parted, in silence and tears...* He listened, mesmerized, all the way through to the end:

"*In secret we met, in silence I grieve,*
That thy heart could forget, thy spirit deceive.
If I should meet thee, after long years,
How should I greet thee? With silence, and tears."

Jamie finished and closed the book, snapping the earl from his reverie.

"Funny how often Jack comes to mind when you're around," Stephen said, giving his head a shake. "I imagine he feels exactly like that. You've read enough—come have tea, Mou—Mr. Riley."

"I'd love some," Jamie said, at the same time that Charles asked

"Jack?"

"Before your time, Charles, but I'm sure I've mentioned him. He was my first lover, and Jamie has his eyes exactly." Stephen paused while he poured Jamie a cup. "Try these almond biscuits, Sam's best, I presume?"

"You're wrong, actually," Charles said.

"I never told you about Jack?"

"Who, your marquess? No, you did. I meant the biscuits, they're Rebecca's."

"Lovely," the earl marveled.

"Who, your marquess?" Jamie parroted, reaching for the plate.

"No, I meant the biscuits, idiot," the earl said. "Not that Jack wasn't a fine looking man, of course."

"Of course," Charles and Jamie chorused together, exchanging a glance.

The earl lifted an eyebrow.

"Well, it's hardly likely you'd be seen with someone who wasn't," Charles said. He remembered something Stephen had once said, and grinned. "Unless he was a cache of hidden treasures."

Jamie looked up. "It can't have ended pleasantly, if that last was the poem that brought him to mind."

Stephen nodded. "It was a long time ago. I was eighteen, he was nearly thirty years older. You never forget your first, do you Charles?"

"Hardly," Charles said. "Especially since he'd smack me if I did. Or worse, stop making me pastries."

"Sam was your first? You're joking." The earl looked aghast, and that piqued Charles enough to rub it in.

"Some of us get it right the first time."

"Good for you, Charles," Jamie said with a smile.

"Yes, well, some of us aren't so lucky. In my case, my first lover and I had a serious difference of philosophy." The earl paused, setting down a third biscuit untasted. "I didn't see any reason to hide what we were to each other. Jack insisted on secrecy."

"There are laws against it," Jamie offered. "People get hanged."

"And when does that happen? When someone is stupid enough to annoy the wrong person. And not even then, if you're a person of rank." Stephen broke his biscuit in halves, then quarters. "Once," he continued, "exactly once, Jack let me hold his hand during an opera." He shook his head. "It wasn't like people couldn't guess— a man in his forties starts to spend all of his time with a boy less than half his age—"

"A beautiful boy, at that," Charles added. Jamie silently nodded agreement, which did not escape his lordship's notice.

"But Jack said as long as we didn't rub their noses in it, people wouldn't notice unless they had to—and as far as I know, they didn't. But it wasn't the way I wanted to live my life."

"Society doesn't seem to have shunned you after all," Jamie mused, "At least judging from the number of invitations you receive."

"Oh, believe me, there are a number of hostesses who won't let me in their door," Stephen said. "As for the rest—some people tolerate me for the sake of my family, especially Aunt Matilda. She's been the reigning queen of financial advice for decades. And I have any number of cronies who'll take my money at cards, but would hesitate to call me their friend—in case people thought we were, you know, *too* close. But my trump card, as far as society is concerned, is that I am an earl, and unmarried. As long as the *ton* still thinks I'll make one of their own a countess someday, I could roast children for breakfast and still be invited to at least half of the balls in town."

"But you will, won't you? Marry someday?"

The earl laughed shortly. "Why? Because it's my duty?"

Jamie frowned, looking down. "Well, there is the title."

"So I should get myself a son to carry it on?" His lordship's tone was deceptively soft. "On a woman I don't love, who would suffer a lifetime of humiliation that I preferred other beds to hers?"

Jamie lifted his eyes. "That would hardly be unique. And you know that there are plenty of women who would consider your infidelities a small price to pay to be a countess."

Stephen settled back in his chair. "Fine. I tie myself to some avaricious bitch, and get her with child. How many sons should I get on her, to make sure the title is secure?"

Jamie swallowed, sensing too late where the earl was heading. "Oh God. I'm sorry—" he began, but Stephen cut him off.

"One? Children are so fragile, you'd need at least a second: an heir and a spare. But anything can happen, so two isn't enough. Three," Stephen said, "now that would be especially safe. Wouldn't you agree?" His dark eyes blazed with pain.

"I'm so sorry. I wasn't thinking," Jamie laid his hand on the earl's arm. "Please. I'm sorry."

Stephen softened. "No, I'm sorry, little one. It's just—I never intended to marry, and while Robert and his boys were alive there was no reason to. Then, after—Christ, what's the point? There's no such thing as 'securing the title.'" He smiled crookedly. "And oddly enough, that philosophy exactly justifies me living as I please. Here's to aimless pleasure and dissipation. And I don't even have to pretend to give up boys."

"Do you regret it?" Jamie asked. "Your decision to live openly?"

"No, I don't." The earl was silent for a moment. "I can't imagine living in fear." And then, "For the love of Christ, Charles, deal the cards. Care to join us, Jamie?"

"I'm not very good at cards, and I don't have any money."

"Nonsense. You're good at everything." Stephen's eyes twinkled. "And how does that go? Cupid and my whoever?" He pursed his lips suggestively.

Jamie laughed. "*Cupid and my Campaspe played at cards for kisses*? I don't think so, my lord."

"Campaspe. I always wondered how you say that."

"One of the many benefits of learning Greek," Jamie said primly.

"Oh, I could give you Greek lessons," the earl said with a slow smile.

"This from a man who's never declined *o kouros* in his life," muttered Jamie.

"Ho what?" asked Charles, who lacked a classical education.

"A youth, Charles, and I can't say I've ever declined one if offered," said his lordship with delight. "But, while I agree there are many interesting nouns I can't decline, I must say my conjugating skills are among the best. Or do I mean conjugal? Either way, I'd be happy to demonstrate with some of my very favorite verbs."

Jamie reddened. "Knowing you, they're quite irregular."

"Oh, yes. But that's the essence of fine scholarship, isn't it? Getting a firm grasp on the unfamiliar. Assuming it is unfamiliar? After all, all sorts of things happen when the lights go out at school, if I remember correctly."

"I didn't go to school, the vicar taught me." And as the two other men burst into hilarious laughter, "Oh heavens! Not that! I mean, he gave me lessons—now, stop that! If I have any idea of what you're talking about, it's simply because some of the Greek literature is very frank." Jamie paused, then admitted reluctantly "And besides, one of my friends in the Eboracum Antiquarian Society had a collection of antiquities — I saw a vase once."

Charles wiped his eyes. "A vase?"

"From ancient Greece." If possible, Jamie got redder.

"I think I know the one you mean," his lordship said. "At least, I've seen one with a similar theme, and there can't be but so many in York. Go on, Mr. Riley—what was on yours? Do tell us."

"I think you can imagine," Jamie shot back.

"Oh, I can imagine," the earl said, caressing the younger man with his eyes. "In fact, I'm imagining right now."

"That's quite enough. Good night, Charles. My lord."

"Wait." Stephen jumped up and caught Jamie by the hand just as he reached the door. "I'm sorry. Come play cards — I promise not to tease."

Jamie shook his head. "No, I'm tired, really." He made no attempt to pull his hand away from the earl's large, warm grasp.

"No hard feelings?"

"No," he said, the dimple appearing briefly. "I'm not such a poor sport."

"Well, good night then." The earl squeezed Jamie's hand and let it go. "Sleep well."

When Jamie was gone, Stephen wandered back to the card table, stretched, and sat back down. "It's not so bad, staying home," he admitted.

Charles smiled.

Despite his words to the others, Jamie wasn't inclined to sleep. He fetched his overcoat from his room and wandered into the back garden, telling himself he wanted another look at where the greenhouse should go. The space behind the townhouse was not particularly wide, but it was deep, with plenty of free space between the house and the stable at the far end. But he couldn't concentrate on planning. The sky was filled with moonlight, his head with poetry, and the earl had held his hand.

He sat on the back steps, his knees weak. Silly thing to be excited over, hand-holding. But his lordship had seemed to view him with real affection tonight. Ever since the night of his birthday, when he had realized he was in real danger of falling in love with the earl, Jamie had been acting on the premise that he could be nothing to his employer but a convenient diversion, a few night's entertainment. That Stephen Clair was a careless playboy like his father, incapable of love.

What if he were wrong?

Tonight, he had learned that Stephen had been in love, at least once. Which meant logically that it could happen again. *But with me?*

Why on earth not? There had been times in their brief interactions in the past when understanding had flickered between them: a moment of shared laughter, or grief. But tonight, Jamie had felt a real connection beneath the banter. And he had to admit, Stephen had impressed him with his playful wit, his frank reminiscences about his lost love, and especially with his courageous decision not to hide what he was in a society where everyone seemed to hide behind a polite façade. Stephen, in return, had been attentive to him. Teased him, flattered him, called him 'little one.' Held his hand.

Jamie had known for at least a month that he could fall in love with Stephen. Now, for the first time, he contemplated whether Stephen could fall in love with him. That would change everything, wouldn't it? Jamie could never give himself to anyone for financial gain, nor even for the sheer animal pleasure of the act. But two people, coming together in love? A shudder ran through him as he remembered his mother's story. She had been certain that her viscount returned her love when she had allowed herself to be seduced in the orangery. And she'd been wrong, betrayed. Cast off.

"But if he did love me, Mama," Jamie said to the darkness. Imagine that. Allowing himself to relax into Stephen's kisses instead of resisting them. Letting those large warm fingers that had held his hand so tightly move over his body. Lying safe within his arms. Jamie shivered again. "If I knew he loved me, would that be so wrong?"

Chapter Eleven

"*B*ertie," Julian said, pacing the drawing room of the house on Floral Street, "this is the third night in a row that Stephen's decided to stay home. Why do you suppose that is?"

His dresser, a small dark man with a pug nose, shrugged while he dusted the shelves holding mementos of the actor's theatrical successes. He picked up the collapsible knife Julian had used to kill himself with as Romeo. "Maybe he's tired. The man's hardly stopped for a breath since he inherited the title."

Julian bit his lip. "Or maybe it's that damned secretary."

"Thought you checked him out, and he doesn't hold a candle to you. Not that he could," Bertie added, with an admiring glance.

"If it were just looks, I shouldn't have a thing to worry about. I wonder, though... perhaps he's not the innocent little thing he appears. Suppose he's a man of experience, who deliberately insinuated himself into St. Joseph House to get his claws into a rich earl."

The dresser's eyes lit up. "We could find out. Dig into his background, find all the dirt. Then you can drop it in his lordship's lap and be rid of the pest once and for all."

Good old Bertie, always on the lookout for some way to be helpful. It might be intolerable for Stephen to have a servant in love with him, but Julian certainly found it useful. He smiled. "If we get you on the Mail coach tomorrow morning, you can be in

Yorkshire by the day after." He reached to stroke the young man's face. "But do hurry back. If you have news for me, I'll reward you generously indeed."

Bertie swallowed. "I'll do my best."

The door opened, and Stephen looked up, smiling to see Jamie entering the morning room. It had taken some persuading, but tonight he was going to join them at cards, not just watch him and Charles play or read for their enjoyment. "I don't think I've seen that waistcoat before, Mr. Riley. It's very becoming."

"Well, since it's one of your old ones that Charles made over for me, you probably have seen it, but thank you."

"Good for him. That shade of green is much more suited for you than me—it brings out the color in your hair nicely."

"Again, thank you," Jamie said. "What are we playing, Charles?"

"Euchre is good for three players. Or commerce, if you like, or *vingt-et-un*?"

Jamie grinned. "Depends on how quickly you want me out of the game. I might last longer at euchre. I'm really not very good."

The earl nodded. "Euchre is fine with me."

True to his claim, Jamie proved to be an indifferent player, hesitating to order unless his hand was unbeatable, and failing to crush his opponents when he had the chance.

"Now look, Jamie, if you'd played your highest trump first, Stephen wouldn't have got that first trick, and you'd have a march," Charles explained.

"So? I won the hand, didn't I?" Jamie asked in bewilderment.

"It's quite acceptable to be ruthless at cards," his lordship said with a smile. "We won't take offense."

Jamie tried, but after an hour of steady losses begged to be released from play. "Cards are too extemporaneous," he laughed. "I'm much more competitive at chess, or even backgammon. Something with a more long-term strategy."

"I used to play chess," Stephen offered. "Haven't for some time, but I was credited a fair player at Oxford. Perhaps you'd give me a game tomorrow night, since Charles was planning on spending the evening with Sam?" He kicked Charles under the table, which Charles thought was hardly necessary.

"Yes," Charles said, "we are going to dine, ah, somewhere—"

"Ibbetson's," murmured the earl.

"Yes, at Ibbetson's, where it is rumored that the pastry chef makes an apricot tart to die for. Sam wants to see if he can figure out the recipe." The valet smiled brightly, pleased with himself.

"If I'll need all my wits tomorrow night, perhaps I should retire early tonight," Jamie said with a stretch.

"No, stay and keep us company," said the earl. "Please?"

"All right. Shall I read to you?"

"No, just talk. Did you hear there's a new Byron due out Thursday week? *Prisoner of Something-or-other*, I believe."

"Really?" Jamie's eyes, behind the unfortunate spectacles, lit up. "Quarter day is next month. I might just treat myself."

"No need to wait," the earl said. "I'll have Hatchards send over a copy as soon as it's for sale."

"That's kind of you, but—"

"Oh, come now. What's a new book cost? Ten shillings? Consider it a bonus for all the work you've done."

Jamie smiled shyly. "Well, all right. Thank you, my lord."

Charles and Stephen continued to play in a desultory fashion, while the conversation meandered like an old river. They touched on politics (Jamie was rather more interested in social reform than the earl, who hadn't given it much thought), literature (Stephen had been well-read at Oxford, and still remembered enough to converse with reasonable intelligence about several of Jamie's favorite authors), gossip (here, Charles had the edge, since the servants of all the great houses stopped by Sam's several times a week to pick up confections for their employers, passing him all the best *on-dits*), and more. They circled back around to books.

"When you're done with the library here, I should turn you loose at St. Joseph," the earl said, tossing down a card, and then wincing as he realized he'd played the wrong one. "It's probably in much better order than this one was, but I'm sure it's never been properly catalogued. Huge, too. If you think we're lacking anything here, we could find things there to fill in the gaps. You also might do some work on our family papers, if you're interested."

"Family papers?" Jamie breathed, the historian in him inflamed. "Like what?"

"Oh, the usual I suppose. I poked around in them once or twice when I was an infant. I remember account books, deeds, letters." He reached to pour himself another glass of brandy, hesitated, and poured from the silver-tagged decanter. "Right up your alley, I presume."

Jamie grinned. "You've never been so right in your life. It sounds wonderful."

"I usually go up for the salmon run in the spring. Perhaps you can join me."

"I would love to, my lord. And now, I really do need to get to bed." His smile was warm as he bade Stephen good night, and the earl's answering smile lingered after Jamie left the room.

Charles gathered the scattered cards from the table, stowing them neatly away in their card box. "Offering up your library at St. Joseph's and family papers was a great stratagem. Jamie was very pleased."

"It wasn't strategy, I just thought he'd be interested." Stephen shook his head. "I don't know what's wrong with me."

Bertie arrived back in London within four days, exhausted from the constant jostling of the Mail coach, which frequently exceeded ten miles per hour in speed. His report had not been encouraging.

"Just what he seems to be. He and his mother lived quietly in the countryside. I thought there might be something in the way the local vicar took him up, but by all accounts it was the lad's brains he was impressed with, not his arse. Not even a breath of scandal about him."

Julian's eyes were chips of green ice. "No one is so perfect. You shouldn't have come back until you discovered what it is he's hiding."

"Well, there is one thing." Bertie hesitated. "This old biddy said she heard from a friend of a friend that Riley's mother was gentry, and there was some long-ago brouhaha about her. But I couldn't confirm it. Up there, they take that not speaking ill of the dead bit to heart."

"A long ago scandal concerning the gentry?" A slow smile crept over the actor's face. "I know just who will know all the details. Bertie, I could kiss you. And if I'm right, I will."

That night after dinner, the Earl of St. Joseph met his secretary in the morning room for their game of chess, both men looking forward to the match with great anticipation.

"Lovely set, my lord," Jamie said, fingering the finely-carved pieces in awe.

"Won't you call me Stephen?" The earl's eyes twinkled merrily. "In a very short time, my head is going to be under your heel, figuratively speaking. In such circumstances, it seems ridiculous for you to be 'my lording' me."

Jamie hesitated. "It doesn't seem right."

"Charles calls me by my first name."

"Thus driving Mr. Symmons to drink. He'd have an apoplexy if I started doing it too."

"But when we're alone?" Seeing that Jamie looked uncomfortable, he added "Or at least when we're playing chess?"

Jamie nodded. "I'll try, my—Stephen," he said.

My Stephen. Now that sounds even better, thought the earl, but he just smiled in encouragement, and plucked a pawn of each color from the board. "Right or left?"

Not surprisingly, Jamie won the first game with ease, and a speed that was downright lowering. The second followed much the same pattern, but by the next, Stephen was relearning the skill of thinking several moves ahead. He was much more satisfied with his performance by the time Jamie called "Checkmate" for the third time.

"Ha! Took you nearly an hour to beat me that time," the earl said smugly. He looked more delighted with his loss than many an opponent would be with a victory.

Jamie's dimple flashed. "Well, no one can say you're a poor sport, my—Stephen."

"Your Stephen thinks he has an even chance of winning a game, by the end of the week," the earl said somewhat rashly. "That is, if you'll continue to play me?"

"Charles will miss beating you at euchre, of course—"

"Charles can spend a few more nights with Sam."

Jamie inclined his head. "As you wish, my lord."

The earl lifted an eyebrow. "I thought you were calling me Stephen?"

"That's while we're playing, my lord. We're done for tonight," Jamie said, with a yawn and a stretch.

Stephen watched the elegant elongation of the other man's frame with unconcealed admiration.

"Unless I can interest you in another game?" he asked, deliberately ambiguous as to whether he meant an additional round of chess, or something else altogether.

"Thank you, my lord, but I need to get up early." Jamie softened the refusal with a smile. "Tomorrow's account day. I've finished your schedule for the next two weeks, barring any new invitations from Lady Matilda, so now I have to catch up with the budget. But it will be a long day, if I want to take Sunday off."

"You're working magic on this household, Jamie. I appreciate it. Really."

The smile he received in return mingled joy and surprise. Had he really been so careless with praise in the past? He'd never really thought of thanking his staff before, assuming it was their duty to see to his comforts with a minimum of fuss, and his to leave them alone to do it.

"Thank you, my lord."

"Goodnight, Jamie."

Jamie paused at the door, and looked back at his lordship over the rim of his spectacles, eyes impossibly blue in the soft candlelight. "Goodnight... Stephen," he said, and was gone.

How on earth does he do that? The earl wondered, shaking his head in bewilderment. Not one of his lovers, stretching through time from Jack Carrington and through the lengthy line to Julian Jeffries—not one of those, with their practiced wiles, exotic tricks, or inborn sensuality, could manage to arouse him so. Using just one word.

How on earth had he ever thought his Mouse unappealing? Tonight, with the soft firelight sparking glints of amber and auburn from his hair, cheeks flushed with his latest victory, his Jamie had been almost unbearably tempting. Almost. If he was going to win the young man, he was going to have to take his time, watch for cues. In the meantime, spending time with him was no hardship. He looked forward to these evening games with an eagerness he hadn't felt since childhood. How long had he been drifting along, drugging himself with mindless diversions, when there was such satisfaction to be found merely in the pleasure of another man's company?

Jamie wasn't just an object of desire. He was fast becoming a friend.

The next morning, Mr. Julian Jeffries dressed in his finest morning clothes and called on Lady Matilda Clair.

Matilda was checking over her household accounts in her small business office when Hargreave, her butler, announced Julian's arrival. She set her quill down with a sigh. "After my money again, I don't doubt. Still, I need to keep a close eye on Stephen, so you might as well send him in."

"Here, my lady?" After nearly forty years' service, Hargreave felt comfortable raising an eyebrow at the thought.

She made a face. "You think I should receive him in one of the entertaining rooms? No, I keep those for people who entertain me. Jeffries is just another problem to deal with, so he's best suited to my office."

"As you say, my lady. Shall I bring tea?"

"God, no. I hardly want to encourage him to stay."

The actor's smile froze on his face as he was led to the single straight-backed wooden chair that faced Lady Matilda's working desk. "My, Auntie," he said. "Someone of your years should spend her mornings more comfortably."

Insolent brat. Matilda's own grandmother had perplexed all her eager heirs by living to be ninety-six, and Matilda intended to outdo her longevity. She cupped a hand over her ear and leaned forward. "Eh? Tears, did you say? No, my eyes always water from cheap cologne."

Julian pitched his voice louder. "No, I said—oh, never mind. I just came for a bit of gossip."

"Gossip?" Her eyes glittered. "Can it be that you know something I don't? By all means, spill it. I haven't got all day."

"Actually, I wanted to ask you about a scandal from years past. Twenty, twenty-five years ago, concerning a woman named Maria Riley."

Matilda's curiosity was engaged at last, wondering what Julian's interest could be in that long ago affair. "Maria Riley. You mean Thornleigh's granddaughter? I always wondered what happened to her, after —" She broke off, not having decided how much of the story to share with the actor.

"Thornleigh's granddaughter. The Earl of Thornleigh? How fascinating." Julian leaned forward. "Perhaps we could pool our information. You know her beginnings, and I know her end."

It was tempting. The scandal had not been obscure: if she didn't spill it, someone else would. And perhaps in return she could ferret out why Julian wanted to know. "Yes, I remember Maria quite well. I used to play whist with her parents. Is she dead, then?"

"Yes, I'm afraid so." He shook his head, attempting a look of mournful sympathy. "Just last spring."

"Oh? Where is she buried? I might like to send an offering to the church in her memory."

Julian laughed. "Do you expect me to give out information for free? Why don't you give me something first."

"All right." Matilda thought. "Maria Riley made her debut the same year as the Parker chit, they were thick as thieves. Ninety-three, it must have been. Lovely girl. Very fair. Where did she die?"

"A place called Wheldrake, in Yorkshire. Her birth name was Riley, then? How interesting, so is her son's."

"Then you can guess the scandal. Old story, isn't it? A child born outside of marriage."

The actor reached to pat her hand, and it took all her strength of will not to withdraw it. "I don't suppose you remember who the father was?"

"Can't say. Perhaps if you tell me more about the son, I might recall it."

"Oh, I ran into him here in London. The circumstances aren't very interesting."

The glitter in Julian's eyes told a different story. A rival? But of what sort? Matilda fished some more. "He'd be above twenty by now. Is he in the theater?"

"No, in service, actually. Was his father a handsome footman?"

Matilda considered ringing for tea. An illegitimate scion of the aristocracy working for one of their own was delicious. She had to know more. "He was a viscount. So the boy's a footman?"

"I didn't say that." Julian also appeared to be enjoying the exchange. He sat back, crossing his legs. "A viscount is the son of an earl. Which earl?"

"Not always. In this case, he was the son of a marquess." Matilda suppressed a wince. Too much information—there were only a handful of marquisates in England. But Julian hadn't grown up among the *ton*, and didn't seem to be able to figure it out on his own. "What else can you tell me about Maria's boy?"

Julian's eyes darkened with an unpleasant emotion. "He's a colorless, scheming little brat. Tell me his father's name and I'll tell you where he works."

"All right." Matilda took a breath, aware that this information was her trump card. "Johnnie Carrington, Viscount Summerford."

"So the Carringtons kept the woman and her brat secreted away in Yorkshire?"

"No, someone else took her off their hands, if it matters."

"Who?"

"You haven't told me where the boy is now."

Julian rose to go. "Very close by. Thank you, Auntie, you're a dear. I must be going."

"Wait. How close?"

"Here in Mayfair. Who kept her after Carrington seduced her?"

"George Whitby—Baron Whitby, if it matters. But he's dead now, too. Give it up, Jeffries. Where's the boy?"

The actor's eyes were brimming with amusement. "At St. Joseph House, of course. But not for long. I wager he'll do anything to keep his parentage quiet. Even leave town, if I tell him to."

Stupid man, to tip his hand like that. "But I don't think you will, Mr. Jeffries. Remember, I know quite a bit about your past as well. You'll not interfere in Mr. Riley's business, and I won't remind people exactly which of the stews you came from. And when, for that matter—you're what, eight years, a dozen years older than you pretend? Would you want that information bandied about town?" Matilda stood, ringing for Hargreave, entertained by the sight of the actor gaping like a fish at the sudden thwarting of his plans.

Her butler returned after seeing Jeffries out. "You had best be on your guard, my lady. Vipers are dangerous when stirred."

"Bah. There's little he can do to me. But I won't have him meddling in young Mr. Riley's affairs. His mother was a sweet girl, and I liked her very much." She fiddled with her quill. "You don't suppose Jeffries' animosity toward the boy has anything to do with Stephen?"

"It seems logical, my lady. The lad must be a threat to him somehow."

"Then I'd best meet Mr. Riley, I think. Hargreave, send a note round to the caterer. I think it's high time I planned another party."

Chapter Twelve

O n Saturday, the last night of November, an ornate landau
painted in violent shades of green and yellow pulled up
outside of St. Joseph House in Hanover Square.

"Don't wait up," the Earl of St. Joseph told his valet. "I shan't
be home until tomorrow at least, and with luck I'll be so hung over
then that I won't get out of bed until Monday." His voice betrayed
little pleasure at the prospect.

Charles' face was uncharacteristically sober. "Are you certain
you want to go out? I know tonight will be difficult for you, but if
Jamie and I keep you company—"

Stephen managed a smile. "Thank you, but no. Some nights call
for companionship, and some for utter oblivion. Julian's particularly good at the latter. That's his carriage outside. I'd best not
keep him waiting."

The actor's smile was artificially bright as Stephen climbed into
the landau, settling next to him on the green leather seat. "How
splendid to see you again, after such a long time."

"Please, Julian." Stephen reached for the other man's hand. "It's
been only a few days."

The gloved fingers twitched from his grasp. "Nearly a week."

"Sorry. I did tell you I'd be staying home more often."

Julian laughed. "To save blunt! How ridiculous. You're one of
the wealthiest men in England, at least on paper. How you let that
withered crone get her crabbed fingers on your purse strings—"

"My great aunt has done very well for the family, thank you. I have no reason to break the trust she and Grandfather set up."

"No reason." The sea-green eyes glittered in the dim light of the carriage. "You're being treated like a little boy who mustn't have too many sweets. Be a man and show Auntie exactly who is in charge."

Stephen looked out the window. They were going south on Bond Street and would soon turn onto Picadilly, toward St. James Street and his club. The distance wasn't great, and the last thing he wanted tonight was a scene that continued into White's. "Please, Julian," he said again. "Let's not fight."

"I'm only thinking of your best interests, darling." Julian's tone warmed, and the actor reclaimed his hand. "You deserve control of your fortune, and Aunt Matilda is badly in need of a comeuppance. Don't you agree?"

Of course he didn't. The carriage turned a corner. "Wait, we should be going the other direction on Picadilly. I wanted the club tonight."

"But White's is so boring. I thought Madame Novotny's would be more entertaining."

Stephen struggled with the idea. The last place he wanted to be right now was London's premier brothel, its public rooms a cacophony of sound and color, staffed with an array of painted wenches and sly-eyed young men. He and Julian had enjoyed some notorious nights of debauch with a variety of the latter, but it wasn't the sort of amusement he was looking for tonight. Still, if a compromise would keep Julian sweet... "Could we just drink for a while in one of the quieter parlors? Madame does keep an excellent cellar, and I'm not sure I'm in the mood for anything more. But I might be, later."

"One of the gaming rooms, then. Let's at least play cards."

"If we're going to gamble anyway, then why not go back to White's? It's quieter, has far more congenial surroundings—"

"Because the stewards at your club, charming as they are, aren't available three for a guinea if you decide you want to fuck them senseless."

Stephen sighed, shoulders slumping. "Fine."

Madame Novotny's was a large establishment sprawling the better part of a block, cobbled together from a number of connected buildings with doors knocked here and there to link them up. It was located among the wharves on the river not far south of Westminster, convenient both to town gentlemen and visiting seamen. Like the proprietors of similar establishments, Madame paid generous premiums to keep from being bothered by the magistrates, and had queened it over her thriving realm of vice for nearly thirty years. It was rumored that any pleasure imaginable could be had within its walls, and should one be able to dream up something not currently on offer, a whisper into Madame's ear would make it reality as soon as the necessary ingredients could be procured.

But what it couldn't provide Stephen tonight was a peaceful spot to sit with a bottle of brandy and mourn. Julian insisted on playing faro, a card game so largely dependent on chance that Stephen soon found himself longing for something better suited to concentration. Like chess. The morning room at home, sitting across the table from his Mouse, watching the young man's brow wrinkle in thought... Stephen drained another glass and stared into its empty depths.

"Your bet, Stephen." Julian was annoyed. "Can't you pay attention?"

"Sorry." He was surprised to see how small his pile of remaining chips was. Either they'd been playing longer than he'd realized, or his luck was even more abysmal than usual. Stephen could stay in the game longer by distributing his few chips among the cards on the table, betting that one or more of them might prove a winner over the next few turns, or go for a dramatic win or lose by piling them all on a single card. He thought about it. Jamie had just turned twenty-two, and those two twos had to mean something. Besides, a glance at the casekeeper, a device that tracked which cards had already been dealt, indicated that the odds were in his favor. Recklessly, he placed the entire stack of chips on the two.

Julian raised his brows. "All on one card?"

"No twos have come up yet."

"Meaning there's an equal chance one will come up as the losing card."

The earl shrugged. "I feel lucky."

The dealer began the turn. The first card he flipped, the soda, did not affect the bets except to remove one more possibility from play. "Ace," he called to the table. A second card was placed to the right. "Losing card is a two." There were disgusted mutters from those at the table who'd bet on that card. "And the winner is... four."

"Idiot," Stephen said under his breath, reaching for his brandy, refreshed by an attentive steward. The drink was finally starting to have an effect, and he welcomed its fire. "Two twos is four. Why don't I ever see what's right before my face?"

"How stupid of you." Julian raised his hand, signaling one of the stewards. "Lord St. Joseph needs more chips."

"No, I don't. That's all I brought with me."

"Fifty guineas? You must be joking. Besides, you can sign for more." He nodded to the steward. "Bring a voucher."

Stephen caught at the servant's sleeve before he could leave. "Thank you, but I'm finished."

"Really, Stephen, we've barely started. You're beyond impossible tonight. What's wrong with you?"

He looked into Julian's eyes. "It's... it's Robert's birthday."

"Well, send a present, for Christ's sake." The actor turned to place a new round of bets.

Stephen remained frozen in his chair for the space of several heartbeats. "My brother, Julian." He put his hands on the table top and pushed himself unsteadily to his feet.

Julian finished laying his chips, but caught up with him just as he reached the door to the gaming room. "Hell, wait. Look, I was distracted. Of course it's too bad about dear old Robert, but he'd probably want you to have a bit of fun in his memory. Come back and play."

Men at other tables were looking in their direction, whispering. He lowered his voice. "Can't we find somewhere quieter for another drink?"

"Why? So you can get all mopish and sulk? That might be your idea of a good time, but it's hardly mine."

"Tell me, Julian. Do you have a family?"

The green eyes blinked, for a moment looking confused. "A what?"

"Brothers? Sisters? People you care about?"

Julian's gaze hardened. "That hardly signifies. Listen to me: people come, people go. Deal with the ones standing solid in front of you, not wisps of memory who can't do anything for you."

Two and two was fast becoming four once again. Stephen's smile was tight. "I should have stayed home with—I should have stayed home tonight."

Julian's eyes narrowed. "With who? Your little bastard of a secretary?"

"My what?" Stephen's hands curled into fists.

The actor laughed. "I meant that in the most literal sense. Or has he tried to pass himself off as something more respectable than he is?"

Stephen shook his head. Perhaps he was drunker than he thought. "You're not making sense. Jamie's a paragon of virtue."

"Oh, are you on a first-name basis with the little guttersnipe? But I suppose that's just as well, considering he hasn't got a last name. Can't imagine why a person like that would insinuate himself into your household, can you?"

"I don't know what you're talking about, but you'd best stop now. Excuse me. I'm going to White's."

৵৹   ৵৹   ৵৹

Jamie took advantage of the quiet evening to sit at the library desk and bring the household accounts up to date. The past nights playing cards or chess with the earl had been very pleasant, but he welcomed the chance to catch up. As the hours progressed, he had reason to be quietly pleased with his achievements. Should the household keep to the economies he'd introduced, and his lordship to the proposed schedule of payments he'd worked out, there was an even chance the staff salaries could be paid this Christmas. By eleven o'clock the accounts were in as good shape as he could make them, and he headed to the kitchen for a well-earned cup of tea. With Rebecca's almond biscuits, if there were any.

He was almost back to the library with his tray when he was startled by an uneven pounding on the front door. Everyone else was long abed, and Charles had told him not to expect the earl, and why. Pausing to first set his burden down on a hall table, he crossed to the door, unlocked it and eased it open.

The master of the house fell into the hall. When Jamie put out a hand to help him up, he muttered, "Not drunk, just surprised."

Jamie refrained from commenting on the brandy fumes emanating from the earl. "Shall I help you upstairs, my lord?"

"Where's Charles?"

"At Sam's, I'm afraid. We weren't expecting you back tonight."

Stephen scowled. "Damned bloody Julian. I was too mopish for him. And White's got too bloody crowded." He caught sight of the tray on the table. "Is that tea? Could use a cup."

"I could take it up to your room for you."

"Stop trying to put me to bed. I'm not tired." He looked it though, face haggard, dark rings beneath his eyes.

"As you wish. The morning room?"

"Can't I join you in your library?" The appeal bordered on plaintive.

"Yes, yes of course." Jamie carried the tray into the library, ensconced Stephen, who was somewhat unsteady on his feet, in a chair by the hearth, and went to fetch a second teacup for himself. He half expected the earl to be sound asleep when he returned, but found him staring unblinking at the fire.

"Your brother was a remarkable man, my lord," Jamie said quietly.

"Yes. Yes, he was." Stephen rubbed at his eyes, which looked hot and tired.

"I don't have to ask if you and he were close."

Stephen nodded, looking back into the fire, as if he could see the past reflected in the dancing flames. "Mother—she was an exotic bird, wasn't she? Fly into the nursery, give us a kiss, fly away. And Father... no interest at all till we were old enough to hunt, and me, I'm bloody useless with horses. So..." He shrugged. "But I had—I had Robert."

"Yes. Of course."

"Six years old when I was born. Utterly furious. 'He'll grow up to steal my toys. I think I shall hit him.' And Nurse says, 'No, he's going to grow up to worship you, and I trust someday you'll be worthy of it.' Oh, God. Fetch the fucking brandy."

"Does drinking really help?"

"Does staying sober?" Stephen smiled, unexpectedly, his characteristic good humor winning through even this pain. "Pity I never had a little brother to set an example for."

"No, but..." Jamie hesitated. "You know, you are in a position where people could look up to you."

"To me?" Stephen's laugh was short.

"Yes, my lord. Oh, I know: all of London takes delight in whispering about your misadventures, but you could be talked about for more positive endeavors. As a peer of the realm, your endorsement could be worth hundreds, perhaps thousands of pounds for a charity or two. And there's a seat in the House of Lords waiting for you to take it up. There, you could do worlds of good."

"Think my friends would respect me for that?"

Jamie caught Stephen's eye and held it. "If not, my lord, that would be the fault of your friends."

After a long moment, Stephen swallowed and looked away. "So I've made a fucking mess of my life. Robert didn't, and he still ended up just as dead, and his legacy died with him."

"Did it? I met him, you know. Just a few times, but I'll never forget him. He was filled with amazing zeal. Joy. Curiosity. Kindness. He died by accident, on a journey meant to expose his children to the history and culture of the Europe he loved. He lived his life well, without regrets, and I've no doubt by example made better men of countless acquaintances."

Stephen's eyes spilled over at last, slow silent tears making tracks down his cheeks to drip from his jaw. He searched his pockets, not finding what he sought, and Jamie handed over his own handkerchief.

In good time, he composed himself. "Anyway," Stephen said, "could I have more tea?"

Two days later, Stephen sat across from Jamie in the carriage on the way to Aunt Matilda's, approving of the way his secretary looked in the blue jacket Charles had cut down to fit him. The young man's excitement didn't hurt, adding sparkle to his face. The December rain beat heavy on the carriage roof, causing Jamie to look up.

"I can't believe your aunt is having a picnic in her ballroom. Could she possibly have known it was going to rain?"

The earl grinned. "A woman of her age doesn't leave the fate of her parties up to God. Besides, it's late in the year for dining out of doors."

"Is your—will Mr. Jeffries be there?"

Stephen sobered. Julian had visited him yesterday, all smiles and cajolery, seeming to sense that he'd been out of order in some unfathomable manner on Saturday night. Somehow, he'd failed to invite the actor to today's affair, despite a few broad hints Julian dropped that he'd heard something was in the works. He had yet to puzzle out the actor's vicious words towards Jamie the other night, but it didn't seem a good idea for the two to meet. And Aunt Matilda had been adamant that he bring his secretary along to the picnic. "No, I don't think so. I forgot to mention it to him."

"Well, I'm glad I get to go. Although I would have been pleased to examine your aunt's book without the bribe of attending one of her parties."

Stephen shook his head. "I can't believe she thinks she might have bought a forgery. Imagine someone counterfeiting a book."

It was Jamie's turn to grin, his kissable dimple as deep as Stephen had ever seen it. "We have established that they're worth money, my lord."

"We've also established that you deserve a treat, so enjoy yourself."

Jamie stretched and settled himself against the upholstered seat. "As you wish, my lord."

Abby pulled the carriage up under the portico of Lady Matilda's Mayfair mansion, and soon Jamie was looking around the ballroom in bemused wonder. There was a grove of living trees at one end, their twenty-foot tops easily accommodated by the vastness of the ceiling. The floor was carpeted with blocks of turf, cleverly fitted together to form a seamless green lawn, with low baskets of flowers placed here and there as if they were growing naturally. A line of mirrored tiles crossed the middle of the room to suggest a stream, complete with a rustic wooden bridge. While the trees contained live birds, imprisoned in wire mesh cages so fine as to be almost invisible; the badgers and foxes, thank heavens, were stuffed.

"Do you like it?" Aunt Matilda's smile held satisfaction.

"It's wonderful," Jamie said. "I've never seen anything like it."

"Must have cost a fortune." Despite his own straitened circumstances, Stephen's voice held only admiration, and Jamie liked him for it.

"Hah." Aunt Matilda snapped her fan closed. "Cost me almost nothing. I just happen to have set up a very-well-traveled gentleman with a few woolen mills, right before the war started. He still sends me gifts from time to time in gratitude—this time it was half a dozen live orchids from South America. I let Archibald's Flowers and Landscaping talk me out of them in exchange for this fribble."

"Woolen mills?" Stephen didn't get it.

Jamie did. "Uniforms," he said. "I've never seen an orchid. Were they lovely?"

"Very," she admitted. "Exotically beautiful. I almost built a greenhouse just so I could try to keep them alive myself. Quentin Lowry would have given me a good price on the glass, too, since I'm the one who sent him that émigré scientist a few years back."

Stephen looked interested. "I told you, I'm planning a greenhouse of my own. I don't suppose Lowry would extend that discount to me?"

"Oh, I think he might." Aunt Matilda's words were more encouraging than the glare she bestowed upon her great-nephew. "However, he knows enough about you to insist on a deposit up front."

Stephen grinned. "With Jamie's help, I've been doing much better, Auntie. Do you have any idea the difference in price between wax and tallow candles?"

"Of course I do, puppy." Matilda extended her arm to Jamie. "Walk with me, young man. At least you look like a person of sense."

They began circling the ballroom, keeping to a flagstone path laid among the grass. Jamie tried to ignore the curious glances he received, but felt his color rise anyway.

"Good afternoon, Lady Matilda." One of the other guests was quick to intercept them, a middle-aged gentleman extravagantly dressed in powder-blue satin, with a damask waistcoat in a contrasting shade of cerise. "And who's your young swain?"

"This is Mr. Riley, the noted historian," Matilda said. "He's been consulting with Stephen about his library. Perhaps you read his paper on Roman tesserae?"

"Of course, of course," the gentleman said, nodding sagely. "Immigration is one of England's gravest problems, isn't it?"

"It seems there are more fools on these shores every day. If you'll excuse us, Lord Whinsbeck. If I stand still too long my joints lock up. Popinjay," Aunt Matilda muttered under her breath as they strolled away. Jamie was hard pressed not to laugh. "All the great houses are declining, don't you think?"

"I wouldn't know. I have little experience with the aristocracy."

She patted his arm. "Apart from being the grandson of a marquess, and in love with an earl, you mean."

Jamie's breath left his body like he'd been punched. "How did you —? Why did you say that? No, don't answer. Please don't."

She ignored his plea. "I've outlived my own generation, boy, and most of Jack Carrington's as well. I may be one of the few members of society left who remembers Carrington in his early twenties — you're his spit and image." Matilda studied Jamie's face. "He grew into his looks, and so will you. Good bones tell in the end. And I remember your mother, as well. Lovely girl. You have her mouth. Whitby's mistress, wasn't she?"

Jamie looked toward the door, escape on his mind. "She hoped people would have forgotten her."

"People did. I didn't. What happened to her was a damned shame, and if I were you I'd hold the Carringtons responsible. I'll help you, if you like. There's money to be had there."

He shook his head. "I don't want anything from them. It would make me sick to accept gold for my mother's betrayal."

"Get off your high horse, son. Surely you don't expect much blunt from my grand-nephew."

Jamie stopped, freeing himself from Aunt Matilda's arm. "I'm sorry, my lady. I don't know what you're talking about, and if I did I wouldn't discuss it with you."

"Nonsense. I saw the way you looked at Stephen—you're arse over teakettle, aren't you? And if you have any expectations in that direction, I'm the one in the family who holds the purse strings."

"I'm not in—" He couldn't say it. "I don't have any expectations. He likes me, and maybe even wants—but I can't—there's no future. I'm not his type."

"He's a fool, then."

Jamie met her eyes. "Perhaps. Do you mind if I take my leave now?"

Aunt Matilda smiled, grudgingly. "Yes, I do mind. You haven't eaten yet, and you deserve some frivolous entertainment. But I'll leave you alone if you like, as long as you promise to stay and mingle. If Johnnie Carrington hadn't been an ass, these would have been your people."

Jamie nodded. "I'll stay. You won't say anything to Stephen, will you?"

"Nothing helpful. That pup has to learn to think for himself."

After the group had eaten, the checkered table cloths were removed from the indoor lawn, and a band began playing in a gallery above. Jamie sat with his back against a tree and watched the brightly-clad couples form a set on the grass for a country dance.

"My, you do dress up well." The voice was soft, and poisonous. "I remember when I picked out that coat for Stephen. But don't worry—I doubt many people here will realize it's a cast-off."

Jamie kept his eyes on the dancing. "Good day, Mr. Jeffries. Are you enjoying the picnic? Sorry there was no room for you in the carriage."

"I was going to skip it, but the Allbrights absolutely insisted I join them." Julian settled himself on the grass next to Jamie. "You know, I think I've changed my mind. Remember how I told you that you should just hold out, and Stephen would soon turn his attention elsewhere? Perhaps it would be less trouble in the end if you just let him have you and be done with it."

"I get it," Jamie said. "He's been spending nights at home, and you think it's because of me. It's not—he's trying to save money for Charles' greenhouse."

"Oh, I don't know. You have a certain superficial attraction, based largely on your youth and presumed innocence. But there'll be just one occasion, one night when your clumsiness will seem charming. Perhaps you could stretch it out to two or three, if you're careful to cry out in shock the first time he sticks his tongue up your arse. But once he's satisfied that he's corrupted your innocence, you'll have nothing to hold him. Will you?"

Jamie wished his color didn't rise so easily. "You know him better than I do."

"Perhaps you think you can learn to please him. Idiot. I've trained and studied my craft for almost twen—ten years. I can perform acts on Stephen you couldn't even pronounce. He appreciates sophistication, Mr. Raleigh."

"I'll keep that in mind." Jamie met Julian's eyes at last. "Tell me, Mr. Jeffries. Do you care for Stephen at all? In the least?"

"Are you telling me you do? Go on, what is it about the man you admire so? Apart from his income, of course."

"He's a better man than he gets credit for, Stephen has a wonderful heart. His staff—he gave most of them a chance when no one else would. He's good-natured enough to put up even with *you*, and he's trying — he's really trying to learn to take responsibility for himself and his dependents. That's admirable, Mr. Jeffries, and if you can't find it so, perhaps you can leave him to someone who can."

"My," Julian said, his eyes glittering from some private joke. "You do have a soupcon of passion to you after all. Do us all a favor and let Stephen use you tonight. Tell you what—I'll come over and coach you, if you're worried you can't figure it out. Maybe I'll even let you have a taste of me when he's finished, if you're very well-behaved."

"Thank you, Mr. Jeffries, but I don't think I'm up to your standards. Good day."

"Just remember, that while the way to most men's hearts may be through their stomachs, Stephen's is a rather more southerly route. You'll have no chance at all if you don't give in."

"The very fact that you're advising it must mean it's the wrong thing to do." Or was that the actor's twisted objective after all? To keep him from passion with Stephen by insisting it was his only choice? Trembling with rage, Jamie left the bucolic ballroom, hoping he would soon forget Julian's hateful smile.

Aunt Matilda's butler caught up with him before he could be so foolish as to attempt the walk back to St. Joseph House in the frigid rain. "Excuse me, Mr. Riley. Her ladyship was hoping you might do her the favor of examining her book before you leave."

"Oh." Jamie shook himself. It was why he was here, after all. "Of course."

Hargreave led him to the library, easily twice the size of Stephen's, lacquered floor-to-ceiling bookcases built into the walls. Fireplaces at either end of the room, shielded by painted Chinese screens, gave off a steady warmth. The butler picked up a volume from a japanned table. "This one, I believe. Lady Matilda doubts whether it's truly a First Folio."

"I'll be happy to give my opinion." With effort, he dragged his eyes away from the shelves.

The butler paused. "Should you feel unlike rejoining the party, perhaps you would be comfortable waiting here for Lord St. Joseph to be ready to leave?"

Jamie smiled with real gratitude, the knot in his stomach caused by the actor's venom easing. "Thank you, Hargreave. I would be very comfortable indeed."

A few hours later, they were back in the coach, the slow clip-clop of the horse hooves on the cobbled street lulling Jamie toward sleep. The unaccustomed glass of brandy Hargreave had brought to warm his tea while he waited didn't help.

"Well? Was it genuine?" Stephen asked.

"Sorry?"

Stephen leaned forward, his dark eyes amused. "You look rather relaxed. I was asking about my aunt's book."

"Perfectly genuine, as far as I can tell." He smothered a yawn. "I am a little—drat." Jamie put his hand to his mouth. "Queasy, at the moment. Not so good, riding backward."

"Come sit by me, then." Stephen patted the seat beside him in invitation, his smile mischievous. "I promise I won't bite. Not very hard, anyway."

Jamie hesitated. It was cozy in the carriage, the rain having gentled into a soft patter, hot bricks wrapped in flannel warming their feet. He had managed to avoid intimacy since his birthday kiss on the floor of the library over a month before, which was absolutely the right thing to do, he reminded himself now. Firmly. Because it was so very tempting, the idea of sitting next to the earl, snuggling against him. Just then, the carriage wheel struck a pot hole, and Jamie's stomach bounced toward his mouth, settling the matter. "Well, I can hardly risk throwing up on your boots," he muttered, taking a place next to Stephen.

Stephen's arm instantly encircled Jamie's shoulders. "There. Isn't that better?" Stephen's voice, always plush, was a devastatingly smooth growl tonight.

Jamie bit his lip. Give in to him, the actor had urged. Let him use you. Jamie could hear his own pulse throb in his ears at the thought. It would be so easy to say yes, and so wrong. Not when the earl didn't love him, not when there would be no future to build in the morning. Worse than his mother's experience, really, because he should have learned better from her. "I'm not... I should..."

Stephen nuzzled Jamie's ear. "It feels so good to hold you, Mouse. Don't make me stop."

"Mouse?" Jamie's laugh was breathless. "Did you call me a mouse?"

"It's not an insult." The words were muffled against Jamie's neck as the earl continued his exploration, setting the nerve endings in Jamie's throat ablaze. "Believe me."

Jamie turned his head, to give Stephen better access, then pushed the other man's head away instead. "You shouldn't, my lord."

Stephen gave a little chuckle and settled Jamie more firmly against him. "No, don't go anywhere, Mouse—I'll try to behave."

"Hmph." Still, Jamie didn't move back to the other side of the coach. He knew he should, but it was irresistible, being held like this.

"Unless you'd rather I *didn't* behave?"

"I don't know," he answered honestly. "I don't know what I

want." Jamie shivered suddenly. These thoughts, these feelings needed investigation, contemplation, and he couldn't think with Stephen's hand moving slowly on his arm. "I need—you shouldn't. I'm—I'm out of my depth here."

The earl sighed into Jamie's hair. "There are two of you, you know," he said. "Right now, you're my timid little mouse, hesitant, unsure. Like when we first met. Like the first time I kissed you. Then there's the other Jamie. Confident, in control—the one who puts tallow candles in an earl's bedroom yet gives wax to the cook—"

"Are you still going on about those cand—?"

"—and who'll argue about it 'til doomsday, because he knows he's right."

"Well, I am," muttered Jamie.

"Yes, you are," agreed the earl. "You're just as confident when you play chess."

"Who's not confident, when he knows the rules? When he knows he's right?"

"Not everyone. Not everyone has the courage to stand up for what they believe in, or the stubbornness to hammer their points home until even a thick-headed earl can see them. I very much admire that Jamie, even when he crosses me."

"Yes, well," Jamie said in a small voice. "When you... touch me, there aren't any rules."

"Nonsense, Mouse," the earl said. "The rules of lovemaking are very simple indeed, and no different whether your partner is a man or a woman. It's just a matter of geography, isn't it?"

"What on earth are you talking about?" Jamie said, laughter gurgling in his throat.

"If the landscape you encounter is convex, suck it." Stephen latched his mouth briefly onto Jamie's neck in demonstration, then moved his lips upward and suckled an earlobe. "I'm sure if you think hard, you can imagine other examples." Jamie shivered. "If it's concave," Stephen whispered, "probe it—" His tongue slid into Jamie's ear, and the young man shuddered again. "—using the instrument that fits best. Flat surfaces can be licked—actually, licking is always appropriate, as are nibbling, stroking, and rubbing—but those are the basic rules. Remember to start gently, and end vigorously, and satisfaction is guaranteed."

"Very helpful," Jamie mumbled.

Stephen touched his cheek, which was hot with confusion. "You're blushing again, aren't you? Well, if you're going to be embarrassed anyway, let me put all my cards on the table. I'm considered to be a generous lover, Jamie, in a way that has nothing to do with finances. That's because I do enjoy all sides of the experience—sometimes, it is better to give than receive, if you understand me? No? Well, it gives me great enjoyment to excite a beautiful young man, to pleasure him, to satisfy him."

Jamie shut his eyes, hyper-aware of his own physical being. The solid warmth of Stephen's body beside him. The earl's breath stirring his hair, the pressure of his arm around Jamie's back and shoulders. The ache in his groin clamoring for attention. For release.

"Mouse," the earl whispered, taking one of Jamie's hands and raising it to his lips. He nibbled a finger gently, as the carriage slowed to a stop. "We're home, and it's a damned cold night. Let's go upstairs where it's warm."

Jamie found his voice. "Not in my room, it isn't."

"Mine, then. The fireplace doesn't smoke, and the bed is big enough for four."

"I won't ask how you determined that." A timeless silence. "I can't." Jamie peered up at the earl as best he could in the uncertain light from the carriage lamp outside. "I'm sorry, I can't. It's not—pleasure just isn't enough." He laughed, a little wildly, opening the door. "Now you have no idea what I'm talking about, do you? Goodnight, Stephen."

"Mouse... please." But the carriage light was shining full onto his secretary's face, and it was clear which Jamie he was dealing with. The earl slumped, defeated. "All right then. May I kiss you goodnight?"

"Better not... oh, hell." Jamie grabbed Stephen's lapel and kissed him full on the mouth, thoroughly, not hiding his hunger. He let go without warning. "Goodnight," Jamie said again, and fled into the house before he could change his mind.

Chapter Thirteen

*J*amie sat at the kitchen table staring into his tea the next morning, long after he should have been at work in the library. In anticipation of quarter-day coming up at Christmas, a new batch of bills had arrived with the morning mail, and they had to be figured into his plan for the systematic retirement of the earl's debts.

But last night's carriage ride consumed his attention. It had been utter folly to kiss Stephen again, to express even a hint of the passion the other man had aroused in him. Unfair to himself, and unfair to Stephen, who of course was ignorant of Maria Riley's history and the effect it had on her son. His employer was doubtlessly confused — why wouldn't any young man who was so obviously attracted to the earl leap at the chance to bed him?

The back door to the kitchen shut with a bang. It was Rebecca, her cheeks pink with cold, toting the day's provisions in two wicker baskets. "Hello, Jamie. Any more of that tea left?"

Jamie looked at his cup. "Sorry. It's been cold for hours, I'm afraid."

"I'll make some new, then." She hummed to herself as she set the kettle to boil, then unpacked her turnips and beef.

"Rebecca?"

The cook looked up swiftly at the plaintive appeal in his voice. "What is it?"

"Is a mouse ever anything but a pest?" Stupid question, but Rebecca seemed unperturbed. Trusting, no doubt, that there was a good reason behind the inquiry.

"Well, boys sometimes keep them as pets. My little brother did. It was a lively and inquisitive little thing. He adored it. Kept it in a little box for months and fed it kitchen scraps."

"What happened to it?"

"Cat ate it."

"Oh." For some reason, Julian's green eyes came to mind. "In case you're wondering, it's his lordship."

Rebecca poured them each some tea and sat down across from him. "I was thinking it would have to be, to keep you from your library. Did he call you a mouse?"

"Yes. But not in a mean way. In the carriage last night. We were—he—I—oh, hell, Rebecca. I think I have feelings for him."

"Ah." She added sugar to her cup, stirring thoughtfully. "And is that necessarily a bad thing?"

"He's offered me money. He's offered me rare books." Jamie stopped and swallowed a mouthful of tea, not tasting it. "Last night, he offered me... pretty much anything I wanted in bed. At least I think he did. But he's never once—not once—said a word about how he feels about me. Well, no, that's not quite true. He did say he admires my convictions." Jamie laughed mirthlessly. "If he only knew how close I was to abandoning them last night."

Rebecca took his hand. "Jamie," she said. "It's hard for men to talk about their feelings."

Jamie squeezed her hand. "Especially if they don't have any. Sometimes I think he does, but that might just be because I want him to so badly. Then he tries to seduce me again, and I'm scared it's just a ploy."

"Oh, poppet, give him time. Charles says he likes you."

"Charles is an optimist, and a romantic." Jamie took another sip of tea, then smiled at his companion. "Poppet? I'm—what?—three years older than you, Rebecca."

Rebecca laughed. "Yes, I know. But I have little brothers, and you just seem younger, sometimes, maybe because—" She shrugged.

"Because I'm a timid little mouse." Jamie sighed. "I've heard him refer to Julian as 'the Golden One.'"

"Don't you think it's encouraging that he has a pet name for you?"

Jamie considered it. "Maybe. Maybe it is. But I wish he'd give up that blasted actor. For good, this time."

"He will. Don't give up on him yet," Rebecca said.

"I'll try not to. Will you do me a favor, though? If you see Charles, will you ask him to stay in tonight? I don't think I can handle quite so much time alone with his lordship."

"Of course I will," Rebecca said, rising. "I need to get to work now, poppet, but stay and talk as long as you like."

Jamie got to his feet. "No, I have a lot to do, too. But Rebecca," he paused, then leaned over and kissed her on the cheek. "Thank you," he said.

"Oh, off with you, now," she said, pleased.

Neither noticed the pantry door closing softly.

"Jamie?" Stephen opened the door to the library that afternoon and poked his head in. There was no one at the desk, but there was a clatter and sharp cry over from the fireplace.

"Oh, your lordship! You startled me, and now I've banged my noggin." The young housemaid tittered nervously, rubbing at her head.

"Here, let me see." The earl crossed over to the girl—what was her name? Bess? Betty? no, it was— "Betsy, you've got a bit of a bump. Why don't you go have Mrs. Symmons look at it?"

"Oh no, my lord, 'taint nothing, this, an' I have to finish cleaning the fireplaces by supper time, or Maisie won't tell me a story about Christmas tonight when I go to bed, before she— Do you like Christmas, my lord?" Betsy picked up the whisk she had dropped and continued cleaning the ashes out of the fireplace.

"Um. Yes, I do. I was looking for Mr. Riley, have you seen him?"

"Sam said he'd make us plum pudding. I never had plum pudding, is it nice?"

"Quite nice—especially Sam's. But about Mr. Riley—"

Betsy was not to be deterred. "Maisie's been telling me all about how flash folks like you pretty up their houses with ribbons and holly and mistletoe." She giggled. "Do you put up mistletoe, my lord?"

"I—um—well, I suppose I could. We'll do the house up proper for Christmas this year, but right now I'm looking—"

"Maisie says girls get kissed under the mistletoe. Maybe Jamie would give *me* a kiss, like—like—" Betsy giggled again.

"Betsy," the earl said patiently, smiling. "If you've seen Jamie and me kissing, it's probably not a good idea to talk about it too free—"

"Not you, my lord! I meant Rebecca. Maybe if you put up mistletoe—"

"What? He, who?" Stephen could feel the blood draining from his face, leaving him light-headed and sick.

"Rebecca. I saw him kiss Rebecca just this morning. Well, and before, too, but not really, 'cause the other time she kissed him, but it's almost the same—"

"You've seen them together—more than once?" Betsy didn't notice the change in the earl's demeanor, and laughed.

"They're together all the time! Jamie and Rebecca are ever such good friends. I know a secret that I'm not supposed to know. Well, two secrets, but this one—"

"Do share it with me," Stephen managed.

"Rebecca borrows Jamie's spectacles, but she doesn't need them at all!" Betsy said. "She just doesn't like Jamie to hide his eyes like that—I heard her tell Charles that Jamie has the prettiest eyes she ever saw."

"And where—is—Mr. Riley?" his lordship whispered coldly.

"Who, Jamie? He went out. If we have mistletoe this Christmas—oh. Well. Goodbye, my lord. I'll tell you Maisie's secret later." Betsy shrugged and went back to clearing the grate.

Damn the bitch. Stephen poured a third brandy from the good bottle, and knocked it back neatly. Rebecca, with her golden hair and soft womanly body. And damn the little mouse, too. It hurt, like salt in a raw wound, to think of Jamie kissing Rebecca with the same whole-hearted passion he had shown that second time in the library. More passionately, more whole-heartedly, without doubt. What would constrain him, with her? She was a far more comfortable match—no awkward social differences, closer in age, and of course, of course, of course: a woman. He picked up the bottle again, and a fourth measure soon joined the others in burning a hole in his guts. Oh, damn him for a duplicitous bastard.

But that wasn't fair, and he knew it. Jamie hadn't played him false—all along he had resisted, and protested, and told him that he was confused and didn't want to be involved. 'It just isn't enough,' Jamie had said, last night. Isn't enough to overcome the taboo, he'd meant, especially when there was a more conventional option waiting for him in the kitchen.

Jamie had shown desire for him, it was true. But Stephen was well familiar with men who were attracted to other men, but chose not to follow through out of fear, or self-disgust, or because it felt safer and more comfortable to return to the familiar world of male/female relations. Men who might allow themselves to be kissed, and groped—sometimes more, who might even wake up in his bed with a shamefaced expression and an 'I can't believe I did that' on their lips. Then the excuses—'I was drunk' 'I didn't know what I was doing'—'I just needed to be with someone'—before the flight out the door, away from the temptation, away from the shame, and back to the wife or girlfriend or mistress who would make them feel like a 'real man' again.

Stephen dropped his face into his hands. Sometimes, once at least, it had gone even further. His second year at Oxford, there had been an upperclassman, Mark Gregory. It had been his first serious affair after Jack. For two terms, they had been inseparable. Ate together, studied together, played together. Late at night, crept into each other's rooms, or met in some deserted corner, to make love for hours with the stamina and enthusiasm of the young. Then it came time for Mark to leave, to graduate and take his place in society. A place, it was clear, where there was no room for Stephen.

"Come visit me," Stephen had begged. "Write to me. We can spend holidays together."

And Mark had looked at him like he was an imbecile. "Look. It was fun, but I have to join the grown-ups now. When your time comes, I suggest you do the same."

For Mark, at least, playing with other boys was a temporary measure, a school expediency, something you grew out of.

Stephen had protected his heart after that, seeking his pleasures from the boys offered at the more sophisticated brothels, and eventually buying the little house in Floral Street, near Covent Garden, to keep his more expensive favorites in. He'd been fond of several of them, and even infatuated sometimes—but none of them had the power to hurt him that, it appeared, he had inadvertently bestowed on his little Mouse.

A fifth brandy was spreading its poison through Stephen's veins. If Jamie had been so damned reluctant, why that final, passionate kiss last night? It occurred to him that there was another sort of man he had encountered in the past, men who were thrilled by the sexual response they could elicit, who gloried in their own power to arouse, with absolutely no intention of following through. Cock-teasers.

That time by the fire, when Jamie had allowed Stephen to kiss him until they were both well worked up, then suddenly refused to go any further. (In tears, the rational part of Stephen's mind reminded him, but he ignored it). Last night in the carriage, letting Stephen hold him and feast on his throat. He didn't have to do that. It was difficult, though, even with the help of alcohol, to envision Jamie for long as a cold-hearted, deliberate tease—easier by far to imagine him running timidly to the safety of Rebecca's skirts.

But why not a little of both? The boy might be just a little pleased with himself for inciting the kind of reaction he got from Stephen. "Well, fuck him." Stephen twirled his brandy glass between his hands. Yes, and why not do just that? Show that prudish little mouse exactly what he's missing. Show him what's 'enough.' And if he were lucky, and that bitch Rebecca hadn't bedded him yet, he might be able to steal him right out from under her perfect little nose.

Stephen reached for the bottle again, then drew his hand back. He had a seduction to plan.

The Earl of St. Joseph frowned at his reflection in the glass. "No, Charles, I think a different shirt. Where's that silk one, with the big cuffs?"

"I think we still have it, but the sleeves are too wide for your new coats."

"Then I won't wear a coat this evening. I'm staying in, and I doubt Jamie will mind the informality." The earl stripped off the rejected shirt and regarded his half-naked self in the mirror while Charles rooted in the wardrobe for the desired garment. Not bad — not as lean as he'd been a decade ago, perhaps, but he wasn't running to fat, either. Strong torso, with good shoulders, narrow enough at the waist. Couldn't fault the fit of his trousers, or the long, muscular legs they outlined so neatly. He turned for a side view. Arse wasn't bad either. Jamie had the edge there, but that was because it was so surprising to see such nicely round buttocks on a slim frame like his. Slim, neat, compact frame, fine-boned but not—quite—delicate. Except maybe those lovely hands...

Charles cleared his throat for the second time, and the earl tore his eyes away from the mirror. "Yes? Oh." His valet was holding out the silk shirt, and so he put out his arms obediently and allowed himself to be dressed.

"Now for the waistcoat. No, not the yellow one, it's too cheerful. Something darker. What do you think — would a red be too blatantly seductive?"

Charles was looking at him curiously. "Is that the effect we're striving for tonight? Blatant seduction?"

Stephen grinned. "Let's not scare my little mouse away. Quiet seduction, make it. Which reminds me, your services are not desired tonight — go spend some time with Sam."

The valet blinked in indecision, engaged in some private battle. "I—I was thinking of staying home tonight. Sam has... um... Sam has a big wedding coming up," he improvised. "He needs to work on the cakes. Try this amber one. It brings out matching tones in your eyes—very nice."

The earl slipped the waistcoat over the shirt and narrowed his eyes, considering the effect. "Don't I have an amber pin of some sort? So go over to Sam's and study your garden books while he works."

"Um... he says I'm too distracting. Let me look. Yes, here it is. Lovely."

"Too distracting, and after eight years? My, my." The earl nodded, pleased. "This will do. If Sam doesn't want you tonight, go out somewhere. There must be a play on somewhere, or a friend you can meet for a drink."

"I don't have—I don't have any mon—oh." Charles blinked at the purse the earl had just tossed him, at a loss. "I—I—"

"Did Jamie ask you to stay in with us tonight?" the earl asked.

Charles looked around the room for inspiration, and, finding none, nodded hesitantly.

"What exactly did he say?" There was an edge of hurt in the earl's tones.

"Well, actually, I haven't spoken to him today, but Rebecca told me—"

"Rebecca? Oh, Rebecca told you, did she?" No mistaking the blazing anger here. "I assure you, your little friend will come to no harm. Now, you will go out tonight, is that clear?"

"Stephen—"

"Charles, that is an order."

The valet's jaw snapped shut in surprise. He stared in stunned silence for a moment, then said "Yes, *my lord*," and turned on his heel.

The earl watched him go, then turned back to the mirror, tilting his head this way and that to catch his reflection from all angles. Not bad, really.

There was a knock on the door. Charles must have thought up a suitable retort.

"Yes, what is it?" he called. The door opened, revealing Mr. Symmons.

"Package from Hatchards for you, my lord." The butler proffered his tray, upon which was a narrow, flat object wrapped in brown paper.

"Must be the new Byron—is it Thursday already?"

"Wednesday, my lord."

The earl shrugged. "Privilege of rank, I assume. It's not supposed to be out until tomorrow. Thank you, Symmons." He took the book. "I hope Jamie likes it."

The butler looked pleased. "Is it for Mr. Riley? How kind of you, my lord."

"Not at all," the earl said shortly. "Again, thank you."

Mr. Symmons bowed and left, leaving him alone to contemplate whether or not to bother with a cravat.

Chapter Fourteen

"Good evening, Jamie," the earl said as he entered the morning room after dinner, a flat package wrapped in brown paper in his hand.

"My lord." Jamie glanced quickly back down at the table, which he had been setting up for cards. His lordship was looking especially attractive tonight, and it shamed him that he had striven so carefully for the opposite effect, sporting his oldest, shabbiest garments. But it was better that he keep distance between them, if he could. At least until he could discern the earl's feelings for him.

"You can put the cards away." Setting down his package, Stephen crossed to a rosewood chiffonier and retrieved the chess board. And the tray with the brandy decanters, which Jamie had banished from the table.

Jamie watched him warily. "I thought Charles was joining us?"

"Sam took ill. It's just the two of us tonight." His smile held such promise that Jamie looked away. The earl poured brandy into two glasses. "Here's to Sam's quick recovery."

Jamie took his glass, but didn't drink.

"You do want Sam to get better?"

"I think I had a bit too much last night. I'd rather not make a habit out of it."

The earl shrugged. "Suit yourself. But one little brandy is hardly going to hurt you. Timid little mouse," he added under his breath.

Jamie's head jerked up, a flash of anger in his eyes. "To Sam," he said, draining his glass.

"That's my boy." The earl's eyes glimmered with amusement. "What do you say we make the game a little more interesting tonight?"

"How so?"

"A small bet." The earl tapped his finger on the wrapped package. "I have here a book I believe you are interested in."

Jamie perked up. "Is that the new Byron?" How thoughtful of Stephen to have remembered. He reached for the book.

"Ah, ah—not so fast. Let's play first, shall we? Since I've already promised you this, you'll get it whether you win or lose—we'll just consider it in escrow until after the game, all right?"

Jamie nodded. "You're sure you wouldn't just like me to read to you tonight?" His own voice sounded wistful in his ears.

"Perhaps after."

"So I'm playing to get the book, which you say is already mine, out of escrow?" The earl nodded assent. "And what will you be playing for?"

The earl smiled slowly. "Something you can well afford. Another brandy?" He poured himself another measure.

"No, thank you. The stakes?"

"Kisses," the earl said. "Payable only if I win the game." He was still smiling, and his dark eyes shone with challenge.

"Just kisses?" Jamie asked. "How many kisses?"

"If I win," repeated the earl, "you would owe me one kiss for each piece of yours that I've captured, minus the number you've won from me. I take five of yours, you take four of mine, you owe me one kiss. Plus one for the win, of course—just in case we end up tied for pieces. Come on, Jamie, the risk on your part is quite small. How many games have I won so far?"

"So far... none. But you are getting better." Jamie considered. "Suppose I decide not to play?"

"Your decision. But the book stays in escrow until you do. If not tonight, then some other time." The earl made a show of checking his pocket watch. "Do let me know. If you decide not to play tonight, I can just make the Johnston's card party."

Jamie took a breath. "I'll play. I just—you're in an odd mood tonight, my lord."

"Stephen," the earl reminded him, placing a pawn of each color behind his back. "Choose."

Jamie ended up with white, and opened with pawn to king four. The earl moved in classic response: pawn to queen four. Jamie moved his queen's pawn up to the third space, opening a path for his queen side bishop. The earl took his first pawn.

Jamie frowned. "That doesn't really help you. Right now you should be trying to develop the center of the board—" he stopped, suspicion dawning, and looked up.

The earl batted his eyes at Jamie, and blew a kiss.

Jamie flushed. "You can't just play for pieces. It doesn't matter how many you win, if you don't win the game."

The earl inclined his head. "Your move, sweetheart," he said, his voice rich and caressing.

It was an absurd game. The earl's moves were wildly unpredictable, literally all over the board, and Jamie's efforts to force the game back into the classic patterns he knew so well hampered his own ability to second-guess what outrageous stratagem his opponent might come up with next. In desperation, Jamie resorted to playing to protect his pieces, and at that point effectively lost the game. As he himself had said, Jamie was no good at extemporaneous play. His inability to plan ahead leveled the playing field, and unbelievably, incredibly, the earl pulled off his first win.

"Well, will you look at that?" marveled the earl, counting. "Twelve for me, eight for you. That's four, plus one for the win. Five kisses, sweetheart." He patted his knee. "Come here and pay up.

Jamie swallowed and looked away. "I—suppose we go out on the veranda?"

"Right here is fine. Unless you'd rather get a little more comfortable on the sofa?"

The sofa was low-backed, soft, and wider than Jamie's bed. "No, I don't think so. Just kisses, right? You're not going to—going to try to touch me, are you?"

The earl sighed. "I can't kiss you properly if I can't touch you. Pull you close, stroke your hair, cup the back of your head."

"I—but—"

"Shall we say above the waist only? Would that make you feel better? But for the love of God, don't try to constrain me more than that. It was," he added softly, "a fair win."

Jamie nodded, too nervous to speak.

"Come here then."

The young man rose and walked slowly over to the earl, whose expression softened. "Come on, love, you can handle a few kisses." Stephen reached for Jamie's hand, and pulled him gently down onto his lap. He removed Jamie's spectacles and laid them aside, stroked his hair, soft as silk. "All right, my little Mouse?"

Jamie, feeling naked and vulnerable without his glasses, perched awkwardly on the earl's knee. "I can handle a few kisses."

The earl laced his hands behind Jamie's head, and brought him down for their first kiss. Jamie parted his lips, and the earl kissed him gently but thoroughly, exploring Jamie's mouth at leisure. He ran his tongue over Jamie's teeth, and across the sensitive roof of his mouth, teased the inside of his lips; stroked the other man's silken tongue with his own, not rushing, not pushing, taking his time. When he pulled away at last, Jamie took a deep breath.

"That wasn't so bad." He relaxed in the earl's arms, slouching down a little, snuggling closer.

For a moment, his lordship rested his face on the top of Jamie's head, breathing in the scent of his hair. "Not your worst kiss ever?"

"One of the best," Jamie admitted. This wasn't a conversation he wanted to explore, however, so he lifted his head for the second kiss he owed Stephen.

It quickly dawned on Jamie that he was in trouble. Because, of course, their second kiss was not a repeat of the first, but picked up where it had left off—starting deeper, growing more and more urgent. Then, feeling a tugging sensation at his waist, he broke away and looked down to find the earl had untucked his shirt, and was now unbuttoning his waistcoat. "What are you doing?"

The earl slipped his hand, large and warm, under Jamie's shirt and rested it on the bare skin of his back, just above his trousers. "I'm allowed to touch you above the waist," he said stroking his hand slowly up Jamie's back. "So... I'm touching you."

Jamie shivered at the unfamiliar sensation of skin on bare skin. It was unbelievably arousing. He was in trouble indeed. "Maybe we should —" But the earl had his other hand on the back of Jamie's head, and was guiding him back for kiss number three.

The earl claimed his mouth with undisguised hunger, and Jamie, rudderless, held on for dear life, clutching at the earl's shoulders as if he'd be lost if he let go. The hand at the back of his head disappeared, then joined its mate under Jamie's shirt, caressing the naked flesh of his back, drawing patterns on his skin, up, down, around.

Jamie moaned helplessly, his whole body throbbing with desire. The kiss went on and on. Hotter. Harder. Jamie realized he had shifted again on the earl's lap, and could feel the other man's arousal pressing against his buttocks. His own trousers were uncomfortably tight. The earl was sucking on his bottom lip, biting down gently at the same time. It was too much. With a cry, Jamie pushed away from the earl, overbalancing and landing in an awkward sprawl on the floor.

In a flash the earl was beside him, gathering Jamie back into his arms, making soft shushing noises against his hair. Jamie was trembling. "You set me up, didn't you? You planned this."

"You're mine," the earl whispered into Jamie's ear. "Mine, and no one else's. Don't fight me, love."

Love. It was the second time Stephen had used that word. Was it just a meaningless endearment, or— Jamie looked for the answer in Stephen's eyes, dark and glittering in the candlelight. He shivered again, caught in their ebony depths, and his hand rose of its own accord to touch the other man's face. The earl responded by pushing Jamie gently to his back on the floor, and covering him with his own large, strong body, resting some of his weight on one elbow.

Their mouths met for the fourth time. The earl's hand crept under Jamie's shirt again, this time stroking the front of his torso, wandering over his chest. Combing his fingers through the light fur there, stopping to feel the rapid pounding of Jamie's heart beneath his palm. A thumb brushed over one nipple, sending fire shooting directly to Jamie's groin. Jamie moaned again, unable to keep his body from arching up into that touch. The thumb moved away, just a little, drawing a light circle just outside Jamie's aureole, and Jamie squirmed, trying desperately to re-establish contact. The earl teased him some more, moving his hand across to the other nipple, circling slowly around that one as well, coming close without quite touching it. Then, suddenly, the earl relented, rolling the hardened nub between his finger and thumb.

Jamie cried out, and stumbled to his feet. He looked gloriously disheveled to the earl, panting, clothing awry, lips swollen and red, eyes wide with confusion and desire. He looked down at the earl on the floor, and back over to the door. "I—I don't—" Jamie turned his back and started from the room.

"Jamie," the earl called. "A gentleman never welshes on a bet."

Jamie paused for a long moment with his hand on the doorknob, then opened the door and fled up the stairs.

Stephen listened to the unsteady pounding of his prey's progress up the steps and got to his feet. He collected Jamie's spectacles, the decanter of good brandy, and the book. Then he followed, stopping briefly in his own room on the way.

In a very few minutes he was outside Jamie's door. He knocked softly. "Mouse? Are you all right?"

Silence.

"Please, love, answer me. I need to know you're all right." With a start Stephen realized his words were true. What if he'd pushed Jamie too far? He pictured suddenly the long drop from the window to the street. Stephen rapped harder on the door. "Please, Mouse!"

"It's open." The words were barely audible through the wooden barrier. Stephen pushed the latch, and the door opened easily. The room was cold. Jamie was standing next to his desk by the open window, lit only by the full moon outside. His back was to the earl, arms wrapped tightly around himself.

"I always blamed her," Jamie said.

"Who, Mouse?" Stephen asked, crossing the room and laying his burdens on the desk. Jamie didn't glance at them, lost in his own thoughts.

"Someone it turns out I'm just like. I should have walked away sooner."

"But you did walk away."

Jamie turned then, eyes huge in the moonlight, brimming with what looked to be equal parts passion and terror. "Yes. But I knew you'd follow. And I still owe you a kiss. And if you kiss me now..."

It was on the tip of Stephen's tongue to release Jamie from the debt, to tell him not to worry, that they could take things more slowly, give him time. But Rebecca was waiting in the wings, wasn't she? And the thought of anyone, anyone else touching his Mouse was unbearable.

"Yes, you do." The earl placed his hands on Jamie's hips and pulled him close so that their bodies were touching. Jamie's cock was hard against Stephen's thigh, and he knew the younger man could feel his excitement as well. Slowly, he pushed Jamie's waistcoat down his arms, then unbuttoned the young man's shirt. Jamie shivered as the cold night air touched his bare torso, and the earl reached past him to close the window.

"It's warmer in my room, love."

"No. Here. Is that brandy?"

"Yes. I forgot the glasses, though."

"It doesn't matter." Jamie took the stopper from the decanter with unsteady hands and put the bottle to his lips. When he had drunk, the earl took it from him and echoed the action, then set the decanter back down with a thump.

"Why not my room, Mouse?"

"Because—because it's always cold up here. Unless I light the fire, and then the smoke is unbearable. There have been nights when I was tempted to go and knock on your door, just because I was so cold. If you want me, it has to be here. Don't you see?"

The earl didn't see, not completely, but he wasn't going to ar-gue. "Why open the window, then?"

Jamie laughed shortly. "I thought it might cool me down. But there's only one remedy for this fever, isn't there?"

The earl hesitated, and this time compassion won. "There's another, actually. Time. If you want me to, I'll go," he said, amazed at his own words.

"No," Jamie said, with a trace of desperation in his voice. His hands went to the button flaps on his own trousers, and began fumbling with the first of the closures. "You've brought me this far. I want to know. Show me the rest. Stephen, please."

The earl led Jamie to his narrow bed, where he joined him under Mrs. Symmons' warm quilts. Quickly and efficiently he stripped Jamie of his remaining clothing, cursing the cold that kept him from a lengthy perusal of the younger man's nakedness. With equal alacrity, he removed his own clothes, thrilling to Jamie's gasp as the lengths of their bare bodies met for the first time. The earl pulling Jamie down on top of him.

Jamie's head was spinning. Skin on skin. Who knew it felt like this? *Everybody but you, idiot*, Jamie thought, and then thinking was impossible as Stephen's hands began to move over him.

"Oh Stephen," he moaned. "Oh my—" *love*, he thought, but couldn't say the word. *Oh, my love.* Tentatively, Jamie's own hands explored the other man, mapping the curves and valleys of the earl's splendid form, smooth skin, resilient muscle, unyielding bone. The hair on his arms was silky, coarser on his legs, nearly non-existent on his chest. Just below his navel, though, a line of hair led directly down to—Jamie's fingers brushed the thick thatch of Stephen's pubic hair and he snatched his hand away in confusion.

He heard Stephen's soft laugh and felt himself blushing. "Remember, Mouse, stroking and rubbing are always appropriate. No? Well, we've got plenty of time for that later. Right now —" Stephen's large hands left their delicate play at Jamie's nipples, slid around to his back and down to knead the firm globes of his arse. Jamie shuddered as one finger insinuated itself between his cheeks.

"I don't—couldn't we just?—oh God, Steph—" Jamie broke off with a cry as the finger reached its destination, rubbing gently at the sensitive entrance to his body.

"Shh, Mouse, it's all right," crooned the earl. "Let me just finger you, hmm? If you don't like it, or you're too tight, I'll stop."

Jamie nodded abruptly, face buried against Stephen's chest, trying to slow his own breathing. The earl rolled them to their sides, still facing each other, and reached for something from his clothing on the floor.

"What's that?" Jamie whispered.

"Oil, Mouse. It makes it easier for my finger to get in." The earl's slick digit returned, massaging carefully. "Relax, love. Let me in."

Jamie made an effort to relax against the earl's probing finger, and the tip of it slipped gently inside. Jamie whimpered.

"Am I hurting you?"

"N—no, I just—"

The earl was relentless. "Does it feel good?"

"I—yes, it's—"

"Good," whispered the earl, pushing further. Again he paused to let Jamie relax a little more, then began moving his finger gently in and out, going deeper and deeper with each stroke.

Jamie moaned, and Stephen muffled the sound with his own mouth, stroking his tongue into Jamie's mouth in time with the finger plunging in and out of his body. The finger was moving easily now, and Jamie's hips had begun to move as well. Then suddenly the earl's hand withdrew, and Jamie whimpered wordlessly.

"It's all right, I'm just—" The hand was back, two slick fingers pushing their way inside. Uncomfortable at first, but Jamie's body soon adjusted. Within a few minutes he was again moving eagerly against his lover's hand, the pressure and friction inside him driving him toward climax.

Then the fingers were gone again, and Jamie found himself rolled onto his back.

"Knees up, love," the earl commanded, and Jamie obediently raised his legs. Then something that was decidedly not a finger was pushing against his opening, and Jamie cried out in protest.

"Wait! You said you were just going to finger me."

"Come on, Jamie, sweetheart. You're ready for me—opened up nicely. Let me in, love, let me in."

"But—oh, God. Oh, God, Stephen." Stephen rubbed the head of his well-oiled cock against Jamie's entrance, and the boy pushed back against him uncontrollably.

"That's it, love. That's it," whispered the earl, sinking his length slowly into Jamie's well-prepared body. "Hold on tight."

This last command was unnecessary, as Jamie dug his nails into Stephen's shoulders hard enough to leave marks. Stephen was impaling him, filling him, *inside him*. The unexpected intimacy of the act seared his soul, and tears welled up in his eyes.

"Shh, love, it will pass. We'll give you a moment to adjust," Stephen said, mistaking the reason for the tears. "I'm in—you've taken all of me now, sweetheart. Oh, God, Mouse, you are so sweet, so sweet, so tight." He ground his hips against Jamie's arse. "Better now, love? I can't hold back much longer."

Jamie nodded wordlessly, and Stephen kissed him briefly, then buried his face against the other man's neck with a deep moan and began to move.

Start gently. The earl followed his own advice, at first stroking slowly in and out of Jamie. A slow, gentle rhythm that built steadily. He reached once between their bodies to caress Jamie's cock, but his hand was pushed away.

"No—I don't need—that's too much. I'm too—too close."

Stephen took that information as a definite sign that he could increase the pace, thrusting harder into Jamie's heat.

Finish vigorously. Jamie was moaning steadily now, crying out with each powerful thrust. Stephen trusted that the cries were of passion, not pain, but it was impossible for him to stop now anyway. He had to grit his teeth to hold back until Jamie suddenly threw his head back and convulsed against him, hot liquid shooting out between their tightly joined bodies. With an answering shout, Stephen let himself go, waves of pleasure contracting through him as he came deep inside Jamie. The contractions seemed to go on forever, suspending him in a state of ecstasy that had no beginning and no end, and no reality outside that of Jamie's sweet, yielding body.

When it was over, Stephen slumped onto his lover's body. "Mmm. Sorry, Mouse," he said, when he realized that Jamie was supporting his full weight. Rolling off him, he groped on the floor for something to tidy them up with, and came up with a shirt. He cleaned Jamie's ejaculate from their stomachs, then wiped his cock, finally pressing the white cloth between Jamie's still-spread legs and examining it in the moonlight.

"No blood," he said with relief. "Still, we'll take it slowly for the next few days, Mouse."

Jamie shuddered. No going back now.

Stephen tossed the soiled shirt back to the floor, but Jamie caught it by one sleeve. "Oh, hell, it was mine."

The earl laughed. "No worries, Jamie. I'll buy you a dozen shirts. A hundred."

"I don't want a hundred shirts, Stephen," Jamie said, fear shooting through him.

"Oh, come on Mouse, you have to let me spoil you a little." The earl licked Jamie on his nose. "I have a feeling you haven't been spoiled much in your life."

"Please, don't."

"Don't what, this?" The earl laughed and lapped at Jamie's nose again.

"Don't spoil me. Don't give me anything, please. It would ruin it."

"Oh, Mouse, Mouse... let's argue about it in the morning, all right?" He spooned up behind Jamie and pulled him close. "Definitely a bigger bed..." he murmured.

Within a few minutes, the earl was asleep, but Jamie lay staring into the moonlight for a long time. 'A hundred shirts, a bigger bed, let me spoil you.' Stupid fool. Jamie cursed himself. Not only wasn't Stephen in love with him, the earl was already trying to adapt their relationship into the form he was most familiar with. Commerce. Jamie shuddered again in the darkness. Maybe he was wrong. Maybe the older man had spoken without thinking.

Stephen had called him 'love.'

Chapter Fifteen

*J*amie awoke, cold and alone. His room was bright, too bright, he realized. What time was it? His clothing and Stephen's still lay on the floor where they had been discarded last night, but the earl was gone. Jamie huddled back beneath the quilts, feeling empty. Soon he would have to get up and face the household, everyone aware by now that the earl hadn't slept in his own bed, and snickering over the fact that Jamie himself was still abed so late into the morning. Rebecca and Charles, at least, would be pleased, and encouraging. 'Don't worry, poppet,' Rebecca would say, 'he'll come around.'

"But why should he, Rebecca?" Jamie wondered aloud. "Now that he's got what he wanted. My father never came around, did he?"

Charles, ever the optimist, would beam happily. Jamie wasn't sure he could take that today, nor Betsy's giggles.

And the Symmonses, who openly disdained the earl's preference for men. What would they think of Jamie now? It would be hard to face their stares of cold disapproval, or worse — disappointment. Jamie's stomach felt like he had swallowed lead. What had he done?

Without warning, the door opened, and the earl entered, wearing Jamie's own dressing gown. He sat on the bed and smiled cheerfully.

"Well, good morning, sweetheart." He leaned down for a brief kiss of greeting.

Jamie sat up to meet him, and winced involuntarily.

"Sore?" the earl said. He reached under the covers and slid an exploratory hand between Jamie's buttocks.

Jamie slapped the hand away. "You might ask first," he said, drawing his quilts tight around his nakedness.

"What is it? Regrets?" Stephen's rich voice was still sympathetic, but his eyes now looked wary.

Indeed: lots. But Jamie couldn't say that, so he said instead, "I'm just not used to being touched, that's all."

Stephen grinned. "That's easily remedied." He pulled Jamie, quilts and all, onto his lap, wrapping his arms firmly around him. It was hard not to feel better, being held like that, and Jamie couldn't help relaxing a bit.

"Where were you?" he grumbled, while Stephen stroked his hair.

"I had to piss, sweetheart. Did you think I left you alone?"

Jamie didn't answer, but he flushed beet red.

"You did, didn't you? Oh, Mouse." Stephen kissed the top of his head.

"What time is it?"

"Oh, early. It can't be much past ten."

"Ten o'clock?" Jamie sat bolt upright. "Oh, blast."

The earl was amused. "Well, it's early for me." He pulled Jamie back into his arms. "What time do you usually get up?"

"Six thirty. Even if I linger over tea with Charles or Rebecca, I'm usually working by eight." Jamie stirred restlessly.

"Good heavens. There'll have to be some sort of compromise from now on."

Jamie was sure he knew which of them would be expected to compromise.

"Well, come on then," Stephen said. "If you're determined to get up, come down to my room and keep me company while Charles shaves me. He can shave you, too, while he's at it."

"God no." Jamie disentangled himself from the earl and rose, wrapping the quilt around him. "I can shave myself."

"Of course you can," the earl said. "But the thing is, you don't have to. Charles won't mind."

Jamie shook his head, mutely but emphatically.

Stephen glanced at Jamie's ruined shirt on the floor. "I'll have him send for the tailor—we need to get you some shirts."

"No! Stop that! Stop trying to give me things." There was a note of desperation in Jamie's voice.

"Be reasonable, sweetheart. I owe you a shirt," the earl said, rising to put a hand on Jamie's shoulder. "And I can hardly ask him to come here for just one, can I? You could use a few extras, and you have to admit your coat's a bit shabby. Suppose we felt like going to the theater? You'd want something a little nicer to wear."

"*Please,*" Jamie said. "If you have to, couldn't Charles just re-make some of your old things for me? He's done it before, and he's very good at—"

"For Christ's sake, Jamie!" The earl sighed with impatience. "It's good of you to want to save the household money, but I can hardly take you out in public wearing my own castoffs. I'd be the laughingstock of London. For heaven's sake," he said in softer tones, "don't be so stubborn. Besides, you let me give you the book."

Jamie shook off Stephen's hand and crossed to touch the flat package on his desk. "You said it was a bonus. But it was part of your plan, wasn't it?"

"Well, you might not have agreed to play me for kisses without some incentive."

"I suppose I can admire your economy. That is, providing you got at least ten shillings worth of entertainment for your invest-ment."

The earl laughed. "You're worth much more to me than that."

Jamie looked him in the eyes, serious, pulling the quilt more tightly about him. "Why last night?"

Stephen met his gaze. "Too much was uncertain. Some things had to be made clear between us."

"I don't understand. What things?"

"You're mine. Mine." The earl's voice softened, and he pulled Jamie close.

This time, Jamie failed to relax into the other man's arms. What did Stephen mean by *mine*? His love, or his possession? "Let me go. I have to get dressed."

"I won't have anyone else touching you, is that clear?"

How absurd. Who else, in all of Creation, did Stephen think might touch him?

"Jamie?" The tone was grave. "Is that clear?"

"Yes, of course it is, Stephen."

"Good." The earl nipped Jamie gently on the ear. "I'm going downstairs. Have a wash and a shave, then join me in my room for breakfast. And sweetheart—" he licked Jamie's neck. "About getting dressed? Don't bother."

The earl kissed Jamie on the lips, twice, and was gone.

When Jamie was alone, he sat on the edge of his bed, with his head in his hands, stomach knotted with a combination of fury and despair. Well, what did he expect Stephen to say? "Oh, darling, be mine, and I'll love you forever, live with you in perfect harmony." Not when the two of them didn't even keep remotely similar hours. Or that Stephen would be embarrassed to be seen in public with him because the only coat Jamie could afford was shabby-but-respectable, when the earl himself flaunted that hideously— but expensively—dressed whore Julian Jeffries all over town. They were from different worlds.

Jamie shook his head impatiently. He'd made this bed, but he was damned if he could lie in it. What was he going to do? Unable to think of anything, he rose and picked up the wrapped book from his desk. At least the new Byron would prove a distraction. Jamie unknotted the string that held the paper together, and stared in blank horror at what was revealed. Acid bile rose in his throat.

"Some things had to be made clear between us," Stephen had told him.

Oh, they were clear, all right. Jamie barely made it to his wash basin before his stomach emptied.

Charles was indeed beaming as he shaved the earl.

"Have some breakfast sent up—something hearty," Stephen said. "Jamie's going to need his strength. And then make sure we're not disturbed."

The valet grinned. "If I have to guard the door myself."

"No eavesdropping, Charles." The earl laughed. "I doubt Jamie would appreciate it. Although if things go anything like they did last night, you're likely to hear him no matter where you—"

He was interrupted by a knock on the door.

"Oh good, that must be Jamie now." The earl made to rise, but Charles pushed him firmly by the shoulder.

"You're covered in lather, Stephen. Let me get it."

It was Mr. Symmons. "Another package from Hatchards, my lord."

Charles took it. "Oh, it must be the new Byron, for Jamie. Thank you, Mr. Symmons." The butler bowed and left.

The earl frowned. "There must be a mix-up. They sent one yesterday as well."

"Can't have. It wasn't out until today."

"I know it wasn't supposed to be. I thought getting one early was just a benefit of rank."

Charles hooted. "Prinny himself couldn't get an advance copy. And I know for sure the Duchess of Devonshire didn't get one yesterday, because her kitchen girl was talking about it when she picked up an order at Sam's this morning."

"Open it, just to be sure."

The book was revealed indeed to be the new *Prisoner of Chillon.*

"Then what the deuce did they send me yesterday?" puzzled the earl.

Charles' face cleared. "Oh, I know," he said, picking up his razor and resuming shaving his employer. "It must have been that book you had me send out to be rebound. I did send it to Hatchards, now that I think of it."

"What book?"

"Oh, you remember. That Book of Hours."

The earl blinked. "The one I had you offer to Jamie if he'd sleep with me? Oh, hell. He wouldn't think I still—would he? I'd better go explain."

But Jamie was already gone. So were all his things, barring the clothing Charles had made over for him. The Book of Hours, with its exquisite new binding, lay on its wrappings on the desk, next to a note.

My lord,

I can't stay. I know you don't understand, but I can never be yours on these terms. The price is too high.

James Riley.

Chapter Sixteen

O n the evening of the day that Jamie left him, the Earl of
St. Joseph sat at the huge mahogany desk in his library,
staring at the stacks of paper lined up in an orderly fashion. Here were his own engagements for the next two weeks, there
a stack of incoming mail that had yet to be sorted. A ledger con-
taining the schedule Jamie had worked out to pay off his creditors,
a growing stack of receipts marked 'paid' in a folder in the back.
The household account book. Stephen rifled through the pages,
covered in Jamie's careful script: *Item, to six quarts dried pease
for soup 18p...to three pounds of wax candles 6 shillings 6d...to
twelve pounds of tallow candles 7 shillings 4d.*

His first impulse when he had found Jamie gone had been to
bolt out the front door and search for him, but even a few minutes
lead into the warren of London streets was enough to make pursuit
impossible, especially if one had no idea which direction one's
quarry might flee. Stephen had never felt so foolish in his life,
standing blinking in the street, turning this way and that on his
heel, trying to decide which way to go. Charles had retrieved him,
leading him gently back into the house.

He'd then thought to visit Aunt Matilda, for advice, for the blunt
to bribe watchmen or hire thieftakers to find Jamie, for a little
family sympathy. The latter two were sadly lacking, and the advice unpalatable.

"You want him to come home to you?" his great-aunt had raised a formidable brow. "Be the sort of man he'd want to come home to."

"Oh, God," he said out loud now, hand hovering over one of his secretary's neat stacks of paper. "Jamie, I don't know where to start."

There was a soft knock on the library door. "My lord?" It was Rebecca. "I thought you might like some tea."

Stephen's back stiffened. "You thought wrong."

"Could I —"

"No. Leave me alone." He knew he sounded churlish, but really, it was all her fault. If the lovely young cook hadn't been pursuing Jamie herself, he wouldn't have been forced to move so quickly to secure the lad. And the blasted mix-up over the books would never have happened.

She withdrew, and almost instantly Charles appeared, bearing the good brandy from the morning room.

"Is there anything I can do?" his valet asked quietly, pouring them both a glass.

Stephen drained his and rose to pace the room. "Help me figure out where Jamie could have gone. Back to Yorkshire? He probably knows someone there who would take him in. That vicar?"

Charles shook his head. "I think the vicar died before his mother did. And even if there's anyone else, he hasn't the money to get there. As far as I know, he hasn't any money at all."

"Oh God." Stephen knew all too well the dangers abounding in London for penniless young men — after all, he'd spent years being one of them. Not that Jamie, unlike many a cheerful country lad on his first visit to the big city, would be glad to trade a few hours of his time for a warm meal and a place to stay for the night. But what would he do when he was desperate? Or if he didn't recognize the peril in some respectable-looking man's seemingly kind-hearted offer of assistance? Stephen suddenly recalled titillating stories that had circulated some years before, of a rich eastern potentate whose procurer had dressed like a clergyman, and had lured dozens of young girls and boys alike off to their fate. Not that his Mouse was likely to end up in a harem, but still —

"Charles, we have to find him. Now."

The valet hesitated. "Bow Street Runners? They found Lady Ashby's son, when he ran away."

"Unlike the Ashby twit, Jamie's of age. Unless I tell them he absconded with the silver, they have no reason to help me find him. And I certainly can't afford to pay them privately." Stephen paced some more, biting his fingernails.

"Let me get Rebecca. She'll have some ideas."

"Rebecca!" The earl's head snapped up, eyes blazing. "If it

weren't for that bitch, I wouldn't be in this situation."

Charles gaped, stupefied. "Stephen? What in blazes are you talking about?"

"She and Jamie. Betsy saw them kissing. That's why I had to seduce him last night."

"Rebecca and Jamie? That's absurd," Charles protested. "They're like brother and sister. Betsy was wrong, or misinterpreted something."

"Ha!" Stephen turned to face Charles, lips in an ugly twist. "Did you know she'd pretend to need his spectacles, just so she could look at his eyes? But you did know, didn't you? Wasn't it you that she told he had the prettiest eyes she ever saw?"

Charles blinked. "We all admire Jamie's eyes. But the spectacles, she borrowed them so that *you* could see his eyes."

"Me? Why the hell would she do that?" demanded the earl.

Slow color crept up Charles' neck, suffusing his face. "Um. We thought if you just got interested in Jamie, you might get rid of Julian that much faster. That's why I made him the blue waistcoat, and Rebecca cut his hair. And got him to lend her his spectacles."

"At first?" The earl's tone was dangerously soft.

"Yes. Well. Then we got to know Jamie better, and like him. And we thought if you could just spend more time with him, um..."

The earl paused to digest this information. "Are you saying there was a backstairs conspiracy to make us lovers?"

"We... um... thought it would be good for both of you."

"Oh Jesus." Stephen sat back down at the desk, putting his head in his hands. "From now on, let me handle my own *affaires de coeur*, all right?"

"Since you do such a fine job of it," murmured the valet.

Stephen whipped his head up, stung. "Maybe without your *help*—oh, hell. This is getting us nowhere. There's just no way to find him, is there?" He stared down at the account book, trying to imagine himself taking his aunt's advice and becoming the sort of man Jamie would want to come home to. Totting up these bloody accounts, taking responsibility for the people under his roof.

Another knock on the door. "My lord?" Symmons had returned to the lands of frost: if his nose were any higher in the air it would brush the chandelier. "A Mr. Jeffries to see you."

"Tell him I'm not—wait." Stephen closed the household account book and put it face down on the desk, not looking at Charles. Who was he fooling? He would never be the sort of man Jamie wanted, not when all he wanted right now was to go out and get stinking drunk with Julian, and stagger home unable to remember his own name, much less the responsibilities the fates had been so foolish as to put in his way. "Tell him I'll be right out."

~ ~ ~

At precisely that same moment, in a tiny, unheated bedroom in Bloomsbury, Jamie Riley sat on his bed and stared at the floor. There was a grate set in it, in case any warm air wanted to rise up from below, but none seemed to be taking advantage of the opportunity. Apart from that, there was nothing else of interest to look at beneath his feet, just bare boards, naked of rugs or even paint. The walls were a little better, although they had been painted at some time in the distant past. From the squares of different colors where the pigment had faded unevenly, someone had once hung a few prints or paintings to liven the room. He tried to imagine anyone finding pleasure in such a dreary place, humming to himself while he decorated his surroundings. Dreaming of a better life, no doubt.

Jamie shivered, and not just with cold. The worst thing he had to face about this room was that he couldn't afford it. He'd had only a few shillings in his possession when he'd fled the townhouse this morning, and technically, they belonged not to him, but to the earl's household money. Either way, they wouldn't go far. He'd been able to pay in advance for a week's lodgings, but if he didn't find employment within that time he would have to seek out a much cheaper room than this. The mere fact that they existed depressed him enough.

"You should have taken your payment," he jeered to himself. Even rebound, that Book of Hours was probably worth over a hundred pounds. He could be sleeping at a fine hotel tonight. Or in Stephen's arms, of course. He wrapped his own arms about himself now, in a futile attempt to stifle the longing that wouldn't go away. The urge to go back to the warm, safe townhouse, to say he was sorry, that he wanted to be with Stephen no matter what the cost in self-respect, in pride. No matter if it left his soul in tatters, and his mother sobbing in her grave.

He looked at the window pane, cracked and dirty. Today, when he'd barely left and still had coins in his pocket, it was easy to resist the hateful temptation to creep back to Stephen. But tomorrow? Time would tell.

Chapter Seventeen

*J*amie smiled at the man behind the desk early the next day, trying to emit an air of calm competence. If nothing else, the two months he'd spent at the earl's had given him practice in hiding his feelings, and he was fairly certain now that no hint of desperation was visible. Haskins Employment Agency was among the most respected in the City, and he had hopes of making a favorable impression on its proprietor. He glanced around the office while he waited, liking it very much. The furniture was solid and practical, but well-built and not unattractive, and he felt he could search the shelves and cabinets for hours and not find anything out of place.

Mr. Haskins adjusted his own spectacles as he perused Jamie's qualifications, plump fingers twirling the ends of a ginger moustache. "You've had little in the way of paid employment, Mr. Riley."

"That's correct, sir. But I did act as secretary of the Eboracum Antiquarian Society for several years." He leaned forward and pointed at another paper on the desk. "It's in the letter of recommendation from the head of the society, Mr. Caswell, who was also the vicar of my parish."

"He describes you in quite glowing terms." Mr. Haskins regarded the letter again. "We do confirm recommendations, of course, so if we think we can place you we'll be writing to Mr.—ah—Caswell ourselves."

Jamie's stomach tightened. "I'm afraid Mr. Caswell has passed on."

"Oh, dear. How... inconvenient. Have you other references?"

The current chair of the antiquarian society had been the vicar's bitterest enemy, long covetous of the post. He'd be unlikely to recommend Caswell's protégé to anyone. Jamie shook his head. "I do have a letter from... from a high-ranking gentleman, offering me employment as tutor to his sons, but I was unable to take up the post."

"I do have a gentleman seeking a tutor. Let's see your letter." Mr. Haskins frown suggested that he was wondering why Jamie hadn't produced this credential at the start. He scanned the letter briefly, finding his answer almost at once. "Ah. The last Earl of St. Joseph. He, too, seems to have been impressed by you. But coincidentally, he, too, is unavailable to confirm his impressions, isn't he?" The employment agent read the missive more carefully, his eyebrows slowly drawing skyward. "Mr. Riley, when did you say you arrived in London?"

"I..." Jamie felt warmth creep into his face.

"I was under the impression that you'd recently come here, but it wouldn't have been as far back as October, would it?"

The date he was supposed to have begun working for Robert Clair's family was clear in the letter. Mr. Haskins' eyes narrowed. "Let me put it another way, Mr. Riley. If I were to write to the Eboracum Antiquarian Society for information about you, when would they tell me you'd left Yorkshire?"

There was no sense in lying now. "I did come in October, sir."

"To St. Joseph House?"

"Yes, sir. I didn't know that the former earl and his family were gone. His lordship asked me to stay for a bit, to catalog his library."

"The *current* earl. Ah." Mr. Haskins gathered Jamie's papers together and collated them with a brisk snap, his moustache bristling. "Mr. Riley, I don't believe I have any openings that would suit you at all."

Jamie stood. "Please, sir—the gentleman you mentioned who is seeking a tutor—"

"For a young and impressionable son. I'm sorry, but I have other appointments to prepare for. Perhaps you can see yourself out?"

"Then perhaps you know of someone without children—a single man?" Too late, he realized how that must sound.

Mr. Haskins' face turned to stone. "I do not make placements of that sort. Good day, Mr. Riley."

Jamie retrieved his documents, his hands shaking. You're wrong about me, he wanted to say. But Mr. Haskins was all too right, wasn't he? He had succumbed to the earl's seduction, quite easily, in fact. What could be winked at among the aristocracy was intolerable in a servant.

"Good day, Mr. Haskins," he said with as much dignity as he could muster.

There was no reply.

Outside on King Street, Jamie stood for a moment, trying to regain a sense of confidence that he would soon procure employment. Watching the steady stream of traffic, on foot, horseback, by cart and by carriage, it was impossible to think that among so many people there wasn't someone who would hire him. He looked down at his meager sheaf of references. Mr. Haskins had certainly not been impressed.

"Meat pies! Who'll buy my pies?"

Jamie's stomach rumbled at the street vendor's cry. It had been hours since the cup of tea and small bun he'd allowed himself for breakfast, but with the few coins he had, he'd best tighten his belt and hold off until evening. He could make up for it when he found employment.

If he found employment.

"More brandy?"

Stephen shook his head, but Julian filled his glass anyway. And since it was there, why waste it? The liquor burned its way down his throat, settling uneasily in a molten pool in his stomach. He had talked the actor out of a more athletic evening with the rent boys at Madame Novotny's, but even this quiet card room in his club was too public, too noisy. At another table, there was commotion as someone won an enormous pot, and he closed his eyes, wincing.

Julian reached to pour another measure, but Stephen put his hand over the glass to forestall him. "Please. I have a headache."

"Wouldn't have anything to do with your servants, would it?" The actor topped up his own drink. "When I came by for you tonight, that young maid of yours was crying, and your valet— what's his name?"

"Charles." *As you should bloody well know, after all these months.*

"Whatever." Julian waved his hand in dismissal. "If I were charitable, I'd say he was too preoccupied to give me the respect I deserve. And your butler! Not that the man hasn't always walked as if he has a stick up his arse, but today he stalked off as soon as he opened the door, and left me to your valet. It was intolerable, Stephen. You should do something."

Stephen changed his mind and poured himself another brandy. "I'm afraid we're at sixes and sevens since Jamie left."

"Jamie? The mousy little secretary?" Julian smiled with pleasure. "Did you frighten the wee rodent away?"

The earl's hand tightened on his glass. "It seems I did."

"Ha." The actor leaned close, tickled Stephen's neck. "Tell me all about it. What did you do to scare him, put your hand on his bum?"

"Rather more than that." He met Julian's eyes. "I slept with him."

Contrary to all expectations, Julian wasn't angry. His eyes softened, and he placed a hand on Stephen's forearm, squeezing gently. "Some men don't take to it, darling. They think they might enjoy being with another man, but when, um, push comes to shove," he raised an eyebrow at his own cleverness, "they just don't."

Stephen ran fingers through his dark curls. "It's not—not a question of enjoyment." He struggled for a way to describe Jamie's reservations to someone like Julian, but the actor was perfectly capable of carrying on a conversation whether he understood it or not.

"Physically and mentally, he just wasn't right for you. Perhaps he took all that fire-and-brimstone nonsense to heart, or just thought himself less of a man. Or..." Julian's cat-like eyes glowed clear green in the candlelight. "Or perhaps he just doesn't appreciate you the way I do."

Less brandy, less hurt, and Stephen might have laughed. Instead, he blinked. "What do you mean?"

"You're a better man than you get credit for, Stephen. You know, you have a wonderful heart. That *unusual* mish-mash of servants you have. It was so good of you to give them a chance when no one else would. And darling..." Julian lowered his eyes, artfully long lashes brushing his cheek. "I've been watching you grow these past few months. You've been trying, really trying to learn to take responsibility for your household." He laughed, looking back up with mischief in his eyes. "I know, we behaved badly when you first came into your inheritance, but Stephen—you were so upset I felt you needed the diversion. Together, I'm sure we can do better in the future."

Stephen stared in bemusement. "You've never spoken like this to me before."

The smile he received in return was uncharacteristically tentative. "I—I've had to think about it, Stephen. I was afraid I was losing you."

"I didn't know you felt like this."

"I don't wear my heart on my sleeve," the actor said. "I can't.

I've been hurt so badly in the—but now I've got you." His voice dropped an octave, and his fingers, playing along Stephen's thigh beneath the table, made the earl's blood course. "Come home with me now, and let me show you how I feel."

"Yes," Stephen whispered. "Oh, yes."

Chapter Eighteen

"Now what?" Jamie said it out loud as he descended the stairs of Montague House three days later, rejected for a position at the British Museum. His credentials weren't good enough to even assist in the Antiquities Department, and when he'd tentatively mentioned that he'd be content to sweep floors, Mr. Peake had tut-tutted that such a thing was no job for a gentleman. He'd spent every available hour searching for employment since Friday, and it had been the same story everywhere. Too inexperienced for clerical work; too refined in appearance to be taken seriously as a menial laborer.

Outside the Museum, he paused, looking wistfully at the temporary structure that had been built to house the Elgin Marbles, purchased last summer by the Museum and scheduled to go on display next month. Although workers must already be busy preparing the exhibit, right now the shed was quiet, the men probably at their luncheon. He wandered close enough to set his hand against the door, a huge padlock barring him from the merest glimpse. On the other side were magnificent sculptures from the frieze of the Parthenon herself, just feet away yet as inaccessible to him as if they'd been on the moon.

"Here now, what're you up to?" The voice was rough, the man large and glowering.

Jamie flushed with consternation. "I'm sorry, I didn't mean any harm. I just... I just..."

The worker's eyes flickered with understanding. "Bloody marvelous, they are. Care for a peep?" His hand curved, palm up.

Jamie jingled the few coins in his pocket, tempted beyond reason. "I can't," he said at last. "I don't have a job. There's nothing to spare."

His misery must have been clear on his face; the worker hesitated, then said, "Bloody hell, what's the harm? Come on, then."

He unlocked the shed and waved Jamie in, cautioning him to be gone before the other laborers returned from lunch. Inside, the work of Phidias cast its two-thousand-year-old spell. The fluid grace of the battling soldiers and centaurs; the stately magnificence of the seated gods in council; the sensuality of the nude, reclining Dionysos inspired him nearly to tears. The Museum had done nothing as yet to restore the statuary, but its rough condition, pitted and scarred, only served to remind Jamie of its antiquity, that these were no modern copies but the very stones gazed upon by Plato and Euripides.

If only Stephen were here to share this. The longing came out of nowhere, and he smiled to himself ruefully. The Earl of St. Joseph was no scholar. Such an exhibit would only bore him. Then Jamie's smile broadened to a grin as he considered the beauty of Dionysos, and the soldiers' physical strength. Stephen would enjoy the Marbles after all.

His smile faded. The exhibit would open in January, and was already the talk of London. Stephen would almost certainly go, perhaps in the company of the classically-handsome Julian Jeffries, who might himself have been one of Phidias' lesser works. It was pure conceit to think that if Stephen were with him today, Jamie could lead him to a finer appreciation of the sculptures' beauty. He dragged his eyes away from a headless youth, perhaps a river god, wet draperies clinging to one arm. There was no denying their erotic appeal, either, despite the artistic convention that left their genitals seemingly underdeveloped. How Julian and Stephen would snicker over those.

The mood broken, Jamie was somber as he walked back to his lodgings. With no employment yet in sight, he would be forced to move to worse within a few days. He shivered in his overcoat, despite its warmth. It had been given to him for his birthday by the Symmonses, replacing the one he'd sold to help pay for his passage to London from Yorkshire. He supposed he could sell this one, too, but the winter cold made that prospect unappealing. Yet what else did he have? The portrait of his mother was very well done, but it was unthinkable to let it go. He thought of his books, worth at least a few shillings, and had to swallow past the lump in his throat.

M.J. Pearson - 141

No. He would bury his pride first, and go back to the earl's town-house. Not to stay, of course, and at a time when he'd be unlikely to run into the master of the house. But Charles would lend him a pound or two, wouldn't he? There were only two things wrong with this plan. First, Charles might be willing to help him, but the valet didn't have any money of his own, and wouldn't until (and if) Stephen paid him his quarterly wages at Christmas time, still over two weeks away. He might be able to procure a loan from Sam, but Jamie was reluctant to involve people he barely knew in his difficulties. Second, he was afraid that if he visited St. Joseph House, his resolve would crumble.

Stephen, he thought. *Oh, God, how I miss you. I wonder if you even think of me.*

"His aunt refuses to help," Charles said, picking apart one of Sam's finest rolls at lunch that day in the kitchen at St. Joseph House. "And he's spending more time with that blasted whore." He cast an apologetic glance toward Mrs. Symmons. "Sorry. I meant to say 'that perfidious actor.'"

"But why?" Rebecca appeared ready to fling her soup spoon in frustration.

Charles shrugged. "Jamie's gone, isn't he? Stephen is hurting, and Julian's been sweet and smooth as custard. I think he realizes how close he came to getting the boot this time, and isn't about to let Stephen get away."

"Yes, well, Julian's bad temper is legendary," Rebecca said. "There's no way he can keep that up for long."

"But he doesn't have to, does he? Just until he's sure his contract is renewed on quarter day." The valet dropped all pretense of eating, leaning forward over the table. "Julian's got that charity performance tonight, and his lordship sent me out for tulips for him."

Betsy frowned. "Tulips ain't so fancy, is they?"

Mrs. Symmons pursed her lips. "Not in springtime. But in December, I should think they'd be more expensive than roses."

"Exactly." Charles nodded. "Besides, Stephen was going on about how the first time he saw Julian on stage, he was holding an armful of pink tulips, and he thought he'd never seen anything so beautiful in his life. If Jamie stays away much longer—"

"But why won't Jamie come back?" Betsy's young face looked on the verge of tears. "Jamie didn't just disappear, like Maisie's — he didn't," she protested. "Couldn't he still come back?"

"Perhaps it's time to speak of something else, Mr. West." Mr. Symmons stirred his soup with his spoon, but little of it seemed to be reaching his lips. "Remarkable cold spell we've been having, isn't it?"

"Winter's early this year," his wife said, lines of worry creasing her forehead. She gave an involuntary glance at the window, where a few dry snowflakes swirled against the glass.

Abby Sawtell looked up from her soup plate. "Smart lad," she said. "Find a stable."

Her son Alex nodded, washing down a large mouthful of food with a hearty swig of ale. His appetite, at least, was unaffected. "Horses throw off a lot of heat. It's warm as toast out in the stables. As long as he—"

Mr. Symmons' face was stony. "Excellent soup, Mrs. Wyss. You've come a long way in your cooking."

Rebecca pushed her own plate away. "Oh, lord: let him be getting enough to eat."

Across the table from her, Betsy began to whimper.

Mrs. Symmons bit her lip. "Perhaps this afternoon, you might go over the household budget with me, Mrs. Wyss. We need to—"

"Please call me Rebecca, Mrs. Symmons. You always have."

The housekeeper's back stiffened. "As cook of this household, you are due the respect of a proper title."

"Even if it's against my wishes? Mrs. Wyss! Heavens! It sounds like a sneeze."

"If you dislike your name so, you could marry that footman of yours and change it." Mrs. Symmons sniffed. "I heard you sneaking out again last night, like a common—"

"I did no such thing!" Rebecca's mug sloshed ale onto the table as she set it down with force. "And keep to your own business, Mrs. Symmons!"

"The way you kept to yours? You and Charles tarted up young Mr. Riley on purpose to catch his lordship's eye—that's clear enough, looking back. Here I though you were being kind to him. Kind!" Mrs. Symmons' eyes flashed with sorrow. "Like a babe to the slaughter he was."

Mr. Symmons tapped his spoon against the edge of his plate. "Here now! That is enough. We will not speak of that—that man at this table again."

Charles stood up, dropping his napkin on the table. "His name is Jamie, and he was always kind to *you*." Hurt warred with anger on his face, its round lines so much better suited to good cheer. "And if his name is unspeakable, Mr. Symmons, why isn't mine?"

The butler lifted his chin. "It's not in me to approve of you and your Sam, but the differences are clear. You've been with each other for years, and had the decency to keep to your own kind. Dallying with the master of the house, especially one such as *he*, is something else entirely. You know what his lordship is."

"Stephen—*his lordship* was better since Jamie came," Charles said, still standing. "More responsible, more thoughtful. There's always been a lot of good in him, with Jamie's influence it was just coming to the surface."

Mrs. Symmons' voice sounded mournful. "Was," she said, shaking her head. "*Was.*"

Julian Jeffries regarded his face in the glass backstage at the Ivy Lane Theatre, which Lady Parkhurst had engaged tonight for her charity benefit. His contribution wouldn't tax him: he and Melinda Phelps were to perform a scene from *Much Ado About Nothing*, which he'd done at least a thousand times before. But if the material was stale to him, the opportunity was fresh.

"Perfect, Bertie," he said to his dresser, reaching to hand the younger man a pink bouquet. "Now, go fetch some water for these flowers. And don't come back until curtain time. I need to concentrate."

"Yes, sir."

He had been between productions for nearly three months now, since his backstabbing understudy, George Fulston, had stolen the lead of his last play from him. So what if Julian had been late for the first act? It was understood that the curtain would be held for him, always. And if by some chance mixed signals had allowed another actor to begin the performance, obviously he should have been allowed to resume the role at the next scene change. But no, Fulston must have come up with a whopper of a bribe: when Julian had arrived backstage, the theatre manager had escorted him to the door.

It still stung. If he could only attract a backer tonight, Julian had many ideas for new productions in which he'd be stunning. Oh, he knew his limits: Julian Jeffries was a competent enough actor, but his real fame (and fortune, for that matter) had come from his exquisite looks, and he hungered for the continued adulation of the crowds. He turned his head, inspecting himself carefully at the mirror. Thirty-eight years old, and in full stage makeup he still looked as fresh as one of those damned tulips Stephen had heaped upon him. Tulips! They made him sneeze. Nevertheless, he had managed to smile and thank the earl graciously. The man was still moping over the loss of that colorless little bastard of a secretary, and the merest threat of a rival was enough to put Julian on the alert.

Because Stephen Clair was perfect for Julian Jeffries. Relatively undemanding, never violent, easily led. And while the earl's current allowance of twenty thousand pounds was eclipsed by that of quite a few members of the *ton*, there wasn't a soul in London richer than his great-aunt, Lady Matilda Clair. It had been a mistake to antagonize her, but who knew that she'd come up so protective of the Riley by-blow? Well, he could mend that fence. Little old ladies loved him.

And if he couldn't? The bitch was eighty years old. She had to kick the bucket soon enough. Leaving everything to Stephen Clair, her only living relative. Julian had been careless with Stephen, and almost lost him. He couldn't afford to make that mistake again. It should be easy enough to keep Stephen eating out of his hand, as long as James Riley cooperated by remaining out of sight.

If only there were some way to ensure it.

Chapter Nineteen

*F*ive days. Jamie had fled St. Joseph House on Thursday, and tonight it was Tuesday already. He had been gone for the better part of a week, penniless and alone on the streets of a filthy and dangerous city. Rebecca shivered to herself and sipped her tea, staring down at the bit of scrap paper in front of her, a stub of a pencil in her hand. The whole household was worried about him, but no one had seemed to have the gumption to do anything about it. They needed someone to take charge, to think the problem through logically and come up with a plan of action: in short, what they needed was Jamie. In his absence, Rebecca was trying her best, but inspiration was slow in coming.

Charles entered the kitchen, home from an evening out with Sam. "You're up late, Rebecca. What's that, the household budget?"

"Hang the budget. I'm trying to figure out how to find Jamie." She turned the paper towards Charles, revealing nothing but aimless cross-hatches and curlicues on the page. "Do you have any ideas?"

The valet fetched a cup, and poured himself some tea from the pot at Rebecca's elbow. "Boarding houses. They must be listed in the City Directory."

Rebecca made a note. "Good idea. They advertise in the newspapers, too. We can make a list and start calling on them."

"Starting where? There must be hundreds."

"I suppose—" The kitchen door swung open, and Mr. Symmons stalked in, ignoring them as he proceeded to the cook stove and poured milk into a pan to warm it. "Sleepless night, Mr. Symmons?"

The butler grunted, stirring his milk to keep it from scalding.

Charles shrugged. "I suppose we should start nearby, and work outwards from there. He can't have gone far."

"But he wouldn't stay too close, either," Rebecca said, pushing her long blonde hair behind her ear and frowning. "He wouldn't want to run into his lordship by accident, would he?"

Charles nodded. "You're right. I suppose we can rule out anything too close to White's, or the theater district as well."

"Or the brothels," came a mutter from the direction of the stove.

"That still leaves..." Rebecca bit her lip. "Far too much of London to search."

Mr. Symmons poured his warm milk into a mug, rinsed the pan and started for the door. "You might try Bloomsbury," he said in passing.

Charles and Rebecca gaped at the kitchen door as it swung shut.

"Bloomsbury?" the valet said. "Why?"

Rebecca groaned and slapped herself on the forehead. "The British Museum. The British *Library*. We're idiots not to have thought to look in that area first."

"Well, thank you, Mr. Symmons!" Charles said. "It's a start."

Julian Jeffries exited a bookshop in Soho two days later, staring down at a scrap of paper in his hand that made him believe once again in the existence of God. For the first third of his life, he had prayed assiduously for heaven to avenge the authors of his wretched childhood. Even during the more cynical years that had followed, he had looked over his shoulder from time to time, waiting for the thunderbolt from the blue that would put paid to his activities, which could not possibly be approved of on high. When neither of these things occurred, he had given up on the Almighty altogether. Until today.

On the paper, carefully written in the rodent's own hand, was the current address of a certain James Riley.

He grinned to himself. Not so miraculous, really, that the little bookworm had surfaced in a bookshop. Julian had dropped by Botherton's Fine Imported Books this afternoon, to check on the status of an item he'd had specially shipped for him from Florence. Italian pornography was much superior to the French trash most of his circle settled for. And much more expensive, to be sure, but since Stephen was soon to receive his quarterly funds, the few guineas this latest trifle would cost him would be utterly unnoticeable.

The clerk, a fetching thing named Shelby with hair black as coal, had regarded his client with an admiration bordering on awe, but Julian didn't have to consult the mirror in the lid of his snuffbox to know he was looking particularly well today. "Yes, sir, it's in, and very impressive it is, too. I'll bring it right out for you."

Julian retreated with the volume to a quiet corner to preview it, deciding almost immediately he wasn't even going to try to talk the price down. Damn, the book was fine, the illustrations erotic enough to fire an urgent itch. Easily fixed, if the clerk were as willing as he appeared. There was no one else in the shop, was there?

But there was. Julian peered between the shelves, noting a young man, painfully neat but rather shabby around the edges, standing at the counter. With a snort of surprise, he recognized Stephen's missing secretary.

What was he doing here?

Whatever it was, Shelby's interest was not engaged. The clerk's gaze kept wandering over to the nook where Julian still stood. He nodded a few times, and Julian heard him say, "Yes, yes, perhaps. I'll tell Mr. Botherton." Shelby's impatient air discouraged the Riley brat from browsing, but the clerk did accept a small piece of paper from Stephen's former employee.

Oh, my. How interesting. Julian emerged from behind the shelves, approaching the clerk with sinuous grace. "What did he want?"

"Looking for employment. If Mr. Botherton will take someone else on, I'd have more time to devote to our best customers." The look he shot Julian crackled with heat.

"I assure you, the man who was here is not at all an appropriate choice." He reached to pluck the paper from Shelby, who stuffed it into a trouser pocket instead.

"Please, sir. I need to keep that. Mr. Botherton would be furious if I didn't at least—"

The actor raised his brows, moving near to the clerk, close enough for their bodies to touch. "Bother Botherton," he murmured, his hand moving to rest on the young man's hip, pulling him even closer. "Suppose you put a sign on the door that said 'Will return shortly' or some such, and then we go to the back so you can devote some time to me?" He leaned in, lips grazing Shelby's ear. "Please?"

Shelby shuddered with desire. "I suppose... a few minutes..." He broke free, scrabbling hastily for a pencil and piece of paper. In the back room, dark and crowded with boxes and trunks of books, the clerk wasted no time dropping to his knees and reaching for the buttons of Julian's trousers. Under normal circumstances, this adoration would have been exactly to the actor's taste, but today other tactics were in order.

"No, my dear." He raised the young man to his feet, pulling Shelby into his arms for a lingering kiss. "I want more than that." His hands trailed down to cup the young man's buttocks, squeezed gently. "I've wanted your sweet little arse ever since the first time I saw you—didn't you know that?"

"I—I shouldn't, sir." Hunger in the clerk's eyes, but he shot a nervous glance towards the door. "It'd be quicker if you let me use my mouth. If you wanted more, we could meet outside the shop later."

"Shelby. My Shelby." Another kiss, longer, deeper. Julian slipped his hand down the back of the clerk's waistband, parting Shelby's cheeks and stroking between them. "I need you. Now." This time, there was no resistance when Julian opened the young man's trousers and pushed them down. Shelby didn't even notice the slight detour the actor's fingers made along the way, dipping briefly into the clerk's pocket. By the time Julian had finished with him, he barely remembered his own name, and certainly didn't recall that of the man who had so briefly visited the shop, seeking a job.

Julian was very pleased with himself as he left the shop, clutching his new book in one hand and Jamie Riley's address in the other.

What was he going to do with the brat? He considered the matter while his coach wended its way through the city streets. Van Dieman's Land was a distinct possibility. Prison ships left the docks at least once per week for the penal colonies in Australia—how hard could it be to bribe the ship's master into taking on an additional convict? But sometimes, long-lost people come back. And point fingers.

Did the solution need to be more permanent, perhaps? Julian chewed thoughtfully on his bottom lip. It had been necessary to remove people before, during his long climb from the dank pit of his beginnings to the bright lights of the London stage. Squeamishness wouldn't stay his hand, but he was a well-known figure now, and had to be careful. If he could find someone else to do the job... Julian leaned back against the leather seat and closed his eyes, the better to collect his thoughts. A name floated in the shadows of his mind, amid the whispers of darkness, and he snatched at it greedily.

Cosgrove.

A wealthy merchant, accused of ghastly crimes. Four or five of his servants, both male and female, had disappeared from the face of the earth, and only one body had ever been found. Ripped apart by wild dogs, Mr. Cosgrove had insisted. Palms were greased, a jury faltered, and the judge dismissed the case for lack of evidence. In the years since, it was rumored that the merchant had not ceased his activities, only become much better at hiding them. No one grieved for the playthings he chose now, as long as he was careful to keep himself to prostitutes, vagrants and urchins of the streets. A young man with no family to inquire after him, who was already missing from his few acquaintances, would be a grand opportunity for such as he.

Julian opened his eyes. Perhaps even Riley didn't deserve that, was already fading from Stephen's mind, soon to be forgotten. No matter how tempting, he would have to think it over before delivering the brat to a creature like Cosgrove. He should call on the earl, find a discreet way of measuring whether he was still pining for his lost secretary.

Julian reached up and rapped on the roof of the coach, stuck his head out the window when the horses slowed. "Take me to St. Joseph House."

The winter afternoon was already darkening when Charles launched into his description for the seventeenth time. With Stephen's blessing, he'd spent every free minute since his conversation with Rebecca two nights before searching the boarding houses of Bloomsbury. They all ran together after a while: tired-looking buildings with sagging roofs, often displaying a few touches that demonstrated a struggle to remain within the bounds of respectability. On this porch a pot of petunias fought for life against the rank London fog, added fading color to the surroundings. He was barely halfway into his piece when the landlady, Mrs. Ormsby, nodded.

"Oh, Mr. Riley. Yes, yes, I know him."

"He's here?" His round face beamed with relief.

The landlady, a stout middle-aged female whose starched and pressed apron covered the worst stains on her threadbare dress, sniffed. "Not anymore. Seemed respectable enough at the first, but in the end he was no better than the rest of them. Tried to cozen me out of my proper due, he did."

"Oh. Perhaps we're not talking about the same man. My Mr. Riley would never cheat a soul."

"Well, this one did. Tried to get me to accept half for next week's lodging, didn't he? Said he'd pay the balance once he'd found employment. And what would happen to me if he didn't find work next week, either? I'd be out of my rightful rents, wouldn't I?" Her watery eyes hardened. "Just like the rest of them, he was."

Charles' hands clenched at his sides. "No, Mrs. Ormsby, he wasn't. Now, do you have any idea of where he's gone?"

Stephen stood for several minutes with his hand on the knob of the library door. If only he could open it to find Jamie at the desk, puzzling over columns of figures or sorting the incoming post. The dimple would flash in his cheek as he saw Stephen standing there, and he would offer some pleasantry that would make the earl smile in return. Jamie had spent too much time at that blasted desk. Stephen should have taken him places, given him the sorts of treats the young man would have enjoyed. Not things he didn't want, but experiences. A few hours wandering the Tower of London. A boat trip to Hampton Court. The city was full of historical sites, museums and galleries, not to mention private collections off-limits to most people but easily accessible to someone of his rank. He ached that he hadn't thought of this when Jamie had still been in residence.

No wonder he thinks I just wanted his body. Did I ever show him different?

He opened the door and entered the empty library, crossing to the desk and sitting down. Where was the household budget? He reached for the ledger, feeling inadequate to the task. Perhaps he should find Mrs. Symmons or Rebecca, see if they could help.

Out in the hall, he could hear the butler at the door. Julian? He perked up, glancing at the clock. Still time for a few drinks and a hand or two of *vingt-et-un* at White's before dinner. Stephen rose from the desk as the actor swept into the library, ashamed at how much he wanted to leave his responsibilities behind yet again.

"Good heavens, Stephen, what are you doing in here? Ghastly room—all dark and tomblike." Julian kissed him on the cheek. "I can think of several more cheerful places to take you. Get your gloves, darling."

Stephen opened his mouth, fully intending to agree, but found himself staring back down at the papers on Jamie's desktop. No. It wasn't fair to just dump a portion of his quarterly allowance on the staff and leave them to fend for themselves. "I really should stay in tonight and take a look at the household budget."

"Budget?" Julian's carefully-shaped brows arched skywards. "Don't you have servants to take care of things like that?"

The earl's mouth tightened. "I had Jamie. And now, I don't." He sat slowly back down in the desk's leather chair.

Julian was quick to join him, leaning over the back of the chair and kissing Stephen's neck. "You're not still moping about that boy, are you?" He gave a little laugh. "I could almost be hurt, if I didn't know how unsuitable he was for you." His fingers walked down the front of the earl's chest.

Stephen couldn't speak for a moment. Unsuitable. Jamie, with his warm good sense, quick flashes of humor, that surprising streak of sensuality... "If by 'unsuitable' you mean he was too good for me, you're probably right." Julian's hand paused in its journey southward, and Stephen pushed it away gently, waiting for the inevitable explosion of jealousy.

But the actor appeared unperturbed, settling on the desk just in front of Stephen, and reaching to stroke the earl's hair. "I sympathize, darling, really I do. But what I mean is that I know what you need. You're a sophisticated man, Stephen—you need someone who appreciates that. Honestly? I don't see how your Jamie, no matter how charming he seemed, could have pleased you in the long term. Perhaps it's best if you just forget about him."

Stephen blinked. Julian had turned over a new leaf in earnest, hadn't he? The actor deserved candor in return. "I don't know what would have happened in the long term. I never had the chance to find out. But there's no way I can forget Jamie."

"It's likely that he's already moved on, found other employment, someone else to... But perhaps he'll come back." Julian's hand, still stroking Stephen's hair, wrought a soothing magic on the earl. "If he cared for you at all, he will. But if he doesn't..." The actor's smile was wistful. "...you'll still always have me."

Stephen reached and caught the other man's hand, raising it to his lips. "Thank you. I never expected you to be so understanding. If I find Jamie, I swear I'll do my best to help you out until you can find a new benefactor."

Julian's smile never faltered. "You are looking for him, then?"

"Charles and Rebecca have started canvassing the boarding houses, but with no luck yet. We may have to try something else."

"Poor love. At least I'm here for you."

"Thank you, Julian. I so appreciate this." The earl squeezed Julian's hand and released it. "But I really have to stay in tonight. Please don't be angry."

Julian leaned forward, kissing Stephen warmly on the lips. "It's all right, darling. There was someone I was thinking of calling on anyway."

"Anyone I know?"

The actor's eyes seemed to glow, cat-like, in the cool dimness of the library. "No, just a merchant with whom I'm hoping to strike a deal."

Stephen smiled at Julian. "As long as it doesn't cost me too much in the end."

Charles' feet dragged as he climbed the steps to the servants' entrance at St. Joseph House shortly after, worn out from a long day's searching. He opened the kitchen door and gaped with astonishment at the sight of his master in his shirtsleeves at the kitchen table, ink stains all over his fingers, caught in the act of crossing out a list and flipping the paper for another try.

"I think we're on the right track," the earl was saying to Rebecca, seated beside him, as he looked up and saw his valet in the doorway. "Oh, hullo Charles. You might be interested in this: whatever else happens, you're all getting your quarter's wages on Christmas Day. We're trying to figure out the best division between household expenses and outstanding debts after that."

Charles stared, fascinated. "Don't forget your own spending money. And the greenhouse. I mean, if there's—"

"There is. That is, there will be. We already have the money I'd put aside for staying home with you and—with you those nights, and I think we can wring out enough to get started if we stick to some of Ja—if we stick to some economies."

"Jamie." Charles looked stricken. "I came so close, but I didn't find him."

Rebecca got up and led him to the table. Maisie and Betsy, who had been cleaning the cook stove, stopped dead to listen, and Rebecca motioned them to join the group at the table as well. "Tell us. Tell us all."

Briefly, Charles related his encounter with the self-righteous landlady. "If I'd worked from east to west instead of vice versa, I would have reached that street yesterday. He didn't leave until this morning."

Stephen's face was pale. "Do you think she really had no idea where he went? Surely a landlady would be aware of the competition."

Charles shook his head. "She made it clear she didn't have any truck with those sorts of places."

"Sorts of places?"

"The sort Jamie can now afford."

"Rats." The whisper came from Betsy, who was staring at something beyond the others' field of vision. "They come through the holes in the walls, and God help you if you scratch your chilblains till they bleed. It's cold, and it smells so bad, but you think you can stand that, if only there wasn't the rats. There was this man that coughed, and his handkerchief was always bloody." She put her hands over her face, thin hair flopping forward as if attempting to veil her from her memories. "They like blood, the rats. One night, they... they..."

With a sob, Betsy fled from the kitchen. Maisie rose slowly to follow, blinking back tears.

Stephen shook his head. "Jamie would never end up in a place that bad."

None of the others looked at him.

Maisie alone spoke up, pausing with her hand on the door. "You don't know," she said, pulling her shawl tight across her thin shoulders. "You don't know where people will end up if they're desperate enough."

Chapter Twenty

*J*amie sat on the edge of his bed in his new home in Lomber Court and wept. There was no bed frame to lift the stained mattress above the things that crawled on the floor at night, and just one tattered blanket to stave off the bone-deep cold of the unheated Seven Dials tenement.

"Sheets is extra," the slattern who had rented him the room yesterday morning stated, her breath reeking of onions and gin. So were additional blankets; a towel; and even a chamber pot, to keep one from having to assay several flights of rickety stairs in the middle of the night to reach the convenience out back.

But the week in the boarding house in Bloomsbury had eaten up the bulk of his few shillings, and Jamie had no extra.

"The lock is broken," he'd observed at the time, fingering the splintered wood of the door frame. Someone had kicked his way into the room—although kicking one's way out made more sense, he thought, looking around the grim chamber. His earlier lodgings were a veritable palace compared to this. The lack of a window might have been useful in this wintry weather, if the wind hadn't whistled in anyway between the cracks of the ill-built tenement. A previous occupant had stuffed them with bits of rag and newspaper, at least around the bed. Perhaps he could do better. If he could afford a newspaper. He pictured himself clawing through the gutters in search of stray bits of cloth or paper to chink the cracks with, and shivered.

"And who needs a lock?" The landlady's eyes were beady and suspicious. "You bring trade home, the house gets a cut. Them's the rules, or you can leave right now."

It was ridiculous, the speed with which he hastened to assure her that he was not of that kind, especially when her demeanor showed only disappointment that he wouldn't be paying her additional for the privilege of whoring himself under her roof. But he had dropped the subject of the lock, and that was unfortunate, and the reason for his tears now.

Because rodents and bugs were not the only creatures of the night to creep into his room in the darkness. Someone with human intelligence had entered while he was asleep, and stolen nearly everything Jamie hadn't been wearing: his overcoat, spare clothing, and books; even making free with his ancient valise in which to haul them off. Worst of all, the thief had absconded with the portrait of his mother, and that grieved him unbearably. He supposed he was lucky the miscreant had left him his shoes, and was apparently unable to pick his few remaining coppers from his pockets.

Luck. It occurred to Jamie that today was Friday the thirteenth, notorious for bad luck, and damned appropriate. "Stephen," he whispered to himself, rocking back and forth. But now that the time had come when he longed desperately to return to the safety of St. Joseph House, by all accounts the earl had forgotten him. Lord St. Joseph was the subject of lively gossip, and current tales depicted him as once again happily infatuated with his companion, the actor Julian Jeffries. The news had hit Jamie hard, and at this moment he couldn't imagine feeling any lower.

He swiped at his eyes savagely. "I have to get out of here. I need to pull myself together and make a plan."

But he couldn't, not just yet, not when the release of tears felt so unexpectedly good.

"Ah, lad." The voice was raspy with some combination of age and drink, and the old woman's steps were uneven as she entered the room without knocking, leaning on a stick and dragging one leg behind her. "Poor laddie. Can't be but so bad, can it? Not whilst ye're so young and bonny." She sat heavily on the mattress beside him, skirts releasing a cloud of dust, and patted him on the arm. "Ye be needing a bite to eat, and then ye'll feel better. Come on, preacher man's coming with the victuals." Her smile was as encouraging as it could be, with so few teeth to aid it.

"I... thank you, Mother. What preacher man?"

"The one as comes with the victuals," she repeated patiently, reaching for her stick to rise again. "Come wi' me, ye won't want to miss a meal, ye being as scrawny as that." Her shawl swung away from her skirts for a second, revealing a glimpse of what

156 - The Price of Temptation

looked like the blue cover of the book of poems Rebecca had given him, tucked into the old crone's waistband.

Jamie wiped his face on the back of his sleeve, not having had the foresight to tuck a handkerchief into his pocket before going to sleep last night. "Tell me, Mother—do you think someone who took a small painting from me, might return it, if he or she knew how important it was?"

She patted his arm again. "Nay, lad, that's not the way of it, is it? Not that I would know about such things, but if I were you, once I got back on me feet I'd be lookin' for her under the golden balls."

Jamie blinked. "I beg your pardon?"

"Askin' Old St. Nick about it," she said, lifting her brows. "No? The pop shops, lad, the pop shops."

"Pawn brokers." Jamie nodded. "Again, thank you."

The old woman studied him. "Ye're not from these parts."

"No. Yorkshire."

"That's not it, lad. I've known Yorkies who fit in just fine at a place like this, and none of 'em was high-spoken like you."

"Trust me, Mother: there are not many places I do fit in. But even a misfit needs to eat, so where can we find your preacher man?"

"Sinners! Sinners, all of us, shaaamed before God." The price of a meal, on this fetid Seven Dials back alley, was to be harangued by Holy Joe, the preacher man. Wild of hair and eye, his voice hoarse with shouting, the man was quite unlike any of the clergymen Jamie had ever met, and quite possibly not ordained by any established church at all. Still, steam rose from his soup pot, and a pile of bowls stood on a box at his elbow. Spoons were not an option: those who had received their portion seemed to get along by picking chunks of meat and vegetables out with their fingers, then drinking the broth.

Jamie's companion had the timing of the preacher man's visit down to a science: Holy Joe's unsavory, rank-smelling constituents were just beginning to crawl from their holes and shake off the effects of last night's gin, drawn by the shouting and smell of the soup simmering sullenly over a smoldering pile of rubbish. Jamie and the old woman were able to find a place near the head of the line forming for what might be the only meal most of these people ate today.

"Confess yer sin!" Holy Joe barked at the man just ahead of them in line. This person, swaying on his feet despite the early hour, admitted to drunkenness.

"Demon rum!" The preacher's eyes lit up. "It reduces the strong man to infancy, drooling and puking. Unable to walk or speak, as helpless as a babe in arms. Who can drive away the devil in the bottle? Who, I ask you? Who can redeem the drunkard, bring him—"

"Jesus?" said the man, holding his still-empty bowl in shaking hands.

The preacher's eyes spat hellfire. "Of course it's Jesus, you stupid sod." He ladled soup into the bowl, and called in disgust for the next sinner.

The old woman who had brought Jamie to this place, stepped forward. "I been taking the Lord's name in vain," she offered, failing to mention anything else she might also have been taking lately.

This transgression, apparently, held less fascination than drink. Holy Joe exhorted her to watch her bleedin' mouth, and motioned to Jamie, his demeanor hopeful that the young man's sin would be more interesting.

"Confess yerself," he demanded, stirring the soup with his ladle.

"I've had some unkind thoughts," Jamie said, having some now.

The preacher narrowed his eyes. "You think I'm a fool? With young men, it's sins of the flesh, ain't it?"

Jamie felt his color rise, it was inevitable, but he was hardly going to admit any such thing to this suspect pastor of the streets.

"I said, sins of the flesh." The preacher rolled the words in his mouth, savoring them. "The animal pleasures of the night. You're no stranger to them, are you? Confess it!"

"I'd rather not," Jamie said steadily, his hackles rising.

"Shame!" thundered Holy Joe. "Shamed before God, before us all! Filthy and unclean, greedy and lascivious, grunting and groaning like pigs in the trough. The widow's nakedness uncovered, the lass's maidenhead beguiled away."

Jamie wasn't sure which he wanted more: to laugh, or to hit this false prophet. "I assure you, I've ruined no virgins. I admit to sins, sir, and am duly shamed. May I have some soup?"

"Confess, young man! I smell the stink of it on you, the rank and fetid desire of the youth. When was the last time you wallowed in the muck and slime of unlawful fornication, shivered and moaned all blinded by lust, while God's eyes bled with sorrow? Slack-jawed and uncaring, defiling the body God gave you—"

"It wasn't like that!" Jamie, pushed to the edge, exploded. "I was in love with h—" He bit off the pronoun just in time. "I was in love."

The preacher's lips curved in a smile of satisfaction. "I knew it. Give us your bowl, and be ashamed before God."

"Keep your soup," Jamie said, "I'm not ashamed." He dropped the bowl on the ground and walked away, curiously lighter at heart. He had loved Stephen—and he still did, and probably always would. And despite his clumsy behavior, Stephen had felt something for him, too. The earl had just been proceeding along the lines he was used to. Now Jamie made a decision: love was too rare and sweet a thing to give up without a fight. He was going to win Stephen back.

Not yet, of course—he could hardly creep back to St. Joseph House in this condition, and he would never be Stephen's whore. He would turn his mind to finding a job, bettering his position first, and then he would call on Stephen and see if there were something they could build together. More slowly this time, and with greater care. "Stephen," he said out loud. "You're going to be mine, and on my terms, too."

"He'll be all yours." Julian leaned back in his chair, crossed his legs elegantly. He had been unable to find the merchant at home the previous evening, but had better luck this morning. "To do with exactly as you please. He has no family, no friends, no one to give the slightest damn."

"But three hundred pounds?" Mr. Cosgrove raised both brows in incredulity. The merchant was a large man, solid but not fat, dressed soberly in clothing cut from plain but exquisitely-woven fabric. His drawing room reflected a similar aesthetic, the simplicity of the furnishings belying the care and expense that had gone into crafting them.

Julian smiled. He'd had the measure of the cit the moment he'd walked in the door, and noted the man's only obvious extravagance: the portraits crowding the walls of the hall. They did not depict the Cosgrove family; but had been snatched up from indigent aristocrats, lords and ladies with blood so blue the upstart merchants of the world could only moon with envy. Julian, recognizing several of the subjects, had tripled Jamie's price accordingly. "Ah, but he's descended from the peerage on both sides. His mother's grandfather was an earl; and his father was a viscount, son of a marquess."

Cosgrove licked bloodless lips, and leaned forward, interest awakening in the cold behind his eyes. "But how is that possible? Surely such a one would be missed."

"He's a bastard, Mr. Cosgrove. The mother is dead and the sire has no interest—may not even know he exists. And he's only recently come to London, so there's no one close enough to care. You'll not have a chance like this again, I think."

"Is he a virgin?"

"I can't promise you that. In fact, I'm rather sure he was used, once." Julian smiled. "But as he fled the household the next day in horror, I think we can assume he didn't enjoy it. That may even work to your advantage."

"Hmph. Let me think." Cosgrove tapped his chin with one finger. "I have to stay in London through mid-February, but if you could have him delivered to my country estate after that, I think we can come to an arrangement."

Julian shook his head. "No, I'm afraid not. It must be soon, or the deal is off." Stephen must not be allowed to locate his insipid darling. Julian's hand clenched at the thought.

"But I can't leave town, and my house here is unsuitable. Too small, too many servants, too crowded a neighborhood in case there's... noise."

"Might I make a suggestion?"

"Go ahead."

"Are you familiar with an establishment called Madame Novotny's, near the docks?"

"I believe I've heard of it," Mr. Cosgrove allowed cautiously.

Julian rather thought he had, and was almost certainly well-versed in the workings of his next suggestion, too. But it was best to keep to a façade of ignorance, when such delicate matters were involved. "Of course, you're probably not aware that Madame keeps a dungeon below stairs. Very Gothic, but equally appropriate to both frivolous play-acting and... more serious endeavors, if you understand me."

"I understand you quite well." Cosgrove was obviously tempted, but still showed a certain amount of wariness. "From what I remem—from what I've heard, it's soundproofed, isn't it?"

"Yes. The walls are several feet thick, and the ceiling baffled. There are drains in the floor for easy clean up, and at least one of the rooms contains a tunnel that leads to the river, in case... anything... might need to be disposed of. You could rent a dungeon chamber for as many days as you like, and are guaranteed that no one will dare disturb you." There was a glitter in Julian's eyes as Cosgrove considered the prospect.

The merchant, who hadn't amassed his riches through foolishness, watched him carefully. "And what's your stake in this, Mr. Jeffries? How do I know I'm not being set up by my enemies?"

"Oh, no," Julian protested. "The only enemy involved is the young man, I'm afraid. For my own reasons, I look forward to seeing him humbled. Among other things, of course."

A smile spread across Mr. Cosgrove's face. "Then perhaps I might persuade you to accept two hundred pounds, if you were allowed to watch?"

He shouldn't. The whole point of getting someone else to dispose of Riley was to keep his own hands clean of the matter, wasn't it? But oh, the temptation, to see the brat's terror and degradation, to let Riley know who had brought him to his end... Hell, Julian was well-known at Novotny's, it would be utterly unremarkable that he be on the premises during the time Cosgrove played with his toy in the dungeon. Why not enjoy the spectacle? "I think you might," the actor said. "I think you might, indeed."

"I have things to attend to first, before I can free myself for such entertainments. Shall we say next Friday night, Mr. Jeffries? One week from tonight. I insist the boy be undamaged and fully conscious, and in return, you'll have your money. And your fun."

"Thank you, Mr. Cosgrove. I knew I could count on you."

Chapter Twenty-one

*S*tephen pushed the ledger away from him and rose from the kitchen table, where the whole household had been gathered for a meeting. "That's it for today, I'm falling asleep. Tonight's the Allbrights' ball—if I'm going to make it, I need a nap first." He gave a short laugh. "I was out too late last night."

With Julian, of course. He didn't have to say it. "Yes, my lord." Rebecca's voice was cool and Mrs. Symmons pursed her lips as they gathered loose sheets of paper and stowed them within the cover of the budget ledger.

Even Charles wouldn't look at him as he'd offered to put his master to bed. "Not necessary," Stephen said curtly. Damn it, why did the servants have to judge him for his continued association with Julian? He fumed about it as he ascended the stairs to his chamber, undressed and climbed into his huge Egyptian bed, its finials carved with the Eye of Horus. Was he supposed to spend all his time brooding over the things he had lost? It should be enough that he was being so attentive to the business of running his household.

And what a headache that was. After several sessions spent puzzling over it, the budget was coming along, but it was lowering to discover just how many quarter-days it would take before all of the debts were settled. He'd asked for suggestions from the servants for where else they could save money, and Charles had very

161

nobly said that the plans for the greenhouse could be abandoned for now. Stephen, reluctant to give up on Jamie's plan, contended in return that eventually, growing their own roses would save so much money that it would be foolish to forsake the greenhouse now. They had argued it back and forth, finally agreeing to move ahead on the structure, but that while it was being built, Charles would do without his daily roses.

"That will help," Rebecca had said, pointing out that roses were especially expensive during the Christmas season, when everyone wanted them for entertaining. That had silenced them all, and for a long moment the whole lot of them had stared at the table.

Christmas. Stephen tossed himself on the bed. Just ten days, now, until Christmas Eve. Stephen pulled the covers over his head now, trying to block out the thought of it. Intolerable that Jamie was out there in some miserable hell-hole, but to think of him hungry and cold at Christmas was like taking a cheese-grater to his soul. Thinking of Aunt Matilda's Yuletide feasts, with their enormous barons of beef and tables of clove-studded hams, made him ill. More tables bowing under the weight of rich plum puddings and brandied fruit-cakes, pyramids of exotic oranges imported from Spain when the local orangeries couldn't keep up with demand, great bowls of sugared nuts and trays of marzipan molded into amusing shapes...

Betsy had begun to cry. "What if Jamie comes home, and we hasn't got any Christmas for him?" Only the intervention of Maisie and Mrs. Symmons, who promised to help decorate the house for the season, had dried the young girl's tears, but the group had remained sober after that. It was clear that they all missed Jamie, who had managed to earn a level of respect in just two months that their master had yet to gain.

Well, no mystery there. Stephen was trying, but so far all he was doing was picking up after the mess he had made of his life. There was no faith, from any of them, that he would change substantially in the future, and he knew why.

Julian.

He sighed. The actor had surprised him with his affectionate ways since Jamie had left, providing not just distraction but a solid shoulder to lean on. The servants didn't see all that, of course, didn't know Julian's good side the way he did. Stephen would have to make a decision soon, about whether to continue the actor's contract. But suppose he dismissed Julian, and they never found Jamie? Worse: suppose they did find him, and his Mouse, still offended, refused to return. In that case, it would be galling to lose Julian as well.

But Julian wasn't Jamie. Even on his best behavior, Julian

lacked the younger man's warmth and sweetness, and especially the inner core of strength that made Jamie so appealing. Stephen smiled wistfully, remembering. It had taken such a short time for his secretary to see what was wrong with Stephen's life, roll up his sleeves and start fixing it. Julian didn't care about such things.

But it was better to have Julian than no one. Of course it was.

Jamie had a job.

He laughed to himself, tempted to skip through the streets back to his Seven Dials lair. It had happened so unexpectedly. Today was Sunday, the one day all businesses closed. Unable to continue his search for work and unwilling to stay in his ghastly room, Jamie had spent the morning wandering from church to church, seeking warmth as well as peace. He'd been on a quest for a cheap meal before seeking out afternoon services when a brougham, over-laden with baggage, took a corner too fast. The restraining rope broke, and trunks and portmanteaus flew, littering the street. Horses whinnied as traffic ground to a halt to avoid the obstacle-ridden roadway. He had leapt to help restore the baggage to the carriage, and in gratitude, the coachman flipped Jamie a coin.

"You're a good worker, son. Thanks for the help."

Jamie looked at the sixpence in his hand. He spoke quickly, as the coachman was remounting his box. "I'm not afraid of hard work. Do you know anyone who's looking to hire?"

And the coachman had. His brother was a foreman at the docks, where there was a solid need for laborers to haul boxes between the warehouses and ships. A quick visit to the coachman's brother, at home enjoying Sunday dinner, confirmed it.

"Can't promise as it'll be regular." Mr. Binks, the foreman, stood in the doorway of his modest flat, obviously eager to get back to his meal. "Some days there's more lads than ships; some days I can keep you 'til midnight if your back holds out. Four pence an hour either way — on a good week you'll make a whole quid."

For sixty hours worth of back-breaking labor. Jamie swallowed, the rich scent of roast beef making him dizzy. It would have to do, until he found something better. "I can do it, sir. Thank you."

"All right, then. Come tomorrow at dawn, and we'll see what we've got."

Jamie was elated as he carefully assayed the rickety front steps of his tenement. "Manual labor," he muttered to himself. "Now there's a step up in the world." It didn't matter what it was — it was a job, and however meager the wages, they would soon have him out of this horrible place, which stunk of urine and despair.

He reached for the doorknob, only to have it open suddenly, the man hurrying out of the building bumping into him.

"Sorry!" the stranger said. He was young and healthy, compared to most of the denizens of the tenement, and had a cheerful face.

"No matter. I wasn't paying attention," Jamie said. "Do you live here? I don't think I've seen you before."

"Just moved in today." The young man's eyes glimmered with mirth. "Hope to move out tomorrow, but I'm waiting for an emergency bank draft from my mother. It could be a week or more before she sorts it out."

"I hope to be away shortly, too." Jamie grinned. "In the meantime, it's nice to see another reasonably sober face around here. I'm on the fourth floor, first on the right if you want some intelligible conversation sometime." He put out his hand. "My name's James. Call me Jamie."

The other man grinned in return as he shook Jamie's hand. "I'm Bertie."

Chapter Twenty-Two

"Go on, one more pint won't hurt. It's on me." Bertie grinned at his new friend in the smoky dimness of the Hanged Man, a dank cave of a public house not far from their Lomber Court tenement. Thank God the lad liked a drink; he'd been afraid Jamie Riley had no vices at all. Didn't whore, didn't gamble—Bertie had been despairing of how the hell he was going to get Jamie to Madame Novotny's on schedule. But perhaps the brothel's reputation as a fine place for a drink would prove the excuse he needed. "Besides, after three days on the bloody docks, you deserve a bit o' relaxation."

"Don't I just." Jamie flexed his shoulders, wincing. "Well, if you're buying." A look of concern crossed the young man's face. "I mean, if you can afford..." He had almost shout the words; it might be a weeknight, but in this part of town all the pubs were crowded nightly with patrons, on a never-ending quest to dull the pain of poverty.

"'S all right, Jamie. I found some coins outside the Red Lion last night. Some bloke must have tripped over his own feet and spilled his pockets when he fell. It's not enough to get me a better place to stay, so why not spend it on good company?"

"Oh. Tha's all right, then." The dimple the young man flashed was so appealing that Bertie was sorely tempted to ignore his master's strict instructions to keep his hands off James Riley, if he knew what was good for him. He patted Jamie on the leg, letting

165

166 - The Price of Temptation

his hand linger on the other man's thigh. Jamie raised his brows, seemingly amused. "My beer?"

"Right." Bertie hurried to the bar to place the order, his feet sticking unpleasantly to the floor as he pushed his way through the crowd. Bah. They all stank, but after three nights in the slums, with no way to wash properly or a fresh change of clothes, he figured he didn't smell so good himself. Another couple of pints, though, and at least he'd have a warm bed tonight. Mister Julian need never know a thing about it. As long as he followed his master's most important order, and got Jamie to Novotny's on Friday night, there was no harm in a little fun along the way. He winked at the bartender. "Throw a bit o' gin in the one on the right. Our little secret, aye?"

Ah, here it was. With a jerk, Charles pulled the pages free from the mess in the Earl of St. Joseph's bedside table. The drawer contained a jumble of miscellaneous keys, calling cards, playbills, a small edition of John Wilmot's filthier poetry... and one contract, duly signed and witnessed, between Lord Stephen Clair and Julian Jeffries, actor.

The valet had taken it upon himself to search for the document tonight, when Stephen was out at his Aunt Matilda's for cards. December was progressing, Jamie had not been found, and Stephen still spent enough time with his poisonous snake of a lover that it seemed increasingly likely that this contract would end up renewed for another year. It was worth taking a look to see what it actually said, and whether there was an easy way out of it if Stephen could be persuaded to take it.

Charles genuinely liked his master; they were as close to friends as their difference in status would allow. But where Stephen insisted on seeing Julian's recent sweetness as genuine, Charles could only see it as a deliberate ploy to get another year's commitment out of the earl. Just this morning, while the valet was shaving him, Stephen had commented on Julian's new attitude. "I always thought there had to be more to him, that he kept locked away for safety, and now it's coming out at last." He'd paused for a second. "I suspect Julian had a beastly upbringing, you know."

Charles struggled with this while stropping the razor, not inclined to sympathy for the actor. "We play the cards we're dealt. And given past history, I'd want to be very sure there aren't any up his sleeve."

"Isn't it just possible Julian really has had a change of heart?" The earl had looked so wistful that Charles decided to shut up and keep shaving.

"Change of heart?" he muttered to himself now, shaking out the pages and carrying them over to his own room next to the earl's to take a look. "Only possible if he had one, and that bloody actor doesn't."

Julian was cold, through and through. He might be all kissy-kissy with the earl when he wanted to be, but the real measure of a man was how he treated servants, and the actor failed every test there: alternately demanding and dismissive of the staff at St. Joseph House, and even more openly abusive of his own man Bertie. Charles frequently delivered flowers to the actor's dressing room before performances, and on several occasions he'd been horrified to observe Julian screaming, throwing things, and even striking Bertie across the face. The young dresser seemed to accept the mistreatment as his lot, though, his eyes gleaming adoration even when puffy with bruises. Stupid boy.

Charles scanned the document quickly, smiling to himself at the necessary obfuscation of what was being sold. Although rarely prosecuted unless an assault was involved or the act occurred in public, buggery was on the books as a crime punishable by death. The earl had thus contracted for "exclusive rights to the private performances of one Julian Jeffries, actor," at a price of... Good lord. Charles' lips formed a silent whistle. Five hundred guineas per quarter, plus related expenses and the right to occupy Stephen's house on Floral Street. Should the earl be in arrears at the end of the year's term, the contract would be automatically extended for another year to allow his lordship to catch up on his payments, and so on into perpetuity. Damn. Julian wasn't so dumb: Stephen's carelessness with money all but guaranteed that he would be tied to the actor forever.

There must be something... Charles went back to the beginning and began to read again. Exclusive rights, the contract called for. Julian, faithful? He snorted. The man would fuck a goat if it would agree to back him in a play. Even Bertie's devotion suggested the dresser might be getting a bit on the side—lord knew it wouldn't occur to Julian to give the lad praise or a few extra coins now and again.

But how to prove the actor had transgressed? Charles frowned. All the household's efforts were being spent trying to locate Jamie. There was no one to spare to shadow Julian right now, no time to dig into any possible indiscretions. He needed someone with resources to spare, someone who might also have an interest in freeing Stephen from his entanglement with the perfidious whore.

He needed Lady Matilda Clair.

                    ❧   ❧   ❧

Later that evening, Jamie was on his knees, rocking back and forth and moaning. The tableau, however, was not quite as Bertie had imagined it.

"For Chrissake." He nudged the suffering young man with the toe of his boot. "Ain't you done casting up your accounts yet?"

Jamie staggered to his feet in the street, wiping at his mouth with a borrowed handkerchief. "Oh, God. I hope so. Told you I wasn't much of a drinker, but I've never had beer affect me like this before."

Bertie scowled. If only he hadn't got greedy and doctored Jamie's drinks with stronger liquor. There'd be no fun to be had off him tonight. "Come on. Let's get you home." Another night in the filthy, stinking, bloody cold tenement, and without even the solace of his doomed companion's body. There'd best be a sweet reward in it for him. *Doomed.* He shivered at his own thought, wishing that he didn't know what was in store for Jamie. Tonight was Wednesday. In two nights, he was to deliver his new friend to Madame Novotny's. Best not to think about what would happen after that.

"You were *where?*" Aunt Matilda's eyes gleamed with amusement. Although they were seated next to each other, she had to raise her voice to be heard. A night of cards at Lady Matilda Clair's was not a casual affair. Tables for play filled just over half the ballroom, while the rest was arranged as if an oversized drawing room, elegant couches grouped together to form a number of conversation nooks for those who preferred gossip to gambling. Buffet tables lined one wall, laden with cold meats and dainties to nourish the players, while another table, discreetly placed in a curtained alcove, served as a bank where ladies and gentlemen could purchase additional chips or cash in their winnings.

Stephen laughed, well pleased with this evening's work. "I said, the Society of Antiquaries. Surely you've heard of them?"

"Of course I have, puppy. One of my uncles was a member when they were chartered, back in the '50s. But I never thought to see you join."

He smiled demurely. "I've taken up an interest in history. Trying to improve myself."

"Good for you," his aunt said, looking smug.

"Hah!" Lord Whinsbeck's face was florid with drink. "History! That's why he looked familiar."

Aunt Matilda played a card. It looked like she and her partner Lady Tuttlehouse were going to win yet another rubber. "What the devil are you talking about, Whinsbeck?"

"That boy you tried to foist off as a historian at your picnic. Interest in history!" He snorted.

Stephen froze. "Looked familiar? Do you mean you've seen him?"

Whinsbeck peered at him in confusion. "Course I've seen him. Didn't I meet him right here, at your aunt's?"

Stephen half-rose from his chair, his voice fierce enough to halt play at several neighboring tables. "You said 'familiar.' Does that mean you've seen him since? Recently?"

"Today. But what do you care—you cast him off like the rest of 'em, didn't you?"

"Where? Where did you see him?" Now people started drifting over from the conversation area, curious as to the raised voices at the one table, and sudden hush from the rest.

Lord Whinsbeck was too drunk, and too foolish, to ascertain the danger he was in. "Hah! Historian my arse. Wanted him for his tight little mind, did you? And once you plumbed the depths of his *intelligence*, out on the streets he goes. No better than the other ones."

Lady Tuttlehouse, the fourth player at the table, leaned forward, her generous bosom nearly overflowing the meager confines of her high-waisted bodice. "Someone told me at the picnic that she thought he might be Maria Riley's natural child. Maria's and—" She glanced around, suddenly remembering that the Marquess of Summerford, father to Maria's seducer, was present somewhere in the ballroom. "—well, remember Maria Riley?"

Someone else sniggered. "Lad came by it honestly, then. No better than his mother."

Stephen's fists clenched. "He's better than the lot of you, damn it! Jamie never had an unkind word for a soul, and has more common sense in one finger than anyone here in his whole body. You excepted, Aunt Matilda." His chair fell over with a crash as he advance on Lord Whinsbeck grasping him by his cravat and hoisting him onto his feet. "Now tell me where the bloody hell you saw Jamie!"

"The dockyards!" Whinsbeck whined, fear blanching his piggy face. "My son—home from India—this morning. Saw your little—saw your friend there."

"Boarding a ship?"

"Peddling his arse to the sailors," a voice murmured in the crowd, and Stephen only just restrained himself from backhanding Whinsbeck in retaliation.

"No! Working—he was working as a stevedore. Loading a cart with crates for a warehouse. I—I knew I remembered him from somewhere, and I've only just now—"

Stephen dropped him, and Whinsbeck tumbled heavily onto the floor. Lady Whinsbeck rushed to her husband's side. "Scoundrel!" she hissed. "To treat a gentleman like this!"

"Gentleman?" Stephen laughed. "He's a drunken sot. James Riley— now *he's* a gentleman."

"Good heavens!" The lady's face was shading toward purple. "What do you care what's said about the boy, anyway?"

"Because I *love* him, that's why!"

There was an appalled silence, and then Lady Whinsbeck, having helped her husband to his feet, turned her back on Stephen. With a nudge, Lord Whinsbeck followed suit. Others followed, first a few, and then a gathering wave of people presented their backs to the Earl of St. Joseph and began to trickle from the room.

Aunt Matilda patted her nephew on the arm. "Now you've done it, puppy. The *ton* will let you get away with all manner of vices with just a bit of teasing, but show an honest emotion and you're excluded from their august company. Playing with other boys is a deliciously scandalous lark, but loving them? Now, that's perversion. Well, you'll not be sent to Coventry in my ballroom." She straightened her back and changed the pitch of her voice to one of command. "You! Amelia Fairway! How dare you turn your back on my nephew, when not two of your children look like each other in the slightest?"

The glittering guests froze in the act of exiting the party.

"Oh, we all have our secrets, don't we? Shall we ostracize Amelia for her bevy of bastards? Stop sniggering, Lady Palmsworth. The only reason your husband's mistresses haven't presented your family with a few dozen by-blow is that they're too young to bear them. And I remember well your own mother's tragic stillborn son — or more likely, smothered before it could draw its first breath. Black as coal, the child was, just like your mother's Abyssinian pageboy."

There were gasps from the company, but no one was going to leave now.

"Not all crimes are sexual, of course." Matilda's bony finger jabbed the air, and a portly gentleman flinched. "How fatherly of you to send your sons abroad for a Grand Tour, before their young friend's death was too closely investigated. It was a relief for everyone to get them out of London, wasn't it? Except, perhaps, for the opium dens that closed from the lack of their custom."

Matilda shook her head with something like sorrow at the Earl of Marston. "The two of you invested heavily in that unlikely scheme I warned you about. I *warned* you, Richard, and both of you still sunk all the family money into it. So how come you were able to recover your funds, and your brother was not? Your own brother, Richard. I'm certain you repapered the study as soon as you inherited, but do you ever imagine that the blood spatters still show through?"

Her eyes traveled the ballroom slowly, fixing at last on Jack Carrington, Marquess of Summerford. The assembled company knew that he was probably Jamie's grandfather. They didn't know he'd been Stephen's first lover. Right now, Jack Carrington stood pale but unflinching, awaiting the blow.

"We all have our secrets," Matilda repeated, her voice falling. "I could go on all night, but I'm too tired, and too sad."

"Just as well you're done casting stones." Lady Elizabeth Blessingham, almost as coldly beautiful at fifty as she'd been at fifteen, stood alone against Matilda Clair's fury. "Are you so without sin yourself?"

"Not at all," she replied, chin firm. "I think if you investigated far enough, you'd find my worst sin against society rather neatly parallels that of my grand-nephew: I loved outside of the narrow confines of where I could marry. So turn your backs on my grand-nephew if you must, but if you do, it's only fair you turn your backs on me as well. Anyone who wakes up tomorrow with the same self-righteous indignation you've demonstrated tonight, can call on me between the hours of two and five tomorrow, and withdraw your funds from my investments. Now, good night."

Only Stephen seemed unmoved by his great-aunt's performance. Looking at his face, alight with an inner fire, she wondered if he'd even heard it.

"I can't believe it," he said. "All this time spent scouring the stews for Jamie, and I find him in your ballroom. Find out how to find him, I mean. He's working at the docks, Aunt Matilda!" Stephen threw back his head and laughed in exultation. "All I have to do is go down there tomorrow and fetch him."

"Best go home and get some sleep then, nephew." She took his arm and walked him toward the door. The ballroom was clearing of people, but a few still lingered, already re-living the scandal of the evening.

He frowned. "When you said 'outside the narrow confines,' what did you mean?"

"So you were listening. Figure it out, puppy. The family's been raked over the coals sufficiently for the night."

"Was he married? A servant? Or... not a he at all?"

"I've kept it secret this long. I will expect at the very least a note from you tomorrow, to let me know if you've recovered your Jamie safely."

"I will. I promise." Stephen's eyes danced as he kissed his great-aunt goodnight.

Matilda turned back from the door with a sigh, to find that there was one remaining guest left in the ballroom. "Hello, Jack."

The Marquess of Summerford bowed with grace. "I wanted to thank you, Matilda. You…could have made things difficult for me, and chose not to."

"I like you Jack. I always have. Still, in my day, the Carringtons were known for cleaning up their own messes."

"You mean Maria Riley's son. Is there really any proof he's Johnnie's bastard?"

"He's the spitting image of you at that age. Maria's dead, but if you do some investigating, I think you'll find your son was the likely father."

"Investigating?" Jack frowned.

"Her friends, her midwife, her priest. I don't think she was one to bear tales, but Maria probably told someone. And if she did, it wasn't for gain — if she ever approached you for money, I'll eat my best bonnet."

"No. She never did." He paused. "As for the young man, what would you suggest? Some sort of settlement?"

"I don't think Jamie would take money. But he could use an education, Jack. Offer to send him to a good university, and then if things don't work out between him and Stephen, his degree would at least give him a leg up in the world."

"I'll do some thinking about it, Matilda." He reached for the door, then halted. "What's he like?" Jack's voice sounded wistful.

"You'll like him. He's a well-mannered lad, and his intelligence is noteworthy. Your son's treatment of his mother is a bit of a sore spot, though. It might not be so easy to get him to take anything from you."

"I'll ponder on the best way to approach him, then."

"You might ask Stephen for help." It was her turn to hesitate. "It would do him good right now, to be seen with someone as well-respected as you. The *ton* follows your lead."

Jack smiled. "Not half as much as they follow your nose for money. I think Stephen was well and truly restored to good graces as soon as you reminded everyone how much they owe to your investments. I don't think there'll be much of a queue waiting outside your drawing room door tomorrow at two."

"Good. I'll take a nap after luncheon instead."

"Like the sweet little old lady that you are." The Marquess of Summerford kissed her hand, and took his leave.

"Good heavens." Julian Jeffries leaned out the window of the Allbrights' phaeton, astonished by the traffic in the streets. Harold Allbright had taken him to dinner with some wealthy cousins of his, who had an interest in the thespian arts. Harold would want a reward if they came through with financing, of course, but that could be negotiated later. Now they were approaching Lady Matilda's mansion for her card party, and while it wasn't unexpected to see a throng of carriages out front, they all seemed to be leaving, not arriving. He recognized an acquaintance in the crowd. "Timothy! What happened? Dear old Lady Matilda didn't take ill, did she?" He shivered with excitement at the thought.

Timothy Swann adored a good gossip, and breaking this news to Julian Jeffries was going to be the highlight of his year. "My poor, dear, Julian... you'll never guess what your Lord St. Joseph just said, and in front of everyone, too!"

Only years of training kept Julian's face from betraying his reaction, but any vestigial qualms he might have had about the cruelty of James Riley's upcoming demise disappeared forever. Tonight, he would force himself to go to Stephen, to coo over how wonderful it was that poor lost Jamie had been found—once, of course, he'd sent a message to Bertie making damn sure Jamie didn't show up at the docks tomorrow. And the night after that, he was going to enjoy seeing the little bastard suffer.

Chapter Twenty-Three

*T*he docks. Stephen bit his lip in frustration. Who knew there were so many of them? Huge wooden piers jutting out from the riverbank, lined with a profusion of enormous warehouses, so many the streets couldn't hold them: some teetered out over the water on stilts to make up for the shortage of land. Every available anchorage was taken by a barge or ship of some sort, and the whole swarmed with people. Sailors, ships' passengers, customs officials, foremen, and most important to his interests, stevedores. Despite the chill and clammy December air, many of these were stripped to the waist, the exertions of shifting heavy cargo keeping them warm. He had yet to see a particular slender torso among them.

"Riley?" Mr. Binks, the umpteenth foreman Stephen had approached, was obviously distracted by the problems of directing his crew. "You there! Have a bloody care, those crates contain *china.*"

"Yes. James Riley." Stephen's heart was sinking into the boots Charles had polished for him so carefully. Three hours ago, when he had left St. Joseph House with a light heart, it had seemed important to look his best, to show Jamie respect. It hadn't taken long to realize that such efforts just made him look ridiculously out of place in this environment. "He's twenty-two years old, and—"

"Step to it, Wilkins, for Christ's sake, or I'll dock your bleeding pay! You were saying, sir?"

Stephen spoke quickly, trying to cover the salient points before Mr. Binks could find something else that needed his attention. "Young, average height. Brownish hair, blue eyes. Spectacles."

"Specs? Why didn't you say? Aye, he's been here this week. Didn't show up today, though—Bloody hell, Jonesie! Move it!"

Stephen blew out a breath, feeling lost. "He's not ill, is he?"

"If you'll excuse me, sir, how the hell should I know? Good lad, hard worker, but I never thought he'd stay. More like a clerk than a laborer, ain't he? Likely he found something more suited to him. Good day, sir. Jonesie! What the hell did I just say?"

"Do you know his direction?"

"His what? Jonesie!"

"Where he lives. Please, Mr. Binks, it's important." It was impossible, simply impossible, that he had come so close to Jamie, and missed him.

"Sorry. He never said, I never asked. Not the talkative sort, thank God."

"Should he come back, will you ask him to contact me?"

Mr. Binks gave the distinct impression that his patience was under attack. "Aye, aye. Good day, sir!"

Stephen proffered a coin. The size of it regained the foreman's attention nicely.

"*Sir?*"

"Should Mr. Riley return, ask him to get in touch with Stephen. Will you remember that? Please?"

Mr. Binks took the coin. "Yes, sir. Of course I will. Good day, sir. There, Wilkins! That's my lad! Jonesie—see there—that's how to pick up the pace!"

Stephen, not entirely convinced that the foreman would remember his message even if Jamie did come back to work at the docks, took a dejected leave.

Bertie listened to the clock striking twelve with satisfaction. His master's instructions to keep Riley away from work today had been redundant—Bertie's ploy to get the lad drunk may not have provided the sex he'd hoped for, but it had kept Jamie out of commission this morning. The lad was just now beginning to stir beneath the dirty blanket that covered him.

Bertie clapped his hands loudly. "Come on, lad, some food will do you good."

"Bertie!" Jamie groaned, pulling his meager covers over his head. "Leave me alone."

"Let's get you over to Mrs. Perkin's bakeshop for some tea and a bit o' toast, shall we? The air will make you feel better, and so will the victuals. Trust me, I know."

"What time is it?" With effort, Jamie made his way to a sitting position. "I have to get to the docks."

"Too late, lad. It's past noon."

"Noon! Oh, Christ." He put his head in his hands. "So much for proving how trustworthy I am to Mr. Binks. Told him I didn't drink, too."

"Nah, lad. Tell him it was your back—you're not used to this work yet, he knows that. Ten or twelve hours shifting crates would put me to bed for a week."

"Fourteen hours on Tuesday," Jamie muttered. "But never mind. The more hours I put in, the quicker I'll be out of here." He wrapped the blanket more tightly about him, shivering. "I can't believe I've lost a day's pay through my foolishness."

"Oh, well," Bertie said, looking away. "I heard something this morning about another job that might suit you. Come on, I'll tell you about it over tea. Rumor is the pay's good."

Jamie rose and straightened his crumpled clothing as best he could, running his fingers through his hair to smooth it. "Really? Whatever it is, I'm interested. I can't believe I've been in this hole for a week—the quicker I'm out of here the better."

Tomorrow you're out of here. The thought pricked at the remnant's of Bertie's conscience. *By next Thursday, you'll be*—He couldn't finish that notion, even to himself. Why couldn't Julian's prey be the prissy little bastard the actor had made him out to be? The lad wasn't half bad. They'd had some laughs at the pub last night. *Mister Julian.* The dresser forced his thoughts back to his employer. The most gorgeous man in London, and Bertie got to see him naked daily. Better yet, play with him, too, whenever Julian was bored enough. He'd be a fool to risk losing his post. No matter what it meant for someone, who, after all, he barely knew. And would hardly miss.

Bertie cleared his throat. Jamie had nibbled the bait, time to hook him. "Come on, lad, let's have some tea. Now, about that job. There's this foreign lady who runs a business, needs help with her accounts..."

The weak winter sun was in Stephen's eyes as he exited the coach, drawn up before the stables behind St. Joseph House. "Thank you, Abby," he said. She nodded, silent as usual, and began the process of unhitching the horses. Stephen stared up at the back of the house, feeling sick with disappointment and unbearably tired. He supposed it was proper that he go around to the front door, but it seemed far too long a walk. Blast it, it was his house. If he wanted to use the servants' entrance, he would. He started up the path to the house, barely registering the stakes and twine where the foundations of the greenhouse were being laid out at last, in the back corner opposite the stables.

Stephen was nearly to the back door when the gate behind him clanged loudly, and he turned to see a woman, hooded and cloaked, hurrying toward him with her head down. Not tall enough for Rebecca, too much so for Betsy, far too spry to be Mrs. Symmons. "Careful, Maisie!" He caught her by the shoulders just before she barreled into him.

She gave a cry of surprise, raising her face, which looked even more careworn than usual, the eyes red and hot. "Oh, my lord! Please tell me you found Mr. Riley. Please tell me he's safe."

Stephen tried to smile. "I went to the docks, but he wasn't there."

"Wasn't he?" Maisie swallowed. "I'm terribly afraid that I may know where he'll be tomorrow."

The back door jerked open, revealing an anxious throng of faces. He watched them fall as they took in the fact that Jamie was not with him. Rebecca bit her lip. "You both look like you need some tea."

"She wasn't a bad girl, my daughter," Maisie said, once they were settled at the kitchen table. "Laurie just got tangled up with the wrong lad. He put her on the streets, he did, and then when he left her, she had no other choice. She went to Madame Novotny. And then..." She stared at the table, a single tear trickling its way to drip from the end of her nose. "Then she just disappeared. Nobody cared."

Charles, his warm brown eyes sympathetic, nodded as he figured it out. "You've been going out at night, trying to find out what happened, haven't you?"

"I've been working at the brothel, nights."

Stephen raised his brows. Fascinating, of course, but what the hell did this have to do with Jamie? "You... work there?"

"I clean, my lord, and see to the lads and girls as work there."

"What have you found out?" Stephen tried not to let his growing impatience show

"A little. They don't want to talk about it, do they? But one of the girls told me the last time she saw Laurie, she was nervous. Madame had booked her with a customer who wanted her in one of the dungeon rooms."

"The dungeons." Stephen took a breath. He'd heard rumors that Madame was willing to cater to the darker ecstasies, but surely she'd never allow anyone to go too far. "It's just for playacting. Games. Isn't it?"

"My Laurie went down there, and no one saw here come out.

I've been trying to find out who it was that took her there, and I finally got a glimpse of Madame's books for that night. There were three men that booked dungeon rooms: their names are Harrington, Cosgrove, and Taylor. One of them killed my Laurie."

"But Jamie—what does this has to do with Jamie?"

"Someone's gone and reserved a dungeon room for a whole week, starting tomorrow, and everyone was afraid that meant one of them was going to—to be the one down there. And Madame told 'em not to worry, that the patron was bringing in his own play thing. A young man nobody was going to miss, what had just run away from the Earl of St. Joseph."

Stephen felt his heart stop, for a moment he couldn't breathe. "No," he said. "No. We'll find him first, if we have to—"

"Stephen, pay attention." Charles was shaking him. "If there were a thousand of us, we could search maybe a quarter of the city properly. But we know where he'll be tomorrow. He'll be brought to Madame Novotny's—we just have to get there first, and make sure nothing happens to him." The valet looked around the table. "We can do that. We have to."

"But how?" Mrs. Symmons' mouth quavered. "How can we? What can we do?"

"Maisie," Charles said urgently. "Do you have any idea of what time this is supposed to happen?"

"I don't know when they're bringing Jamie in. But the patron is expected by midnight."

"*By* midnight, or at midnight?"

"I don't know. That's all I could find out—sometime around midnight. And I still don't know who booked the room, but I'll wager it's the same bloke as did my Laurie."

Charles drew a breath. "And we know it's the dungeon, so—"

"*A* dungeon. There's eight different rooms down there. I don't know which one he'll be in."

"Right." Rebecca squeezed Maisie's hand. "That will have to be enough. Now, we need a plan."

Lady Matilda sat at her writing desk, staring at the copy she'd transcribed of her great-nephew's contract with Julian Jeffries. Stephen's valet had brought the original to her a few days back, and she'd agreed that it was likely the actor could be caught breaking the exclusivity clause. As soon as possible, she'd contracted a couple of Bow Street Runners to shadow him, and two more to trace the whereabouts of Jamie Riley. Her tame Runners had just made their daily reports, and their information had been interesting indeed.

Because the two investigations had intersected at the same book-shop in Soho, where a confused young clerk couldn't understand why he was suddenly of so much interest to the Law.

Yes, he'd told the Runners, a young man fitting Riley's description had applied for a position, but he had lost the slip of paper with his address. Mr. Shelby had flushed so deeply at this point that a follow-up was warranted: it turned out that the paper might just be in the possession of a particular customer who had visited the shop at about the same time.

A Mr. Julian Jeffries.

Matilda set down the contract with a sigh and picked up a pen, dipping it in the inkpot and beginning to write a note. The Runners had observed young Shelby's extreme embarrassment at the inquest into Jeffries' visit, but could not get him to admit that anything untoward had happened between them. Not that it mattered. The clerk's word against Jeffries' would not be enough to break the contract. But the larger puzzle was: what could the actor want with young Mr. Riley? Perhaps he just wanted to keep track of a potential rival, perhaps he had worse plans in mind.

Matilda rang for her butler. "Hargreave, take this note to Bow Street. I need the watch on Jeffries tripled." If the actor did try anything, he would lead them straight to Jamie. If not, well, eventually she would catch him with another man, and find the Riley boy some other way.

"Certainly, my lady. I'll arrange it at once."

There was one other consideration, however, and as much as she hated to spend money where she didn't have to, it was best to have a back-up plan. "Hargreave? Would I happen to have a thousand guineas lying around the house?"

"Not at present, my lady. Shall I call at the bank, as well?"

"That would be most excellent, Hargreave." Her lips curved into a smile. One way or another, she was going to get Stephen out of the clutches of that conniving whore.

Chapter Twenty-Four

"Oh, come on, Jamie. Madame needs someone like you!" Even now, making their way on foot to Madame's establishment, Bertie's prey was in danger of slipping the trap. He had to think fast and persuade the lad otherwise. "The operation has grown too large. It's not just the lads and lasses she sells, it's food, drink, gambling. Money-lending. Madame can't keep track of it all anymore."

"Bertie, I know the money's good, but..." Jamie seemed to sink further into himself the closer they got to the brothel. "There's someone I know who frequents the place, and I *cannot* run into him there."

"You could work during the day," Bertie said. "I assume things are quieter then, with less chance of running into your *friend*. And tonight, we'll sneak you in through the servants' entrance, in case your fellow's there."

"I suppose." Jamie pulled at the collar of his shirt, borrowed from Bertie for the occasion. "I wish I could like it better, though."

Bertie shook his head. "Damn! If I could even pretend I had a head for figures, I'd be jumping at the opportunity. She's willing to pay out the arse. Enough to get you on your feet right away."

"It's an ugly business, the selling of flesh, Bertie. I don't mean to be a prude about it, but I suppose I am. Someone—someone I was close to sold herself, and it destroyed her. It would dishonor her memory to—"

"Oh, well. The poor kids, then." Bertie sighed. "I was hoping you could help them."

"Help... who?"

"Who do you think suffers when Madame can't figure out where the money is going? If she thinks she's short, it comes straight from the whores' wages. It's not like they can complain."

"I didn't think of—"

"I wanted to keep my family stuff personal, but I see it's time to put all my cards on the table. My cousin Timmy works there. He came to me just the other day about it, about how Madame docked his pay yet again. Tim works hard for that money—they all do—and there Madame is getting rich off their efforts, while they barely have enough to put food in their mouths. Or their children's."

"Children." Jamie took a painful breath. "Bertie, I—"

"It's not even so much that Madame means to cheat them—she just can't reason from the bar to the beds, if you get my meaning. What comes in from the liquor sales gets mixed up with what comes in from the whores, and when it's time to pay out the vendors..." He shook his head mournfully. "If the sheets don't balance, they all have to spend more time between the sheets."

"Oh, God. I don't know. Maybe I should..."

Bertie put an arm around Jamie's shoulders, giving him a friendly squeeze. "No harm in meeting with the lady, taking a look at her books. You don't have to decide this minute."

Jamie's smile was sheepish. "You're right, of course." He took a breath. "Are we almost there?"

"Almost," Bertie said, looking away. "Almost."

Charles grinned to himself as the hansom cab rolled along through the streets, carrying him and Mr. Symmons to their destination. Such a serious endeavor had no right being so blasted fun. After much discussion, the household had decided to approach Novotny's singly or in pairs. Maisie was going to sneak Rebecca in as a newly-hired prostitute, her job to get information from the other girls while Maisie herself talked to the kitchen staff. Mr. Symmons would meet up with Sam to check out the gossip in the second-class gaming rooms; Stephen would do the same in the first-class equivalents. Abby Sawtell seemed to have a plan of her own, and either couldn't or wouldn't disclose it.

And Charles, lucky Charles, got the job of approaching the young lads for hire to find out what they knew. Of course, he wasn't actually going to have sex with any of them, but it felt naughty just to play the part of an interested customer. "But you know," he'd murmured to Sam before they left St. Joseph House, "I'll expect a suitable reward for my restraint." The baker's reply had been non-verbal, and left Charles weak at the knees. He shook his head. And after eight years, too.

Mr. Symmons stared, stone-faced, out the carriage window, obviously wondering how fate had arranged things in such a way as to send him to a brothel tonight. Charles stifled a smile. The butler must be mortified. Well, they would all laugh about it later.

His smile faded. Assuming everything went well tonight.

But it bloody well had to.

Chapter Twenty-Five

*T*he night was chilly, but not too cold as they made their brisk way through the streets. Jamie hummed to himself. He had all but convinced himself to take the position. Helping the prostitutes was a major consideration, of course, but he also couldn't overlook the benefits of the enormous salary Bertie assured him he would receive. He would move to respectable lodgings, keep himself in clean shirts, find decent and bearable employment. Working at the docks had given him an idea: the port of London was enormously busy. There must be endless need for shipping and warehouse clerks to keep track of the bustling trade.

And then, once he had established himself, proved he could stand on his own two feet, he would call on Stephen. No, he would write first. He was good at letters. *Dear Stephen...*

Bertie nudged him. "That's the place, over there."

"It looks like a hotel."

"I think it was. Come on, servants' entrance is round the back."

Jamie followed him to the back door, where Bertie rang the bell. It was evident they were expected; the girl who opened the door nodded with familiarity to Bertie, and gave Jamie a curious glance.

"Downstairs. Number Three. You know the way?"

"Aye." Bertie jerked his head in a nod, his hands jammed into his pockets. He led the way through the enormous kitchens, where an army of servants labored at the cook stoves and cutting boards. Bertie looked at a rack of knives and shuddered. "Come on, keep up."

"I'm still here," Jamie said mildly, wondering what had gotten into his friend. Perhaps he was having second thoughts about encouraging him to work in this place. They proceeded through a doorway and into another part of the building, older, quieter, cooler. Down a set of stairs was an enormously thick door. Bertie wrestled it open. Inside, more stairs led down.

Jamie held back. "Are you sure this is the right way? This seems to be some sort of sub-cellar."

"Madame keeps her office where it's quiet and out of the way, of course. Can't be distracted by all that upstairs." Bertie waved his hand vaguely.

"I...suppose that makes sense."

Another enormous door at the base of this stairwell, too. This one led to a dark stone corridor, barely lit by flickering torches. The effect was positively medieval. Jamie shivered. It was also much colder down here.

"Number Three," Bertie muttered to himself, taking an audibly deep breath. "Let's go, then." He paused at the third doorway. "Jamie. Remember when I asked you if there was ever something you wanted so badly, that you'd do something bad to get it?"

Jamie thought he understood. "It's all right, Bertie. I've come to terms with the idea of this place."

Bertie pushed open the door.

"You're here early tonight, my lord. It's barely nine o'clock." The front door steward took his overcoat. Stephen had come in the coach, driven by Abby as usual. When she handed him down he had clutched her hand for a moment, staring at the front door of the brothel. His love was in there somewhere, or would be soon. What if they couldn't find him in time? What if...?

Abby squeezed his fingers. "Strong," she said.

Did she mean Jamie was strong, or that he should be strong for Jamie? Either way, she was right, and he smiled wordlessly in appreciation. Abby nodded back. For once, their communication was perfect.

The coachwoman had given the reins to her son, then entered the brothel behind her employer, striding on long legs down the corridor to the left without waiting for the steward. Alex remained outside with the horses, where he could keep an eye on the door and send a message in if he saw anything unusual. The other members of the household were coming singly and together; on foot or by hansom.

Now Stephen looked around the front hall, finding that it all appeared different tonight. The décor hadn't changed, it was still quietly furnished in dark wood and rich crimson fabrics, resembling nothing so much as the foyer of a first-class hotel. But always before, it had seemed welcoming. The idea that Jamie would be in danger within these walls made the darkness threatening, gave a tinge of blood to the red upholstery.

"Early? Yes, but I was damned bored. Any action tonight?"

The steward shrugged. "Depends on what you're interested in." He nodded towards a set of doors on the right that led into the upper-class gaming rooms, where only the titled or very wealthy were welcome. "Too early for much play. We've put together a few tables of out-of-town gentlemen if you'd care to join one of those." Madame kept her patrons carefully segregated by class: the doors on the left-hand side of the foyer went to the second-class rooms, which catered to middle-class businessmen. There was a separate entrance outside for tradesmen and clerks; while common laborers, servants and worse had to go all the way around to the back.

Stephen scowled, waving at another door on the right. "Any one I might know in the bar?"

"Still very quiet. Perhaps you'd care for some private entertainment upstairs while you wait for things to liven up?"

"Not in the mood. Not yet, anyway. Unless...is there anything unusual going on tonight? I'm feeling remarkably jaded."

There was no flicker of knowledge in the steward's face. "Not that I'm aware of, my lord. Shall I let you know if I hear of anything?"

"Please do. In the meantime..." From the corner of his eye, Stephen saw the front door open, and recognized the newly-arrived patrons as his butler and valet. He'd best make up his mind quickly, as Charles couldn't be trusted to keep a straight face at seeing him. "May as well sit in on one of the tables you have going. Anyone playing *vingt-et-un*?"

Jamie was barely inside the chamber when his arms were grabbed by two hulking men.

"About time," one of them muttered.

"I told you I'd be here between seven and eight," Bertie said.

"Well, it's almost eight. We've been waiting."

He struggled, but it was useless. "What's going on? What do you want?" Jamie cried.

Madame's men ignored him, hauling Jamie efficiently over to the wall, where his wrists were pulled above his head. Cold iron encircled them as manacles clicked shut. One of the men tested the length of the chains.

"Can you stand comfortably? We don't want you dangling."

"What does it matter?" his companion asked. "Come on, this place gives me the creeps."

"Could be a few hours before you-know-who shows up. We're supposed to turn him over in good condition—wouldn't do to have his arms pulled out of the sockets."

"Who?" Jamie shouted. "Why am I here? *Bertie?*" But Bertie was already gone, and the two others soon followed. At the last, one of them hesitated, then set his lantern down on a table in the middle of the room. As he looked around the room, Jamie wasn't sure he was grateful for the courtesy.

Think. All right, what did he know? He was chained to a wall, in a small stone chamber somewhere beneath the brothel. The room contained a fireplace—unfortunately unlit—and several sets of chains hanging on the walls, one of which was, of course, attached to him. In the center of the room was a large, freestanding stone block, about four feet in height, holding the lantern the man had left behind. The table—or altar—had stout iron rings sunk into the corners, convenient for chaining someone down. A smaller, wooden cart stood next to it. The tray it held was discreetly covered by a linen towel.

The phrase *torture chamber* came to mind.

Jamie shuddered.

No. There could be anything under that towel. A nice lunch perhaps, for him and Bertie to enjoy once his friend popped back in, grinning, to laugh at the grand joke he'd played on him. For a minute he almost believed it. *Ha! You should have seen your face! What, did you think I was leaving you here? To be...*

"Oh, God." Jamie tugged at the chains. They were real enough. Although there wasn't much strain on them, his arms were tiring of the position. He worked his hands open and closed to force his blood to flow upward.

It was impossible he was here to be hurt. Why? Who could hate him so? But it didn't have to be personal. *Bring me a slender young man, preferably with blue eyes.* If Madame didn't have what was ordered in stock, she would have to get it from somewhere.

Bertie. He closed his eyes. The young man must work for Madame. *Ever want something so badly...?* What had she promised him? Money? Freedom?

The next question was what his buyer wanted from him. This was a brothel. That implied sex. Jamie's stomach tightened. But if that...if that were all, why not tie him to a bed and get on with it? He stared at the covered tray. Monstrous to think that anyone would get pleasure from causing pain, but there was good historical precedent for it. Some of the Roman emperors had been notorious for their enjoyment of cruelty. Caligula. Nero. Panic rose in him at the thought, and he forced himself to control his breathing.

All right, someone wants to hurt you. Then what?

He hadn't been blindfolded. Unless someone came back and performed that task, he would see his attacker. Be able to identify him, press charges. It was possible the person might think he could be bribed to keep quiet. Or be so grateful to be freed that he would just stumble home and try to forget it ever happened. Or...

There were grooves cut into the stone floor, channeling toward a drain at the base of the table. They would neatly dispose of a great deal of blood.

Jamie forced himself to face the simple fact that if someone did mean to...harm...him, the safest means to ensure his silence was to...silence him forever. *You know the words, Jamie,* he told himself savagely, *use them. Not hurt, not harm.*

Rape.

Torture.

Kill.

He said them out loud, and somehow the act made him feel calmer. "All right," he said. "If that's truly what's planned for me, how do I get out of it?"

Useless to shout; he had noted the thickness of the walls when Bertie had opened the door. His chains were too sturdy to break; the iron cuffs at his wrists snug enough to keep his hands from wriggling through. Would it help if he could dislocate or break some of the bones in his hand? He considered the matter dispassionately. Two drawbacks: first, if he could manage to do it, he'd have to work quickly before the flesh swelled and rendered his sacrifice void. Second, supposing he could free himself from the chains, his broken hands would be useless. He wouldn't be able to pick the lock on the door, or work the hinges from it, or pry a rock from the wall and use it to crush the skull of the bastard who had chained him to a bloody *wall*...

Easy, Jamie.

I will get out of here.

If he couldn't free himself physically, he would use his brain. Find some way to work on his assailant, some means of rendering himself worth more to him alive than dead. But how?

Charles straightened his cravat while he and Mr. Symmons waited for the steward to return. Nice place, this. And he felt like a proper gentleman, all dressed up in Stephen's brother's clothes, which he'd been able to tailor to himself quite nicely. He nudged his companion. "So this is how the other half lives, eh?"

Mr. Symmons glowered, and folded his arms.

"Good evening, gentlemen." The steward, a dignified man in his late forties, took their measure with a practiced eye, turning first to Mr. Symmons. "You were a military man, sir? Perhaps you still enjoy disciplining the troops?"

"Certainly not." Charles tried not to laugh at the look on the elderly man's face. "I did, however, pick up some international tastes in the army, if you follow me."

"Of course, sir. We have plenty of ladies trained in the French and Greek arts."

Mr. Symmons harrumphed. "Pedestrian. I was thinking Spanish, perhaps Portuguese."

The steward perked up. "I believe we could—"

"Or Indian, perhaps."

"Red or Eastern?"

"Good heavens! Eastern, my good man. With half Egyptian—my back is bothering me tonight. I assume you can arrange it?"

Charles' jaw dropped, but Madame's employee positively grinned. "That's a challenge, sir, but I believe we can accommodate you if you're willing to wait a bit."

Mr. Symmons nodded. "I wish to play cards for a while first anyway—say, until midnight?"

"That will be fine, sir." He led the butler to the appropriate card room and came back for Charles. "Sir, would you care to meet a young gentleman? I can assure you, sir, that all our staff members are discreet, clean, and very willing to please."

Charles blinked. Damn, he was good. "Er... yes. That is, I..."

"Madame has procured some fresh young lads, just in from the country. If you'll follow me, sir, you can make your choice."

Assuming the young men were newly-arrived, they would hardly have the information Charles needed. He bit his lip. "Um...do you have gentlemen with experience, as well? Not too old, of course, but you know. Been around a bit."

"Of course, sir. This way. I think I have just the perfect companion for you."

"Wait. Would I have to decide right away? I'm—uh—I'm very choosy. I'd like to have a drink with a few of the lads, then pick one out."

If the steward felt like rolling his eyes, he was too well-trained to show it. "At this hour, most of the lads are at leisure in the saloon reserved for...gentlemen's gentlemen. You are welcome to take your time examining them." He led the way to the third door down on the left.

Charles pulled at his cravat, which was feeling tight. "Will I be able to tell who's employed here? I mean, I'd hate to make an offer to another patron."

Now the steward's lips curved into a smile. "I don't think sir will have any difficulty on that account." He opened the door to the bar, and Charles gasped. It was rather obvious, at that. The clients, few at this hour, were the ones who were fully dressed. The others...

"Oh, my," Charles said. There had to be fifteen or twenty of them, ranging from tall and hulking to wispy and delicate, and all in various stages of dishabille. Some sported shirts open to the waist, displaying a tantalizing glimpse of muscled chest, while others, bolder, had dispensed with an upper garment altogether. And one—Charles blushed as a dark-haired young man, sleek and sinewy, approached him sporting only a loincloth.

"Buy me a drink, sir?"

"Yes," Charles said, mesmerized. "God, yes."

Time passes slowly when you're chained to a wall. One learns to cope. Jamie found that by flexing the muscles of his arms, he could lessen the discomfort of their position. Twisting his hands to grasp hold of the chains themselves helped as well, although that shortened their reach enough to put him up on tiptoe, so he didn't resort to that often. The dungeon was cold, and damp air seemed to rise from the drain in the floor, beneath which he could hear the gurgle of the river. But the longer he was in chained in one position, the more the stone at his back warmed from his own heat.

Keeping his mind from wandering was easier than he'd imagined: a lifetime devoted to the pleasures of books gave him riches that he squandered lavishly now: he recited Shakespeare's sonnets; recreated Euclidean proofs; mused over Walpole's defense of Richard III. All of this mental activity kept him remarkably calm and self-possessed, under the circumstances.

Until the old woman came to cut off his clothes.

The worst thing, Jamie thought, was how careful she went about it, her wrinkled face frowning in concentration as she picked apart the seams of his borrowed jacket and shirt so that she could sew them up again neatly later. It was so damned practical. Why waste perfectly good garments, especially when the wearer was unlikely to need them again? Somehow, more than anything, this convinced him that whatever was in store for him, he was not expected to survive it.

She took his spectacles, too, worth a sixpence or two at the pawnshop, and Jamie almost cried. Not being able to see increased his sense of helplessness tenfold, especially when she lit the fire, turning the room into a place of menacing shadows. At least the fire gave the promise of heat, although the cold stone walls would be slow to warm up.

The old woman refused to respond to his queries for information, so assiduously that Jamie began to wonder whether she was deaf. Or again, just very practical. Why speak to a dead man? No good could come of it. Once he was naked, she washed him down with impersonal efficiency, then dried him off, still without a word spoken.

He tried one last time as she was bundling up his clothes into a neat parcel. "Please, madam. He'll pay you well for this information. The Earl of St. Joseph, in Hanover Square. Or any member of his staff. Please. It will be well worth your—"

The door closed behind her, and the enormous lock clicked.

Jamie shivered, with cold and creeping fear. What a difference in morale a measly few layers of cloth makes. An accoutrement of civilization, a badge of one's rank and self-respect. Without them, he felt less than human, just an animal chained to a wall. He tried to regain the sense of calm he'd managed to find before, even in this place. Before, as long as he was alive, it seemed there was hope. Now, he fought the rising panic.

Soon. It's going to be soon, and I'm not ready. I don't know anything about this man, or how to fight him, and he's going to walk through that door and I'm going to fail, I'm going to die...

Or even worse, maybe it wouldn't be soon. Maybe he would spend hours, half the night, on the knife-edge of terror, until exhaustion dulled his senses to the point where he'd be beyond scheming to save himself. He had to find peace, find an anchor within himself. *Mother.* That helped. She'd been the center of his life for most of it, a friend and confidant, his only family. Jamie closed his eyes and recreated the smell of her, lavender-water and talcum powder, and the anise comfits she'd loved. But his mother was dead, belonging to the past, and he needed to focus on the future.

Stephen.

When I get out of here, I'm going home. Home wasn't the cottage in Yorkshire, long since sold, where he'd spent most of his life. Home certainly wasn't either of the lodgings he'd most recently known. Home was the townhouse on Hanover Square, its warm kitchen filled with conversation and laughter and the smell of almond biscuits. Home was his library, the hours spent working at the desk, or curled up in front of the fire lost in the pages of a book. Home was Stephen, smiling with admiration at him over the chess board, teasing him into mirth in return. What a joy it had been, to find a fine mind within such attractive housing. Stephen, teaching him that there were more pleasures in life than those of the mind. Oh yes, he would live, if he could, for Stephen. Nothing was going to keep them apart after this. The sparks of attraction, of affection the other man felt for him, Jamie would fan until a love grew that matched his own.

Strength blossomed in him. Whatever was to come, he would fight through it.

Stephen.

Chapter Twenty-Six

*S*tephen bit his lip, frowning at the cards in his hand. It was after ten o'clock, and the first-class gaming room was still all but deserted. The influx of *ton* gentlemen would not begin until after the long dinners at the club were concluded to the final cigar; after the prettiest young misses were whisked home from Almack's; after the balls and musicales and other staid society gatherings began to pall. It was useless. He wasn't going to learn anything from the out-of-towners who, devoid of London social connections, spent their evenings in a place like this.

He stood up. "Pardon me, gentlemen, I need a breath of fresh air. If I'm not back within an hour, have Winstone bank my chips for me." Remarkably, his pile of winnings for once was impressive. Like he cared, tonight.

Stephen repaired to the bar, also nearly empty. The publican knew him well enough to reach instinctively for a bottle of French brandy.

"Good evening, my lord. Will this do, or will Mr. Jeffries prefer something from the cellars?"

"Mr. Jeffries isn't here tonight."

"My lord, he's only just arrived. I saw his coach pull up just a few minutes ago, as I was coming in for my shift. If I'd known you were already here, I would have told him."

Julian must be amazingly bored to come to Novotny's this early in the evening. Still, no matter. If they should run into each other,

Stephen would just have to fob him off with one excuse or another. In the meantime, he would have to think of some way to help in the search for Jamie. Wait a second...

"Did you say something about the cellars?"

"Yes, my lord. I wondered if you or Mr. Jeffries might like something fine from the wine cellars."

Stephen reached into his pocket and returned with a gold coin, tapping it carelessly on the polished mahogany surface of the bar. "I've always been curious about your wonderful collection here. If you're not terribly busy, is there any chance I could get a tour?"

"Aye, my lord." The coin was discreetly tucked away. "Follow me."

The barman stopped and took a lantern from the table outside the door to the cellars, pausing to light it before continuing down. "We can't leave lights burning down there, what with all the wooden wine racks and flammable spirits."

Stephen nodded, striving to show casual interest and not worry and strain. "How far do the cellars extend beneath the building?"

"Whole way, and more. They go all the way under the stables, as well."

They proceeded down the stairs, and Stephen suffered through an interminable tour, oohing and aahing over what, in other circumstances, he might recognize as truly impressive vintages. The wine cellars took up enormous acreage. Where were the dungeons? "Impressive," he said.

"Ah, that's nothing. The very best stuff is over here."

Stephen followed his guide through an archway. This was a possibility. The corridor had several doors, locked with padlocks, on either side, and a final, unlocked door at the end. He counted. Just seven, total. Hadn't Maisie said there were eight dungeons? But perhaps there were more in another part of the cellar.

The barman waved his lantern, scattering shadows on the walls. "This is where the good stuff is. Madame has bottles she swears were put up in the time of the Tudors. Spanish wine from the Armada shipwrecks, even. Might even be telling the truth—I once opened three bottles for someone whose name you would recognize, and one of 'em was brackish with seawater. Other two were ambrosia, though—I sipped the last drops from the bottles when they were done." He shook his head. "My God. Only a handful of people get the chance at something like that."

"All of these rooms contain wine?" He tried to keep disappointment from his voice.

"Aye. Well, the finest aged spirits, as well. You want a bottle of Scotch that belonged to Bonnie Prince Charlie himself? We got it. That's why they're locked up, see? If you want something from down here, only the Head Wine Steward has the keys."

"What about that door, there?" Stephen pointed at the unlocked portal.

"Oh, that just goes down to the second level."

His own pulse sounded loud in his ears. "Another level of wine cellars?"

"Nah, that's the dungeons down there. For them as likes the weird stuff."

Stephen swallowed. "How bizarre. I don't suppose you'd show me?"

The barman shook his head. "Can't, my lord. Madame's very strict about privacy for those patrons. The bookings are timed so they don't run into each other, and staff use a separate staircase."

"Does that go to the staff stairs, then? I can't imagine you'd have patrons wandering through the wine cellars."

His guide grinned. "Staff neither. No, this staircase doesn't get used much, but Madame hasn't bricked it up in case there's an emergency. Fire, or flooding. There's access to the river from some of the dungeons, so if the water rises suddenly, they flood. People might need to get out in a hurry. Come on, my lord. I've got to get back." He turned and started back through the maze of cellars.

Stephen took a last look at the unlocked door, memorizing its location, and followed, flicking open his gold watch. It was nearly time for the conspirators to meet and pool what they'd learned.

Maisie, with her inside knowledge of the establishment, tracked everyone down—except Abby, who could not be found—and herded them by ones and twos into an unused parlor on the first floor. "We should be safe enough in here, at least for a bit. Me, I'll start. I don't know which dungeon for sure, but it's either going to be Number Three, Five, or Seven. That narrows it down."

"His name is Cosgrove," Charles said, slipping an arm around Sam. "The lads told me that. Time was, he wasn't quite so bad, but he's got worse and worse over the years."

"Is there any way we can get a look at Madame's books?" Rebecca looked at Maisie. "The girls say she's very meticulous about her records. Now that we know his name, if we can see which dungeon he's booked, we'll know that's where Jamie is. Or is going to be. Does anyone know if he's here yet?"

There was a flurry of head-shaking.

"No," Stephen said, "but if it helps, I've found a rarely-used entrance to the dungeons through the wine cellar. When the time comes, we can get down there without running into anyone on the staff or patron stairs."

If only the others didn't look so surprised that he had been able to contribute.

Maisie spoke up. "If you're going to try for Madame's office, now's the time. She usually takes a break for a late supper about now. You should—"

The door opened suddenly, and they all started guiltily, each instantly groping for a reason for their curious assembly.

It was Abby Sawtell, who didn't bother with any recital of where she'd been, whom she'd spoken with, or how she'd found them. "Lad's here. Eight o'clock."

Stephen swallowed painfully. "Jamie's been here for over two hours? Oh, my God."

"Cosgrove's not. Yet."

"That's amazing, Abby," Charles said. "Have you found out which dungeon?"

She hadn't.

Maisie quickly gave directions to Madame's office. "I'd show you myself, but if I'm gone from the kitchens much longer, I'll be in trouble. If one of you can get to me there when you've found out which room, I'll see if I can get the key."

"Who's going to the office?" Stephen asked. "I'm too well-known here. Charles?"

"Yes, Mr. Symmons and I can do it. We can pretend we're lost if we get caught."

"I have a better idea," Rebecca put in. "I'll go with you—then, if anyone sees us, we can say they're trying to book my time."

Maisie shook her head, looking toward the door. "Any of the stewards could arrange that—you wouldn't need to go to the office yourselves."

"But I'm new—I don't know that." Rebecca smiled. "Come on, lads, fancy a go?"

Stephen chewed on his fingertip. "Maybe the rest of us should just wait in the wine cellar. It's too complicated to gather us up again."

"Good idea." Charles grinned through the gathering tension. "All right, ye piece o' fancy," he said to Rebecca. "Let's just get us put down for a mite o'—how about Portuguese, with a side of Red Indian, Mr. S?"

Mr. Symmons coughed. "If that's where your tastes truly lie, Mr. West. But I should think your Sam would be very surprised."

Lady Matilda waited patiently in her coach outside Madame Novotny's. Once her tame Runners had brought the surprising news that Julian's dresser Bertie had escorted young Mr. Riley to the brothel, she had been quick to follow. Any reason Julian had for wanting Jamie in such a place could not be good.

At last, Mr. Hammond opened the door and leaned in. "Your nephew and Jeffries are here, but not together. Lord St. Joseph has been playing cards since just after nine, while Jeffries seems to be waiting for someone in a private parlor."

"Another lover?" Lady Matilda's eyes gleamed. "We may be able to kill two birds with one stone tonight. But the safety of the Riley boy comes first. Where is he?"

Hammond shook his head. "I don't know, but he's not with Jeffries' dresser. Bertie Ellis is drinking alone in the second-class barroom. Looking very morose, if you ask me."

Lady Matilda collected her gold-tipped cane. "Then it's time you and I had a chat with Mr. Ellis, don't you think?"

Chapter Twenty-Seven

The heavy, iron-banded door swung inward. Cosgrove shouldered Julian out of the way, eager to take the measure of his prey. The first impression was extremely favorable—young men, he had always found, are at their best chained to walls. Naked. Defenseless. Cosgrove moved closer, liking the way this one clung to defiance, his muscles taut as if poised for an escape that was not going to happen. It was so disappointing when they gave up too soon.

The subject gave a cry as he recognized Cosgrove's companion. "You bastard!" It yanked at its chains. "Get me out of here. Your little joke has gone far enough."

"Joke?" Julian smiled. "I assure you, you won't be laughing for long."

Cosgrove glared at the actor. Why wouldn't the man shut up? "It's a much better looking specimen than you led me to believe. Are you certain it won't be missed?"

"No one will care, I guarantee it."

"I'm not an it, sir. My name is James Riley, and—"

"Tell it to shut up, Mr. Jeffries, or the first thing I shall remove will be its tongue."

"Where's the fun in that?" The subject was struggling to keep his voice reasonable, but the stink of fear emanated from him. "Wouldn't it be much more satisfying to hear me plead for mercy?"

Cosgrove was amused. Sometimes they even thought they could outwit him. "Jeffries—there was supposed to be a brazier. Where is my brazier?"

Julian waved a hand. "Bother the brazier. You can heat things up in the fireplace. Aren't you going to get on with it?"

Cosgrove stalked over to the actor. "Mr. Jeffries. You will fetch my brazier, and you will do it now."

The actor stiffened, then shot a glance at Jamie, chained to the wall, and his posture relaxed. It was clear that the entertainment he anticipated was worth a little pride. "Of course. I'll be back shortly."

Cosgrove inspected the room, liking what he saw. The thick stone walls afforded both the privacy he needed for his efforts and the forbidding atmosphere that proved so effective at dampening the spirits of his subjects. Speaking of damp... He frowned. Dungeons should be cold and dank, he supposed, but at his age he really appreciated the fire warming the chamber. Hopefully, the subject wouldn't find it too comfortable—but then again, the boy didn't have the advantage of clothing. Cosgrove tugged at the sleeve of his sober black evening jacket, enjoying the discreet flicker of gold from the buttons on the cuff. It was these small achievements that made his climb to riches so satisfying.

Cosgrove turned his back to the boy on the wall as he lifted the towel from the tray on the cart, grunting in satisfaction at the implements he found there. They were honed to a perfect sharpness: some, he'd heard, appreciated the agony caused by a dull blade, but he preferred to err on the side of precision.

"That was a nice touch," the subject said, still trying to engage him in conversation. "Covering the tray. Bit of a risk, though. If I were a man of little imagination, leaving me here for a few hours in plain sight of your tools would have been more terrifying. But for someone like me, it was much more effective to make me wonder."

Cosgrove ignored the words, holding up a utensil to catch the firelight, angling the reflection so that the light hit the chained young man in the face. "Ah," he said, and smiled. "So few can appreciate the many uses of a sharpened spoon."

The chains rattled slightly as the young man shuddered. "It's so ironic, that I spent all that time in my studies, only to fall into your hands." A note of desperation was already creeping into its voice. Perhaps it was time to play along for a few minutes.

Cosgrove picked up a poker and poked the fire up, adding another few pieces of wood. At the last minute, he slid the iron implement into the coals, leaving it there, half-buried. A little something to keep in reserve until the brazier heated. "Studies? What do your studies have to do with me?"

"Not you precisely, but someone I fancy is very like you. Have you never heard of the Wolf of Wheldrake?"

"Wheldrake? Where's that?" He moved closer, reveling in the young man's increased tension as he neared.

"In Yorkshire. Did nothing make the papers down here?"

"I don't read the papers. People tell me what I need to know." Was there any chance this story was true? "If there is something I need to know, I suggest you tell me while you still can."

"It..." The boy faltered, having to begin again. "It started about seven years ago. A boy was found with his throat ripped out, as if by a wolf or very large dog. I didn't think it was an animal, but no one would believe me. They found and shot a big black dog, and considered it over."

"But of course, it wasn't."

"No. He was perhaps the cleverest human monster to ever walk the face of the Earth."

"Clever? How so?"

"It took a long while to realize the attacks were carefully timed, to build fear in the district. None for months, so that people would pray he was gone at last. Then, a body each month, and then every week, until everyone was terrified that he would strike nightly..."

Cosgrove licked his lips. "And then he'd stop, wouldn't he?" Even as the fiction he took it for, it was an appealing story. He liked that this one was trying so hard. It would be that much more satisfying to break him in the end.

"Yes. For just long enough. Another curious thing—"

A rap sounded at the door, dimly heard through its thickness. Cosgrove turned his dead eyes toward the noise. "Do shut up now." He crossed to the door, allowing Julian back in. The actor's arms were full.

"Here's the brazier, and a bag of extra charcoal that should keep it going for a good long time. Madame apologized in person, and threw in this bottle of wine for our trouble. Care for a glass?"

"No."

"I'll just help myself, then." Julian uncorked the wine and poured himself a measure, carrying it over to enjoy the sight of Jamie, chained to the wall. "Look at you." The lovely green eyes were filled with scorn as they appraised the naked body before him. "How Stephen could ever consider such a scrawny little thing, when he had me—"

"It might be slender," Cosgrove said, "but it is very well made." He ignored the actor's pout. Tiresome man: grating in so many ways, from his preening vanity to the lack of taste evident in his bright yellow waistcoat. His only value was as another instrument to use against the young man on the wall—unless he could use them both against each other? Intriguing thought. "You've made me a rare find, Mr. Jeffries. Tell me, though. Why do you hate the boy so much? Did this Stephen you mention prefer him to you?"

"Prefer him?" Julian's laugh was harsh. "A passing interest, I assure you. Look at him! No one who had ever seen me naked could *prefer* him."

"Perhaps I'm at a disadvantage, then," Cosgrove purred. "Remove your clothes, Mr. Jeffries."

"What?" Julian froze, like an animal finally scenting danger when the wind turned.

"You so clearly hate this rival of yours. Wouldn't you find it amusing to sport with him a little?"

"Oh." The golden haired one relaxed. "You'd hate that, wouldn't you, brat?"

"Of course I would, or he wouldn't be suggesting it." The younger man shrank against the wall, obviously disturbed by the thought of the actor touching him. "He's a very perceptive man, haven't you gathered that?"

Cosgrove narrowed his eyes at such flagrant flattery. Perhaps the tongue would have to go soon after all. "You tell me then—why is it that Jeffries hates you so much?"

"Oh, that's easy," the subject said. "I'm in love with his patron."

"Ah. Stephen Clair, isn't it? I heard the most interesting story the other day, about an outburst at a party…" He stood even closer, watching the boy's face avidly. "Jeffries doesn't hate you because you love his Stephen. Where's the threat in that? He hates you because his Stephen loves you."

Nice. The young body stiffened in pain, and he hadn't even had to touch him yet. Time to turn the knife a little—figuratively speaking, at this point. "Oh, how wonderful. You didn't know, did you? And that makes it so much worse. To die now, with such happiness just beyond your grasp." He waved a hand at Julian. "It's all this man's fault. It was his idea to sell you to me, to wreck any chance you might have had to be with your love. Look at him, gloating at you. How you must despise him."

The actor approached the chained man, smiling. "Shall I hurt him now?"

Cosgrove raised a brow. "You have no instinct for this. Sometimes I wonder if I have the right specimen in chains." Oh, the looks on both their faces. The flare of hope in the one; the unease in the other. He smiled. "You have no instinct for this," he repeated. "Hurt him? No, I want you to arouse him."

"Arouse him?" Julian looked taken aback.

"Yes, you *idiot*. Don't you understand how much more deeply that will wound him?"

Comprehension dawned in the sea-green eyes, and the actor reached out his hand. "Yes, I see. You're really going to loathe this, aren't you?"

"She's still in there." Charles barely breathed the words, peeking out through the door of the closet across from Madame's office. He, Mr. Symmons and Rebecca had been able to get this far unobserved, but were now stuck waiting for the brothel's mistress to leave for her supper. "Oh, bloody hell!"

"What is it?" Rebecca hissed.

"A girl is bringing a tray. Madame's going to eat at her desk. No, wait! Here comes Maisie as well. She must have a plan."

They all leaned forward to listen, barely able to make out every third or fourth word the housemaid spoke.

"...forgot...Jeffries...angry...insists...recompense?"

Madame's voice was clearer, and only slightly accented after so many years in England. "Fob him off with a bottle of wine. Nothing too fancy. He insists on speaking with me? Very well. I can spare a moment."

Charles strained to see the legendary proprietress as she passed their hiding place, but in the dim hallway she was a creature of shadows in her dove-grey silk gown. "She's gone. Come on, we only have a few minutes."

The two men slipped into the unguarded office, leaving Rebecca to watch at the door. Charles was struck by how similar Madame's office was to Lady Matilda's, both of them no-nonsense places of business within a much more luxurious setting. The two greatest financial minds in London seemed to think alike.

"Cosgrove, Cosgrove. I don't see it." There was an edge of panic in Mr. Symmons' voice as he scanned the ledger on the solid oak desk.

Charles leaned over the book and flipped the page. "Today's the twenty-first, not twentieth. I still don't see..."

"There!" Mr. Symmons stabbed his finger on the entry. "She spelled it with a K—look, Kosgrove. But damn it, what does this say? Her numbers are no better. It could be a three, or a five."

"Five," said Charles. "I think?"

"Hurry!" Rebecca hissed from the doorway. "She won't be gone much longer."

"Yes," Mr. Symmons said. "It has to be a five. Let's go."

They paused briefly in the hallway. "I'll get Maisie," Rebecca said. "You two join his lordship and the others in the wine cellar, and wait for us to bring the key."

Apparently, it wasn't unusual for Madame's girls to wander in and out of the kitchens, because no one seemed to give her presence there a second thought. She found Maisie quickly, and it was a good thing.

"He's here!" Maisie was trembling. "Cosgrove. Mr. Jeffries is with him—he was just up here raising hell about a missing brazier, and Madame had to give him a bottle of wine to make up for it."

"Brazier!" Rebecca felt her stomach lurch. "It's Number Five, Maisie. Can we get the key?"

"Yes. Follow me."

They retrieved the key to Number Five and flew through the utilitarian back corridors of the brothel, then down the stairs to the wine cellars. At first they didn't see their colleagues in the darkness, until someone opened the cover on his lantern so that just a gleam showed through to guide them.

"Over here!" The voice belonged to Charles. They followed him to the hallway with the locked doors, and the stairway that led down to the dungeons.

"Cosgrove is here," Rebecca said, whooping for breath. "But we have the key."

"He's here? With Jamie?" Stephen turned and hurtled toward the stairs.

"Wait!" Charles called softly. "We should plan this—he could have a pistol."

"Then he can bloody well shoot me."

There were seven of them crowded around the door in the dim stone corridor: Sam, Charles, Abby, Maisie, Rebecca, Mr. Symmons, and Stephen. With shaking fingers, Stephen extended the key to the lock, only to snatch it back when he heard a noise from one of the other staircases. The torches on the wall flickered in the air disturbed by someone's approach.

They stared at each other mutely. So many of them. Where could they hide?

"Get the door open," Sam said, retrieving his rolling pin from where he'd stashed it in the small of his back. "If there's trouble, we'll deal with it."

Stephen turned back to the door.

"Lady Matilda?" someone said.

He dropped the key.

"Nice little army you've got here," Aunt Matilda said. "And thank God for it—not that my cane isn't a handy weapon. No, don't bother with the key, that's the wrong door. You want Number Three."

Mr. Symmons looked stricken. "It was a three, after all?"

"Yes. We had a nice talk with the fellow that brought your Jamie here, and he delivered him to Three a few hours back. But there should be time—Cosgrove isn't expected until—"

"Cosgrove is here," Stephen said, his eyes full of misery. "And we don't have the key to that door."

"Maisie—are they interchangeable?" Charles asked. "One fitting another door?"

She shook her head. "Not supposed to be. But we can give it a try."

Stephen grabbed the key from the floor and hurried over to Number Three. He eased it into the lock, wary of warning the inhabitants of the room inside. *Some of the dungeons open into the river…* He shivered at the thought of Cosgrove goading into disposing of Jamie at the first sign of trouble. The key wouldn't turn.

"We need the other key. Maisie!"

"I'll try." She turned and ran for the servants' stairs, the most direct way back to the kitchens.

In the meantime, Mr. Hammond stepped up. "If any of you ladies have hairpins or broaches, I'll try to pick the lock. It's big and solid, but probably not too complex."

With trembling fingers, Rebecca pulled some pins from her hair and handed them over. "Hurry!" she urged, as he bent to the task. "Jamie could be..."

They all knew what Jamie could be, and there was breathless silence as they watched Mr. Hammond at the lock. After a moment Abby Sawtell stepped forward and loomed over him, examining the door, running her large, capable hands around the frame.

Hammond looked up. "Please don't block my light. As I said, this is a good lock, and—"

"Good lock," Abby agreed. "Good door." Her hands reached a spongy spot of wood on the doorframe, and she reached out and toppled Mr. Hammond out of her way. "Bad jamb." Her long, booted leg came up, aiming squarely for the center of the door.

"Don't. Touch. Me." Jamie welcomed the rage he felt as Julian approached him, so godlike of form and animalistic of mind. It took his mind off the fear of what was still to come, if he couldn't find some way of getting through to Cosgrove.

"You're not exactly in a position to make demands, are you?" The green eyes glittered. "Poor little Jamie."

Cosgrove stirred. "Get on with it, Jeffries, or I swear I'll chain you up next."

The actor complied, pitting his long years worth of sexual skill against Jamie's resistance to allow this monster the satisfaction of wringing a response out of him. Jamie's mindset was such that at first he thought the crash of the door was that of his world coming to pieces about him, as Julian's wretched attentions began to have their effect. He opened his eyes to find the cause quite different, as person after person tumbled into the room in a cacophony of sound, including, incredibly, Stephen's Aunt Matilda. Julian rose from his knees, swearing, looking for another way out of the dungeon. But Jamie's rescuers blocked the door.

"Julian!" It was Stephen's shout, shocked.

"Let me." A figure he thought was Sam dashed forward, waving something club-like. Julian, raised in the worst parts of London, fought back like a cornered cur, snarling and clawing at anyone within reach.

"Stephen! Hammond!" Matilda called to her nephew and another man Jamie didn't know. "Don't let Cosgrove get away!"

Away? How? Jamie turned his head, for the first time noting the presence of a second door, barely visible in the wall further down from where he was chained. Cosgrove had nearly reached it by the time Stephen tackled him, Aunt Matilda's companion just behind. There were grunts, and the thwack of fists on flesh. A sharp cry, from the man Matilda had called Hammond. "Damn it! He has a knife!"

Hammond clutched at his thigh and fell back, knocking into Stephen. Cosgrove reached the door, and Jamie heard the rush of water as the merchant opened it and was gone.

And then Stephen reached him at last, stripping off his coat and wrapping around Jamie's naked body, tears of anger and relief in his dark brown eyes. "Jamie. Oh God, *Jamie.*" Stephen turned to the room behind him. "I need the key to these chains!"

"Here, my lord." Hammond limped forward, with what looked like hairpins in his hands. "Let me."

It took just a few seconds for him to release the manacles, and Jamie stumbled to the floor, dragging Stephen with him. There was another cry, and a third body toppled into them. It was Julian, stone-cold unconscious. Jamie looked up to see Sam standing over him with a rolling pin and a look of satisfaction on his face. Aunt Matilda came into view. She stared down at the actor's naked form, prodding him about the crotch with her cane.

"Hmph," she said. "So that's why you kept him for so long. But you know," and a smile lit her up from the inside, "I should think this about takes care of that exclusivity clause."

Stephen pulled them both to their feet, unable to resist a small kick into Julian's ribs. "We should chain him up to the wall and see how he likes it."

"Not a bad idea," Charles said, eyes narrowing in distaste. "The staff won't come down here until the week's up. That's not long enough for the bastard to die of hunger, is it?"

Jamie, one arm wrapped around Stephen and the other holding the coat in place around him, stared down at the man who had wanted him dead. "Probably not—he's healthy enough."

Rebecca, cuddled against her Chris, sighed. "Yes, but Cosgrove might decide to come back, and if he finds Julian there..."

"What do we care?" Stephen's voice was raw. "Let him tear him to pieces, the way—the way he—" He buried his face against Jamie's hair.

Just then, someone else rushed into the room. "I've got the key! Oh." The person was too far away to make out, but the voice belonged to Maisie. She looked around. "Where's Cosgrove? Where's the bastard that killed my Laurie?"

There was obviously more to this story than Jamie could figure out just now, but he did have the answer to this one. "He's gone, and I don't expect he'll be back." He looked down at Julian, on the floor, and made a decision. "But Julian doesn't know that. Chain him to the block, not the wall, and let him spend the night thinking that Cosgrove might come back for him, or that he'll be lying there, alone in the dark for an entire week. But we'll tell someone here to let him out in the morning."

"If you say so," Stephen said, and Jamie held Stephen's face in his hands.

"We're not animals, Stephen." He watched as his beloved's eyes slowly cleared of madness.

"No. We're not. There is a chance, though, however small, that Cosgrove might come back before Julian is released. You understand that?"

Jamie shrugged his aching shoulders, and found that there was still a remaining spot of coldness in his soul. Perhaps it was permanent, and if so, that would be a pity. "There's always a certain amount of uncertainty in life, isn't there?" He reached for the actor's discarded clothing. "Give me a second to put these on, and then let's get out of here."

Chapter Twenty-Eight

What do you do once you've been snatched from the very jaws of mutilation and death? Why, you have some tea, of course, and then go to bed. Jamie allowed his friends to fuss over him and replay their roles in his rescue for exactly the space of one cup, then held his hands mutely out to Stephen to be rescued again.

"I'm hoping...will you come upstairs with me?" Stephen asked once they reached the quiet of the hall, the noise and laughter in the kitchen muted by the thick door. He had seemed uncharacteristically shy and uncertain to Jamie since they'd returned to St. Joseph House, perhaps because there was still so much to talk about.

Jamie nodded now, and let Stephen take his arm and lead him up to the Earl's suite. His dimple appeared at the first sight of the Egyptian décor. "Goodness," he said, touching one finger to a lamp in the shape of the Sphinx. "If I move in here, we might need to redecorate."

Stephen wrapped his arms around Jamie from behind, resting his cheek on the top of Jamie's head. "If?"

"I did leave for a reason, you know."

A sigh stirred his hair. "It was a mistake, a misunderstanding. I wasn't trying to pay you with that Book of Hours. I swear I thought the package contained the book of poetry you wanted."

"Oh." Jamie squeezed his eyes closed, thinking about the last weeks of misery. "It hurt so badly, Stephen. My mother..."

"I know. Aunt Matilda told me. I was a fool to try to buy you, but I didn't know about your mother then. And I wanted to spoil you. God help me, I still do. Jamie." Stephen swallowed. "I love you."

But Jamie was tired, and his arms hurt from the chains, and it wasn't enough. Not yet. "So I heard," he said, turning to look up at Stephen, "although I could have found out under more favorable circumstances. But what I need to know is, what does that mean to you? A wardrobe allowance and the house on Floral Street?"

"No! I need you here with me, Jamie. Please. Will you stay with me? Will you share my life?" Stephen's eyes were huge and dark. "I need you. You...you're the only person who's ever expected anything from me, and I'm—I'm trying to live up to it. I'm trying to be a better man, and a better master, and—"

"You fraternize with the servants something dreadful," Jamie said, dimple flickering.

"Well, don't expect that to stop anytime soon. Especially with regards to you." His brows flew up. "Unless you don't think you should resume working for me? I mean, if we're going to be together."

"Of course I will. I don't care whether you call me your secretary, or your steward, or your family historian, as long as the boundaries are clearly drawn between what you're paying me for and what you're *not*. Do you understand?"

"Yes." But Stephen's lower lip jutted out. "And *you* will understand that if I supply you with new clothing, or treat you to a new book, that I am not putting a price on your affection. Clear?"

"I won't take—"

"Mouse. What's mine is yours. We can't build a life together unless that is true." He held the other man's eyes steadily, until Jamie finally nodded agreement, then let out a sigh of relief. Besides," Stephen smiled crookedly, "what's mine won't even be mine until you get me out of debt. And now that I appreciate how much work that is, I'm going to do everything I can to help."

"Then I think that's all I need."

"Shall we go to bed, then?"

Jamie had been worried that the degradation of the dungeon would kill desire for some time to come, but looking into Stephen's eyes, warm with longing, he felt passion kindle within him. "Yes," he said. "I need that. I need you to touch me."

Oh, it was different this time. Jamie had always found Stephen's kisses exciting, but the confusion they used to cause was gone, along with the hesitation, the fear. In the security that there would be a tomorrow, and a next day, and by God, if he could help it a next year and a next decade, Jamie relaxed into his lover's arms. Within a very few minutes he was able to compare the very real desire he was feeling for the man he loved, with the shameful, purely physical reaction Julian had forced upon him earlier, and the sickening humiliation of that moment was gone.

Jamie moaned, in relief as much as pleasure, encouraging Stephen to begin unbuttoning his—Julian's—shirt. He'd almost forgotten he was wearing the actor's clothes. Well, they could burn those tomorrow, too. He helped shrug himself out of them, then reached to undress Stephen.

"Mouse—are we going too fast? Is this—?"

Jamie rolled atop him, kissing him soundly. "This is exactly what I need." And slowly, he coaxed Stephen into forgetting to be careful, touching him with a new-found confidence born of his exile in the harsh streets of London. He knew what he wanted, and he knew how easily it could be lost, or taken from him. But by God, he also knew that he would fight for it to the last breath in his body, with a strength he'd never dreamed he possessed.

And he also realized that he had forgotten to say it. "Stephen. Oh, God." Jamie had chosen a bad time for speech. His lover had slicked himself with saliva, and was now entering him, and the raw pleasure of their joining was making it hard to think, much less form words. Jamie had lived so much of his life in his head, considering himself a creature of intellect. Tonight, after having tasted primal terror, and hatred, and the will to survive, he was all emotions. Now, he shared the passion for life, taking and giving without thought, without reason.

What was it he had wanted to say? They were moving together in a fierce rhythm, Stephen driving into him with long, powerful thrusts. *Mine.* Or perhaps *yours*. Jamie cried out, coming, the force of his release dislodging the words at last. "I love you, Stephen!" It was half-sob, half-laugh, all joy. "I love you."

And Stephen was crying out, too, his body taut and trembling for a long moment before collapsing on Jamie. And then there was peace, and warmth, and the crackle of the fire. And Jamie was home, at last.

AUTHOR BIO

M.J. Pearson's meandering career path has included stints dispatching taxis in Vermont, making pizza in Santa Fe, digging Roman ruins in Israel and studying nationalism in Scotland. Currently residing in Indianapolis, M.J. is hard at work on a new romance novel.